THE WITCH'S KISS

Katharine and Elizabeth Corr have been writing since they were children. They keep in touch any way they can, discussing their work via phone, text and skype, and have been known to finish each other's sentences – and not just when they are writing!

Also by Katharine and Elizabeth Corr

The Witch's Tears – coming soon!

THE WITCH'S KISS

KATHARINE & ELIZABETH CORR

HarperCollins*Publishers*

First published in Great Britain by HarperCollins *Children's Books* in 2016
HarperCollins *Children's Books* is a division of HarperCollins*Publishers* Ltd,
1 London Bridge Street, London, SE1 9GF

The HarperCollins website address is: www.harpercollins.co.uk

5

Text © Katharine and Elizabeth Corr 2016

ISBN 978-00-0-818298-4

Katharine and Elizabeth Corr assert the moral right to be
identified as the authors of the work.

Typeset by Palimpsest Book Production Limited, Falkirk, Stirlingshire
Printed and bound in England by Clays Ltd, St Ives plc

For Laurence, who was my inspiration.

E.C.

In memory of Nana Pat, who really did make our
childhood magical.

K.C.

THEN:

THE KINGDOM OF THE SOUTH SAXONS, 522 AD

WITCHES DO NOT kneel.

They do not grovel. They do not beg favours from any creature, mortal or immortal.

At the most, they bargain.

Meredith knew this; had known it for as long as she could remember. But, as she scrambled up the steep hillside, shredding her skirts and her skin on the long thorns of may trees, the things she had been certain of were no longer enough.

Finally, she reached the summit. This place was not holy, but it was old. Very, very old.

Meredith passed through the outer ring of pine trees, so tall and close growing they blocked out the sun and the wind, walking on until she got close to the single oak growing at the centre of the circle. The oak was twisted and split with age, green foliage flecked with cream. Not flowers, but bones: tied to the branches, littering the ground beneath.

Then, Meredith knelt.

She cleared a space in front of her, sweeping away the bones and dead leaves until the earth beneath was revealed, and pulled a knife out of her belt. She had no offering to bargain with. She had only herself.

'This I pledge—' Her voice was weak; she swallowed, ran her tongue over her cracked lips and tried again. 'This I pledge: by the time the charmed sleep ends, one of my children's children will be ready to face Gwydion, to defeat him and to remove all traces of his enchantments from the face of the earth. We shall have vengeance.' An echo seemed to come from the encircling trees, throwing her words back to her:

… *vengeance… vengeance…*

Without hesitating, Meredith pressed the point of the knife into her palm, dragging the blade slowly downwards to split the skin, allowing blood to drip from her outstretched hand on to the ground.

'I swear, not by the gods, nor by men, but by the bones and ancient soul of this land, to bind myself and my descendants to this fate.'

… fate… fate…

With one finger dipped in the blood, Meredith traced a shape on the ground: a binding rune. For a moment it glowed white against the dark earth, before burning away into smoke.

NOW:

ONE

MERRY WAS DREAMING about blood.

Blood, running in scarlet rivulets across the black tarmac at her feet, pooling around her toes. So much blood that she could smell the coppery-tinny scent of it, like a palmful of coins warm from being clutched in her fist. She put her hand up to cover her nose and mouth, tried not to breathe too deeply. In the distance, someone was screaming.

She looked up. A boy was walking towards her across the flat, grey-lit landscape. Memory stirred in her mind. She knew this boy, and not just from her recent nightmares. She recognised his clothes: a cloak, pinned with a gold-coloured brooch, some sort of tunic and – trousers, she guessed they were, but not like anything she'd ever seen boys actually wearing. She recognised the evil-looking knife he carried. The boy was tall, with long, blond hair tied back – the same colour as her brother's, but straight, not curly – and a handsome, angular face. As he came closer she saw for the first time, or maybe she just remembered, that his eyes were brown; brown, with little flecks of gold. And she gasped, not because his eyes were beautiful, but because they were hard and cold and full of cruelty.

Another memory floated to the surface of her mind. Somehow, she knew the boy's name.

Jack?

The boy smiled at her, and it was like looking into the maw of a shark.

Meredith…

Merry woke with a gasp, swore, rubbed her eyes and tried to remember where she was.

In her bedroom, of course – she must have just dropped off. In the lamplight, she could see nothing had changed. There was no one else there: no strange boy with dead eyes staring down at her, threatening her with a knife.

Just another bad dream, that was all.

It was after midnight now. A quick peek into Leo's room

11

on the opposite side of the landing confirmed that her pain-in-the-neck older brother still hadn't come home; it was just her and their mother's two Burmese cats, and they were probably asleep on top of the boiler in the kitchen. Mum herself was working in France for the rest of the week. A self-employed graphic designer, one of her major clients was in Paris, and she spent a *lot* of time there. But that didn't bother Merry any more. Not really. As she turned back into her own room, Merry's glance took in the half-completed homework on the desk, the half-read magazines piled next to the wicker chair in the corner, the half-reorganised wardrobe. She picked up a couple of pairs of ankle boots and half-heartedly arranged them on the shoe rack, but it was no good. She hadn't been able to settle, to actually finish anything, for days. The restlessness was like… ants, crawling over her skin. But there was definitely more to it than that. A person who was merely restless didn't check under her bed every night before she turned out the light, or sleep with a tennis racket handily positioned against the bedside table.

Unwilling to risk another nightmare, Merry texted and played games on her phone for another hour or so, until her eyelids grew too heavy for her to focus on the screen any longer. She got up to close the curtains and peered through the window for a moment, hoping to see some sign of her brother. But there was nothing. Just the darkness and her own reflection – auburn hair half-falling out of a ponytail, shadows underneath hazel eyes – thrown back in fragments from the uneven panes of leaded glass.

Behind her, something began to rattle. Among the photos of her and her friends, which she kept on the dressing table, the one of her and Leo was shuddering. The motion grew, the frame rocking more and more violently until it hurled itself off the dressing table and smashed into the wall opposite. Merry yelped and flinched.

Oh no, not again –

She inspected the damage: the frame had taken a big chunk of plaster off the wall. That didn't matter – Mum never came into her room. But she felt stupid. It had been four years since her power first began to emerge; eight months since she'd decided it was too dangerous for her to practise any more. Her capabilities were hardly a surprise.

It's these attacks, and the nightmares, that's all. Making me tense.

Ha. That was a lie and she knew it. Sure, the situation in Tillingham was making everything worse – that was obviously why she was dreaming about scary, imaginary blond boys. But the power she had... Recently, in the last

13

few weeks especially, her magic seemed to be developing a life of its own. It didn't shock her any more.

It frightened her.

In bed, Merry pulled the duvet up close around her neck and shoulders, breathing deeply, trying to force herself to relax. The familiar outlines of her room gave contours to the shadows: the bedroom furniture, the laptop open on her desk, the pile of clothes and shoes on the floor. She could hear the usual night-time noises of the house: doors banging slightly in the draft, floorboards and ceiling beams creaking as they cooled and contracted, the wind sighing in the chimneys. But tonight it all felt – alien. Like the recognisable shapes and sounds around her were fakes, put there to conceal something utterly strange, something that was crouching in the darkness just waiting for her to fall asleep…

She shivered, and pulled the duvet tighter.

Yellow light lanced through the curtains. There was the chug of a diesel engine pulling up outside, followed by the sound of a car door slamming – a taxi. Her brother was finally home. Merry's shoulders relaxed and she glanced at her alarm clock.

I can't believe Leo. There's a bloodthirsty maniac running around town, and he decides to stay out until two in the morning? I could be lying up here bleeding to death, for all he knows.

She slipped out of bed. It was time to make Leo pay.

Thirty seconds later she was downstairs in the dark, quietly sliding home the bolts on the front door. She pressed her ear to the cold wood. Leo was stumbling up the path, swearing as he tripped on one of the uneven paving stones. He reached the door and she heard him drop his keys, pick them up, drop them again. More swearing. Then the tapping sound of Leo trying to fit the key into the keyhole, turning the lock. The door shifted in the frame.

'What the—?' Leo turned the key again, pushing against the door, trying to force it open. Merry grinned and ran back up the stairs. She'd let him in eventually, but –

Knock, knock, knock.

Merry froze. That wasn't coming from the front door. That was coming from up above her, from the attic. She reached for the light switch. Nothing happened. She flipped the switch: on, off, on, off – still no light. A fuse must have gone somewhere. Or –

Or the maniac is up in the attic, and he's cut the power –

Knock, knock, knock.

She stared up at the ceiling. And there was that feeling again, the same feeling she'd had in her bedroom but worse, tendrils of fear snaking up between her shoulder blades and giving her goose pimples. And now the unknown presence was right behind her, reaching out to engulf her –

Merry scrambled down the stairs and dragged back the bolts. Her hands shaking, she opened the door just as Leo was trying to ram it with his shoulder. He stumbled forwards and lay on the floor, groaning.

'Leo! Leo, get up. I think there's someone in the attic.' She pulled ineffectively at her brother's elbow.

'Merry, I – couldn't get door open. I'm jus' – jus' gonna lie here for a minute. It's all – dizzy.'

'Oh my God, you're totally wasted.' Merry stopped trying to drag Leo upright and slapped his arm instead. 'I can't believe it. We're probably about to be attacked and you're lying there completely—'

'I had a couple – a couple of pints, that's all. Three, maximum. Maybe six.' He squinted up at her. 'What d'you mean, attacked?'

'The electricity's gone and there's a noise coming from the attic. A banging noise. I think someone's broken in. What if it's the maniac who's been in the news – the one who's been knifing people?'

Leo pushed himself up into a sitting position, cradling his head in his hands.

'Merry, don't be daft. Town's full of police: whoever it was, he's long gone. No way is he gonna be in our attic. Just – go back to bed.' He pressed his hand to his mouth, grimacing. 'On second thoughts, make me some of that mint tea you drink. Then go back to bed.' The lights in the hallway suddenly flickered into life. 'See? It was just a power – thing. Cut.'

Merry looked back up the stairs, frowning.

'I don't know, Leo. When I was on the landing, it just felt really… scary.' The words sounded pathetic, but she couldn't think of another way to explain. 'You're meant to be the responsible one. You should check the doors and windows, that kind of thing.' She paused, and tried to make her voice soft and coaxing. 'Just a quick look? Please? Then I'll make you some tea. You know I don't like being alone in the house. I mean, it's so isolated…'

'Leave it out, Merry.' Leo grabbed hold of the newel post at the end of the staircase and used it to heave himself upright. 'I've got to get to bed; I'm working tomorrow.' He checked his phone and groaned. 'Today, even. You want me to do anything else, you're going to have to get your wand and make me.' He smirked at her. 'Seriously, why don't you go and cast a spell, or something?'

Merry stared at him, eyes narrowed.

'I really hate the way you are when you've been out with Simon and the rest of those idiots. You know we don't use wands. And you know Mum hates us even mentioning the craft.' She started examining her fingernails. 'In fact, when she gets back I might just tell her what you said. And what time you got in. And that you're—' she sniffed and made a face. 'Geez, you reek. Have you started smoking again?'

'No.'

'Yeah, right.'

Leo scowled at her.

'Y'know, if you were the witch in a fairy story, you'd be the kind that eats the children. *Meredith*.'

Merry scowled back.

'Don't call me Meredith.'

'Whatever, Maleficent. Maybe I'll tell Mum exactly how many parties you've been to in the last couple of weeks, and how much time you've spent not studying.' He yawned and started walking up the stairs, weaving slightly, only narrowly missing the cats as they streaked past him. 'Damn cats! Honestly, Merry, I'm knackered.

And you're crazy.' He tapped a finger on his temple. 'I'm going to bed.'

Merry quickly locked the front door, then hurried up the stairs behind her brother.

'But Leo – what about those people who've been attacked? Three couples in two nights, just stabbed and left to bleed to death on the street. What if—'

'Just give it a rest, Merry.' Leo yawned and rubbed his eyes. 'Look, you have got to stop obsessing about that. It'll probably turn out they're connected in some way, like…' He screwed up his face in concentration, 'I dunno, they're all criminal overlords. Doesn't follow whoever attacked them is wandering around town looking for his next victim.' He yawned again. 'But if it makes you feel better I'll leave my door open. If anyone dodgy shows up, scream. I'll come and – and—' He waved his hands around vaguely.

'Rescue me?' Merry guessed.

'Yeah. That.'

'Fabulous. That makes me feel so much better.'

Leo shrugged his shoulders, went into his bedroom and promptly collapsed on to his bed. He almost instantly started snoring – loudly. Merry stood and watched him for a moment. Leo was probably right. The banging noise she'd heard was most likely to do with the central heating.

And as for that feeling she'd had, that horrible, sickening fear – it was probably just stress, or too many late nights. She sighed and went back into her own room. But she left the landing light switched on.

'What the—'

Leo sat bolt upright, pushing the cats off the bed. They yowled and jumped straight back on to it, tails fluffed up like feather dusters.

'What is wrong with you two?' He checked his phone: just after five in the morning. Still dark outside. Collapsing back on to the pillows, he closed his eyes against the pain in his head. It was stupid, to have drunk so much. But being with Simon and Dan and the rest of his old friends, and having to keep pretending... He could understand how Merry felt. He was starting to hate himself, the way he was around them.

Knock, knock, knock.

The sound was coming from the attic. Just the plumbing, or some woodworm in the old timbers. Probably. He glanced at the cats. Both were bristling, their ears twitching back and forth. Leo sighed and got out of bed. This was all Merry's fault, putting ideas in his head. The whole thing was ridiculous. Still, he was awake now. He lifted his cricket bat down from the top of the wardrobe and padded across the landing to his sister's room. She was muttering faintly, frowning in her sleep, her hands clenched into fists.

'Merry? Merry, wake up.'

He shook her shoulder and switched on the bedside lamp, causing her to screw up her eyes against the light.

'Leo – oh, thank God.' She covered her face with her hands for a moment. 'I was having another—'

'Shh.' Leo put one finger on his lips.

'Huh? Why are we whispering? And what's with the bat?'

'Listen.'

Knock, knock, knock.

The knocking was more frequent now.

'That's the noise I heard earlier,' she murmured. 'What is it?'

'No idea. But it's coming from...' He pointed upwards. The noise stopped for a minute. Then it started again, slightly louder. 'I'm sure it's just a squirrel, or a rat, or something. A burglar wouldn't be, you know, tap-dancing on the floor.' He patted the cricket bat. 'But I like to be prepared.'

'Tap-dancing?' Merry yawned and squinted up at him. 'What the hell are you on about, Leo?'

21

Leo straightened up, running a hand through his hair.

'Honestly, I don't know. I've had less than three hours sleep and I'm tired, OK?'

'Hungover, more like.' She stared up at him for a minute. 'Damn. I suppose you want me to come up there with you?'

'Well, you're the one who's making me paranoid. What do you think?'

Three minutes later, Leo was switching on the light in the attic. Merry was standing, shivering, on the bottom rung of the metal pull-down ladder.

'Well, I think we can rule out an intruder,' Leo shouted down at her. 'Unless he's really, really tiny.'

'Huh?'

He poked his head back though the hatch.

'Come on up and I'll show you.'

Merry muttered under her breath, but she climbed the rest of the ladder and came to stand next to him, hastily brushing a cobweb off her pyjamas. It was years since either of them had been up here. The attic – really a whole bunch of attics connected by odd steps up and down – was huge, and just as well. Mum was a chronic hoarder; she never threw anything away, on the basis that 'it might come in handy someday.' Or alternatively, 'this is bound to be worth something eventually.' After sixteen years the attic was crammed with cardboard boxes of various sizes, old pieces of furniture and artwork, unidentifiable things draped in sheets. It would be a tight squeeze for even the smallest burglar. Leo and Merry manoeuvred their way through the dust and detritus. The knocking was getting more frequent, more insistent.

'What the hell is it?' Merry asked.

'I don't know, but it's coming from over there.' He waved a hand towards the corner, where a dark oak chest had been wedged between a broken armchair and an old-fashioned sewing machine table.

The two of them went over to the chest and carefully lifted Merry's old doll's house and a stack of commemorative issues of the *Radio Times* off the top of it. Something inside was banging noisily against the wooden frame.

'Right,' said Leo. 'You open it.'

'How about you open it and I stand over there at a safe distance and watch you?'

Leo sighed.

'No, you need to open it. Then, if anything jumps out, I'll hit it with the bat.' He waved the bat around a bit, to demonstrate.

Merry shuddered and stepped away from the chest.

'But what's going to jump out?'

'Oh, for – something less annoying than you, hopefully. How on earth should I know? Just open it.'

'Ugh, fine. After three, OK?' Merry counted; she got to three, lifted the lid and leapt back quickly.

Nothing jumped out at them. Merry gave a little 'oh' of relief and surprise and went to peer inside. Leo came and craned over her shoulder. The chest was empty, apart from a pile of children's picture books and a seven-sided wooden box, tucked away in the corner.

The box was twitching.

As they stared at it, the twitching got worse. The box started slamming against the side of the chest again.

'What is it?' Leo asked.

'Er, it's a jewellery box?'

'Yes, so I can see. But why is it doing *that*?'

'How on earth should I know?' Merry scowled, then turned away and started fiddling with the dials on an old record player sitting nearby, shaking her hair forwards so Leo couldn't see her face.

Leo rolled his eyes.

'Come on, Merry. This has got to have something to do with your lot.'

'My lot?' Merry swung round. 'You know I've never

been allowed to practise. You know I'm completely untrained.'

'Seriously?' Leo pinched the bridge of his nose. 'Look, I also know you do stuff on the quiet. Or you used to, at any rate. You *know* I know. But I'm not going to tell on you to Mum. Just make it stop – jumping, will you? The noise is really starting to get on my nerves.'

'I still don't know what you expect me to do about it.'

'Merry!'

'OK, OK,' Merry huffed. She reached down slowly, carefully, and picked up the jumping trinket box. It stilled immediately.

Merry looked up at Leo and smiled.

And then she fainted.

TWO

MERRY MUST HAVE been unconscious for all of about thirty seconds. But it was a really intense thirty seconds.

Something had come out of the trinket box. Not a physical something; more a sudden swell of energy, running like electricity up her arms and into her chest. Then everything had gone dark.

And out of the darkness came images. A pair of large oak doors set into the middle of a stone wall that seemed to reach up to the sky and beyond. An endless, winding corridor dimly lit with candles. A chair – no, a throne of some sort – near to a wall lined with shelves, shelves crammed with hundreds of faintly glowing glass jars. And a boy chained to the throne, a blood-red crown upon his head. It was the boy from her nightmares. Merry could hear him struggling for breath, and she thought for a moment he was unconscious. But his eyes focused, and she saw his lips move:

'Help me…'

Merry opened her eyes.

Leo was kneeling over her, his face white and tense.

'Merry? Are you OK?'

'Yeah. I think so. Help me sit up.'

Leo put one arm underneath Merry's back and slowly pushed her upright.

'Here, lean against this.' He pulled an old beanbag over and put it behind her. 'What happened?'

'I'm not sure. I – I saw things.' She shuddered. 'I saw him again.'

'Him?'

'The guy from my nightmares. But he wasn't… killing people, this time. He was chained up somewhere – like, in some old, medieval castle.'

'Jesus, Merry. What the hell's going on?'

Merry breathed out slowly.

'No idea. Where's the box?'

'You dropped it.' Leo gestured towards where the box had fallen, lying on its side on the floor. At least it wasn't moving any more.

'Pass it over.'

'Are you sure? I mean, after what just happened? Shouldn't I be taking you to the hospital or something?'

'I'm fine, Leo. Just give it to me.'

For once, Leo didn't argue; he picked up the trinket box and handed it to her. There was no trace of the 'energy' she'd felt earlier.

The box was quite small, its diameter less than the length of her hand. There was an intricate, fluid design carved on to the lid, interlocking figures of eight curling along each of the seven edges, punctuated at every corner with a triangular knot that looked vaguely Celtic. In the centre of the lid was a circle with a crescent etched over the top of it: the Moon. Merry tried to prise the lid open with her nails, but the box was locked. Absentmindedly, she traced a finger over the design. She'd seen that pattern before.

'Let's go back downstairs. I've think I've got the key that will open this.'

While Leo went to make some tea, Merry returned to her room and started rummaging in drawers and boxes.

Eventually she found it: the charm bracelet Gran had given her for her twelfth birthday.

'What've you got there?' Leo put the tea down and knelt on the floor next to her.

She held the bracelet up to him by one of the charms: a small silver key.

'It's got the same design on it, see?' Picking up the trinket box, she pushed the key into the keyhole. The lock turned with a faint click. Merry lifted the lid carefully and peeked inside. 'Curiouser and curiouser. Look.'

She tipped the contents of the box out on to her duvet: a faded fragment of stiff paper, what looked like a short braid of human hair, and the hilt of a sword. Probably a hilt. It didn't look like it belonged to the type of swords she'd used at fencing club a couple of years back, and it wasn't big and shiny like the swords in fantasy films. The short grip was wound about with worn strips of leather, the guard was a narrow block of dark-coloured metal, the pommel was gold, set with red stones. And the whole thing looked old. Very old.

'This is so bizarre. That looks like it should be in a museum. And what on earth is this for?' asked Leo, picking up the braid of hair and examining it. 'What does it all mean?'

Merry sighed. 'Unfortunately, I think it means that we need to go see Gran.'

Leo groaned. 'What, now?'

'Course not.' Merry locked the three objects back in the box. They couldn't be that important, whatever they were, or they would never have just been left up in the attic. 'I'll call her tomorrow. Maybe I can pop over there after school.' She glanced up at Leo, who was holding a half-eaten biscuit in his hand. His face had gone slightly green. 'We'd better get some sleep.'

Merry just about managed to drag herself out of bed a couple of hours later. The bus journey took forever – the Tillingbourne river, swollen by two weeks of almost constant rain, was in flood for the first time anyone could remember – but at least first period was indoor netball. The match went well: she scored four goals and chatted to Verity from her history class whenever the action moved out of their third. The trinket box was entirely forgotten. But she shouldn't have hung around in the changing rooms after everyone else had left. Immersed in noting down the new timetable for the after-school javelin and track club, she felt a tap on her shoulder. It was Esther Perkins: a minor bully / major irritant since primary school.

'Hello, Meredith.' Esther smirked. 'Haven't seen you around for a while.'

Merry shrugged. 'It's a big school.' She moved to go past, but Esther moved too.

'Really? I thought maybe it was 'cos of Alex. Bet you think you're a real hero, pulling him out of the river. Bet you think you're too good to hang round with the rest of us now.'

Merry took a deep breath.

Here we go.

'Get lost, Esther.'

She stepped forwards, but again the other girl blocked her path.

'But why did he need rescuing, that's what I want to know.' Esther leant closer. 'I've heard what people say about your family. My mum says your gran should be locked up. Says she's a wicked old bag. Only a matter of time before she ends up hurting someone.'

Stay calm, Merry. Keep control...

Another deep breath.

Oh, this would be so much easier if I still did magic.

I could just put a memory charm on you.

I could make you forget your own name, let alone mine.

Just one little spell...

31

But that was where it had started with Alex: one little spell, that had led to another, and then another – Merry had promised herself that she would never, ever let anything like that happen again. So instead, she slung her PE bag across her back and forced her way past Esther.

The other girl's voice followed her out of the changing room, taunting:

'I know what you are, Meredith Cooper…'

The day slid downhill from there. When her friends went out for a coffee at lunchtime, she had to stay in and finish some overdue art homework. She seemed to be developing some kind of hearing defect: there was definitely a random buzzing sound coming from somewhere, almost like the babble of distant voices, but nobody else could hear it. There was no answer when she called Gran's landline – the only number she had – to ask about the trinket box. And everyone at school kept going on and on and on about the vicious knife attacks in town. The fact that no one had died so far was, frankly, miraculous.

It was kind of understandable that people wouldn't shut up about it. Until they started, Tillingham was probably the safest and most boring town in Surrey, if not the country. Gran and the others had made sure of that. The problem now, Merry thought, was the current of excitement running under the fear, the way some people were starting to – well, almost enjoy themselves: dissecting every detail of the attacks as if they were discussing the latest instalment of some gory Scandinavian crime show. After last night's drama, the whole thing set her teeth on edge.

Later that day, as Merry stood stuffing some folders back into her bag, two girls from her art class came down the hallway, chatting loudly. They stopped at their lockers, right next to Merry's.

'So, my aunt called last night – she's a nurse at the hospital, right?' said Eloise. 'And she's been looking after those people who got attacked.'

'Oh my God, really?' exclaimed Lucy.

'Yeah. She said all four of them had lost huge amounts of blood. That's why they're all in comas.'

'That's horrible.' Lucy grimaced.

Eloise leant in closer.

'Yeah. My aunt says the places where they were attacked must have been covered with blood. Running with it, she reckons.'

'Ew, that is so disgusting,' said Lucy. 'Hey, Merry, did you hear what—' She stopped. 'Are you OK?'

No, Merry wanted to say, *I'm not OK. Because I can smell*

the blood, just like in my nightmare, I can almost taste it, and
my fingernails are aching like I'm about to cast a spell right here
in the middle of the corridor, and –

'Merry?'

Oh my God, I'm going to be sick.

There were a couple of Year 11 girls hanging out in the toilets, but after one surprised glance at Merry's face they both left rapidly. Merry held on until the door swung shut behind them then sank to her knees, gripping the edge of the basin in front of her, jamming her fingernails hard against the cold porcelain. Long, slow breaths – that was the key. If she could just calm down, the magic might ebb away again before it could do any damage.

Gradually, the tingling in her fingers subsided. Merry risked relaxing her grip. She stood up slowly, turned on the tap, waited as the water ran over her hands and wrists. As long as she looked more or less normal before she ran into Lucy and Eloise again she could probably –

There was a girl in the mirror. Just standing there, watching her.

Merry jumped and spun around.

The room was empty.

She swung back to the mirror. The girl was still there:

a long plait of dark hair hanging over one shoulder, green eyes, full-length dress belted at the waist. Merry began to tremble. Her brain was screaming for her to run, but her legs just wouldn't cooperate. The girl moved closer, until she stood at Merry's shoulder, so close Merry ought to have been able to feel her breath against her neck – she leant in, as if she was about to whisper in Merry's ear –

Pain lanced through Merry's hands as magic exploded from her fingertips. The large mirror above the handbasins shattered. The girl's reflection disappeared.

Merry staggered into one of the stalls and locked the door.

Fifteen minutes later, the shaking and the nausea had started to subside. She had no explanation for the imaginary girl. Because she must have been imaginary. It was probably just exhaustion. Or – she touched her fingers to her forehead – perhaps she actually was coming down with an ear infection, and it was giving her a fever. But what she'd done to the mirror... Her magic never used to behave like this, never; yet in the last few weeks it had become – unpredictable. Uncontrollable. Spilling out at odd moments, occasionally heralded by a painful tingling sensation in her fingernails. Completely different from the spells she'd managed to teach herself by sneaking books out of Gran's house: no words, no rituals, no music. Just raw power. She hadn't dared try to cast a spell deliberately, to check what was going on. Maybe it was all these months of not allowing herself to practise witchcraft, or the nightmare situation with Alex leading up to her decision to quit. Maybe it was because she'd never been properly trained. She had no idea – there was no one to ask about it. As far as Mum or Gran were concerned, she didn't do magic.

Merry glanced down at her fingers. Her nails still throbbed, but otherwise there was no outward sign of the energy that had surged through her hands. They looked normal, just like she did. Which was a joke, because she'd wanted to be normal for so long. Not in the beginning, not when she first found out she was a witch, but after Alex –

She was desperate to be normal. At least, she'd thought that was what she wanted. It was what she'd wished for.

Well, maybe she was finally getting her wish. Maybe her magic was going crazy because it was draining away. Leaving her. And that was a good thing. The best thing that could be happening to her.

Wasn't it?

★ ★ ★

The bell rang. Merry was still sitting in the stall, staring absentmindedly at some graffiti daubed across the cubicle door, asking anyone who happened to be sitting on the loo with a pencil to 'Tick if you came here to get out of PE'. She couldn't face going to her last class. The day was nearly over, anyhow.

'Merry? Come on, I – what the – what happened to the mirror?'

Merry swore silently. Ruby was her best friend, had been since they both started secondary school five-and-a-half years ago. She should have known Ruby would come to find her.

'I know you're in here, Merry. Lucy said you looked like you were about to faint. Mind you, she also said your fingernails were glowing. Have you bought some of that glow-in-the-dark nail varnish? Can I borrow it?'

Merry emerged from the stall.

Ruby looked her up and down, frowning.

'You look crap. What's the matter?'

'Nothing. Just felt a bit sick. I didn't sleep well last night, but I'm fine now.' Merry walked over to the basin with the least glass in it, ran the tap and splashed some cold water on her face. A glance in one of the mirrored fragments made her wince. Her hair was wrecked: twisted into knotty tendrils where she'd been running her fingers through it – even more of a contrast than usual to Ruby's glossy curls. Her face was paler than normal, her hazel eyes puffy and red-rimmed. The ear infection was obviously some horrible virus. Flu, or something. 'Is there a bug going round?'

'Not that I know of. Morning sickness?'

'Hilarious.'

While Merry dried her face on some hand towels, Ruby took the opportunity to pull out a small mirror and touch up her lipstick.

'So, why aren't you sleeping? Is it because of these attacks? My sister's been having nightmares all week.'

Occasionally, Ruby could be almost too perceptive.

'Your sister's ten. And why would I have nightmares? I can take care of myself, you know.'

'Alright, keep your knickers on.' Ruby started fiddling with the stack of bracelets on her wrist, turning them over and over. 'I heard from Alex, by the way.'

Merry stiffened. Alex would never reveal to anybody what she'd told him. Probably. And if he did, Ruby wouldn't believe him. Probably. She'd never believed the gossip that sometimes got repeated about Merry's family.

Still…

'He says he's doing OK,' Ruby continued. Merry relaxed

fractionally. 'His counsellor's got him into extreme sport, running obstacle courses or something. Sounded a bit of a nightmare, to be honest, though you'd probably love it.' She shrugged. 'I still think you should text him – at least try and figure out what his problem is. I mean, you saved his life, Merry. Surely he must want to talk to you?'

Merry turned away and yanked some more paper towels out of the dispenser. Ruby was right, in a way. Alex had jumped off a bridge into a flooded river, and Merry had gone in after him. She had saved him. Had stopped him drowning, at any rate. But Alex wouldn't want to talk to her again, not in a million years. He hated her, and she didn't blame him.

It was definitely time to change the subject.

'Let's go to the library for a bit. Leo's picking me up around six – he could give you a lift home, if you like?'

Ruby's eyes glazed over.

'Hell yeah.'

As they stood outside school waiting for Leo, Merry wondered if she had made a mistake. Offering Ruby a lift was probably going to land her in trouble. At eighteen, Leo was only two years older than Merry, but he'd gone all superior and grown-up over the last few months since he'd left school; at least, he had when he wasn't hanging out with his best friend Dan. Plus, Ruby had a massive crush on him, and she wasn't shy about letting him know it.

Leo definitely wasn't into Ruby. He wasn't really into girls at all. But only Merry knew. Leo hadn't told anyone else: not Mum, and certainly not any of his friends.

Things had come to a head the previous summer. Leo, Dan and his other close friend, Simon, had spent four months hitchhiking their way around the US. By the time they had flown back to the UK Leo had realised that he liked Dan – really liked him – and not just in a best mates kind of way. Merry remembered the conversation word for word.

'I think you should tell him, Leo. Maybe he feels the same way.'

'Dan? You've got to be kidding me. He's got a serious girlfriend. He's completely loved up. Besides, Simon just wouldn't understand. I don't know how he and the others would react if I told them. I think – I'm not sure they'd think I was me any more.'

He'd had such a dejected look on his face. Merry had hugged him and told him she loved him and supported him, over and over. She had also (in her head) threatened to curse anyone who gave him a hard time, once he'd got up the nerve to actually tell them.

Leo's battered black Peugeot pulled up to the curb now. Merry could see his blue eyes widen in disbelief, then narrow – he shook his head at her. She was probably going to pay for this later. But before she could say anything Ruby had surged ahead and jumped into the front seat. Leo said hello to her pleasantly enough. Then he turned back towards Merry, and glared.

It was going to be a long ride home.

It was Merry's turn to make dinner. Yesterday, Leo had made them sausages and mash, so Merry, who was generally speaking a better (though unenthusiastic) cook, decided to go for something marginally healthier and try a vegetable stir fry recipe she'd torn out of a magazine. She was pretty pleased with it, but Leo spent most of the meal picking out the broccoli and complaining about Ruby, Merry's friends in general, and the fact that he was having to 'babysit' her. It was true that Ruby had been unbearable in the car: giggling at everything Leo said, brushing her hand against his leg at every opportunity. Merry didn't blame him for being annoyed. Plus, she knew he was tired in the evenings; he was working long hours on a local farm, saving money for when he started studying medicine in September. But still, she finally had enough.

'For God's sake, Leo, she was only in the car for half-an-hour. And it's not like I expect you to stay in with me every evening. You're out just as much as I am. Why are you being so obnoxious?'

And that was it. They ended up having a massive row, basically about nothing. Leo spent the rest of the evening in his room, not even coming down for the latest episode of their favourite sci-fi show.

Now Merry was sitting in the bath, watching the ends of her fingers shrivel up, headphones on and music cranked up to drown out the thunderstorm raging outside. Usually she liked to sing along to her favourite songs – loudly – but tonight she just wasn't in the mood.

Geez, what a day. She'd had an uncontrollable magical outburst at school, hallucinated about some strange girl and managed to have a fight with her brother. And it was only Tuesday.

The trinket box was preying on her mind too. She'd called Gran's house again and left a message, but so far Gran hadn't phoned back.

The bath water was cold. Merry pulled the plug and got out; there was no reason to put off going to bed any longer.

Time to man up, Merry. Woman up.

As she passed Leo's bedroom she paused for a moment, tempted to knock and say goodnight, but she couldn't hear any signs of life – no point in waking him if he'd already gone to bed. She crossed the landing to her own room. But at the door, she hesitated.

She couldn't make herself go in.

Something was wrong.

As her hand lingered on the door handle, she felt something. Some kind of energy, similar to the energy that had surged from the trinket box and knocked her out the previous night. But this time, it was far, far stronger.

She drew her hand back.

Magic.

THREE

MERRY PANICKED. FORGETTING her current no-magic policy, she tried to think of a spell she could use against whomever – whatever – was on the other side of the door. She tried to think of any spell at all, but her mind was too full of images: images from when she had first touched the trinket box, images from her nightmares. Almost without any conscious decision, she turned the door handle and stepped into the room.

The boy from her nightmares was standing on the other side of the door. He yanked Merry towards him, pushing the door shut as he spun her round, putting one hand over her mouth and his other arm around her body, pinning her arms to her sides and crushing her against his chest. She kicked backwards with her heels, beat her fists against his legs, but his grip only got tighter.

This was no dream.

'I would not willingly hurt you, maid, but you must be still.'

Merry ignored him and slammed the back of her head against his face.

The boy grunted, but his grip didn't falter. 'I've a blade in my hand. Unless you wish me to use it, be still!' Something sharp pressed against the side of Merry's ribcage. She stopped struggling. 'Now, I am going to take my hand from your mouth. You will not scream.'

Merry tried to remember how it had felt when she'd smashed the mirror earlier that day. If she could summon even a fraction of that power, force him away from her –

The pressure from the knife-point increased. But she couldn't feel the faintest flicker of magic. The repelling charm she was saying in her head might as well have been a nursery rhyme.

'Agreed?'

Merry nodded. The boy lowered his hand, placing it instead around her throat.

'What is this place?'

'Tillingham,' Merry whispered. 'We're just outside Tillingham.' She felt the boy shake his head. He didn't seem pleased by her answer.

'Where is Gwydion?'

'I don't know anyone called Gwydion.'

The boy's hand tightened slightly.

'Then why do I know your face? Why am I drawn to this... this dwelling?' There was anger in his voice, but underneath the anger Merry could hear panic. The boy was terrified of something.

'Please, let me go. I don't know what you want. I can't help you.'

'You're lying. You must help me.' The boy turned Merry around so he could see her face. 'I know you. I remember little else, but I know you!'

The bedroom door burst open and the light came on. Merry tried to duck as Leo took a swing at the boy with his cricket bat. He wasn't quick enough. The boy shoved Merry towards her brother and leapt for the window. He paused and looked back at her, crouched on the sill for a moment, before jumping out into the darkness.

Leo ran to the window and leant out. The next moment he was on his knees next to Merry, his arms around her.

'It's OK, Merry. He's gone. God, I thought – I thought—' He took a deep breath. 'Who the hell was that? Was it someone from school? Did he hurt you?'

'No, he didn't.' Merry clutched her stomach as a ripple of nausea shot through her. 'He didn't hurt me, not really. It was him, but it can't have been. He's not real. At least, I didn't think he was.'

'You're not making any sense. I think you're in shock.'

'It was that man – boy – the one I've been having nightmares about.' She shivered. 'But you saw him too, didn't you? I'm not – I'm not imagining it?'

Leo shook his head.

'Of course I saw him.' He dragged the duvet off the bed and wrapped it round Merry's shoulders. 'I just tried to bash his head in, didn't I? God, this is crazy. Maybe he just looked a bit like the guy in your nightmares?'

'No. His clothes were exactly the same. Every last, weird, detail, right down to the stupid brooch thing he had on.' She groaned, pressing shaking fingers to her temples, remembering how the boy had asked for her help, how certain he'd been that he knew her. None of it made any sense. And why hadn't she been able to cast a spell? Sure it was a long time – at least seven months – since she'd deliberately tried to use her power, but even so…

She swallowed; her throat was parched.

'How did you know he was in here?'

'The cats. The pair of them were on the landing, staring at your room and hissing, with their tails all fluffed up.'

Merry closed her eyes and leant against her brother's chest.

'I'm not sure I can cope with much more of this.'

'Let's call the police.'

Merry sat up again.

'No. Let's not.'

'But maybe you're psychic. Witches are automatically psychic, right? Which means he *was* the one who's been attacking people. It certainly looked like he was trying to kill you.'

'He wasn't trying to kill me. And I'm not psychic.' She winced and rubbed her side where the knife had dug in. 'But—'

'Please, Leo? The police won't be any use.'

'Why on earth not?'

'Because I've never seen the guy before, but somehow I've been dreaming about him. If I tell the police that, they'll just think I'm mad. Or worse.' She yawned, suddenly feeling utterly drained. 'I think… I think he must be linked to that trinket box. Gran will know what to do.'

Leo groaned and ran a hand through his hair.

'Well, if that's true, you have to get hold of Gran tomorrow. This is all getting too dangerous.' Merry could hear the anxiety in Leo's voice. 'And if he comes back, I am calling the police.'

'I don't think he will.'

'Since you've just told me you can't see into the future, you don't know that. Come on.' He gathered up her duvet and pillow. 'You'd better sleep in my room until Mum gets back on Sunday.'

Leo insisted Merry went to school the next day; he said she would be safer there, and he told her to stay at school and study until he could come by and pick her up at six. When they got home he went straight upstairs and nailed her bedroom window shut. Merry, unconvinced that nails would help, went through her mother's address book and found an old mobile number for Gran; the call went straight to voicemail, but she left another message.

Early the next morning, in the dim greyness just before dawn, Merry heard singing outside Leo's window. Chanting, really; voices rising and falling along different harmonic lines that somehow combined into a single, sombre melody. She couldn't make out the words. Pushing the curtain

49

aside and peering through the glass, she saw a group of women standing with their arms raised. Some of them seemed to be holding things: bunches of twigs, stones, a metal bowl on a chain with smoke coming out of it. As Merry watched, one of the women knelt, pulled out a knife and started carving a shape in the lawn underneath the window.

'Oh, my – Leo!' She shook him awake.

'Huh? What?'

'There're people downstairs in the garden – I think they might be witches. They're singing. And one of them's messing up Mum's lawn.'

By the time they had got downstairs and unlocked the back door, the women had moved away from Leo's window and were vandalising the grass at the front of the house. Leo ran towards them, waving his arms.

'Stop! What the hell are you doing?'

The woman with the knife straightened up. Merry knew her: she lived in the old manor house a little further down the lane.

'Mrs Knox?

'A bad business this, Merry. Very bad. We came as soon as we got your grandmother's message.' She followed

Merry's gaze to the large carving knife in her hand. 'Protective runes. If we'd known the counter-curse was going to break down…' Mrs Knox shook her head, sighed. 'Didn't think it would happen in my lifetime. If it happened at all.' There were murmurs of agreement from the other women. As Merry looked at their faces she found more of them that she recognised. One of the checkout ladies from the local Waitrose; the woman who owned the bookshop on the high street; a girl whose name she couldn't remember, who was in the year above her at school and sometimes worked in Zara on Saturdays.

'Are you, um, Gran's coven?'

'Some of it, yes.'

Well. This is weird.

Leo stepped forwards.

'I don't know what exactly Gran has asked you to do, but you cannot go around messing up people's lawns and – and singing at them. Our mum's going to go insane—'

'No need to worry. The runes will have faded by the time she gets back.'

'That's not the point. You're still trespassing.' He blushed and tugged at the hem of his T-shirt; Merry saw the Zara girl staring at him, grinning. 'What's a counter-curse? And what does any of this have to do with us?'

'Ah. Think your grandmother had better deal with that. She's presenting at a conference in Whitby this week, but she'll be back Saturday morning. You're to visit her at one o'clock.'

'But—'

'No more questions.' Mrs Knox nodded to the other women. 'We've one more side to do, then we'll be out of your way. I'd have some breakfast and get dressed, if I were you, young man. You shouldn't be standing around in your underwear in this kind of weather.' After gazing at Merry one last time – such a strange look, it made Merry shiver and pull her coat tighter – she turned away and started shepherding the rest of the coven round to the far side of the house. The conversation was clearly over.

For the next couple of days Merry avoided her brother as much as possible. She knew Leo wanted to talk about what had happened, about the boy in her room and the sudden arrival of the coven, but she didn't. Instead, she spent Thursday evening in her room, trying to catch up on homework, and on Friday she persuaded Ruby to go with her to the gym at the local community centre. Ruby was happy enough for the first forty-five minutes (a drop-in yoga class) but was less keen when Merry suggested working out with some of the weights and exercise machines.

'Can't we go and get some dinner now? I'm knackered. We don't all have your stamina.'

'Just a bit longer, please? I've got a javelin competition on Saturday.' A partial truth: Merry's life seemed to be full of those at the moment. But the whole truth was far too complicated. 'Sit and have a rest while I use the punchbag.'

Ruby groaned, but she sat on the floor and got out her phone while Merry searched for the least rank pair of gloves. She liked feeling that her body was strong, that it would do pretty much whatever she asked of it; she'd started doing more sport a few years back, encouraged by Gran, and kept it up even after she began to see less of her grandmother. Plus, the boxing was therapeutic. Taking out her frustration on the bag, she almost forgot she wasn't alone until Ruby interrupted.

'Merry? Is something up? You're being even more weird than normal.'

Merry stopped and looked at her friend.

'What do you mean?'

'Well, I get that you like to be busy. But at the moment – you never seem to stop. It's either sport, parties or late-night studying. All the time. And you're still not getting everything done. It's like you're...' Ruby's face scrunched up. 'I dunno. I'm just worried about you.'

53

Merry pulled off the boxing gloves and started examining a cut on her knuckle.

Ruby knew, almost. So maybe Merry should actually talk to her. Tell her that she'd come to the gym this evening because she was hiding from her own brother, and because she was trying to forget that someone had threatened her with a knife three nights ago. That when she was exercising, or out with mates, or completely exhausted, she didn't have to think about what she'd done last year, or about what she'd given up. That she had once been a witch, and now she wasn't.

Tell her how hard it was to want something that she knew she shouldn't want.

She might understand, if I explained.

What, like you tried to explain to Alex? And how did that work out for you?

The mixture of disbelief and fear on Alex's face still haunted her. It was too much of a risk.

'I'm fine, Ruby. Just, you know, stuff. School, mostly. I'm not sure I can be bothered to resit chemistry. I know I'm going to fail again, and I've got so much else to do...'

'Then just drop it. You need to stop trying to please everybody, Merry.' Ruby grinned. 'Who wants to be good the whole time anyway, eh?'

Well, I need to be, Merry thought. *Because the alternative to me being good, is me being bad. And me being bad will be terrifying.*

She shrugged.

'Yeah, maybe. Come on.' She held out her hand to Ruby. 'Let's go late-night shopping and try on expensive clothes that we're never gonna buy.'

'Oh, yes – and hats. And shoes.'

'Yeah. Those really hideous high heels with the spikes all over them. And I saw this pair of purple, thigh-high, lace-up boots the other day...'

Ruby giggled.

'That's your birthday pressie sorted then.'

Merry smiled. Tonight, at least, she was going to be a completely normal teenager.

FOUR

SADLY, PRETENDING EVERYTHING was normal wasn't really a long-term plan. Because the trinket box – along with most of its contents, and the key – appeared to be growing.

By the time she got home on Friday evening, the scrap of stiff paper, which Merry now realised must be parchment, had become a couple of blank pages tied together with a strip of leather. The braid of hair had grown longer and thicker, almost long enough to wrap around Merry's wrist. Only the sword hilt was unchanged.

It was all very stressful.

When Leo sauntered into the kitchen on Saturday

morning Merry was sitting at the table, a chemistry revision book propped up against the apple juice carton and the trinket box in front of her, next to a ruler.

'Thought you had some athletics event?'

'Cancelled.' Merry waved a hand towards the window, indicating the rain that was gradually transforming the flower beds into mud soup.

'So what are you doing?'

'I'm trying to catch it growing,' she replied, still staring at the box. 'But it only seems to happen when I'm not watching.'

'Growing? Merry, it's a box. You must be imagining it.'

Merry rolled her eyes at him.

'If you say so.'

'Well, I wish you'd put it away. It's really starting to creep me out. Do you want some toast?'

'Yes, please. And I've tried putting it away.' She sighed and straightened up, shoving the box away from her. 'The damn thing is following me around.'

'Once again—' Leo opened his hands wide, '—it's a box. Not possible.'

'Really? I put it up in the attic last night, back in the blanket box. This morning, when I woke up, it was on my dressing table. Yesterday I locked it in the garage before I went to school. But when I got home last night, I found it in my underwear drawer.'

'Oh.'

'Yeah. Oh.'

Leo plonked himself down on the chair next to Merry and poured himself a coffee. He opened the lid of the box and poked a finger at the contents.

'Is it me, or is that – hair extension – longer?'

'Exactly. See?' Merry snapped the lid shut and turned towards her brother. 'And don't ask, 'cos I don't know. I thought you had to work this weekend?'

'I called in and told them I had a family emergency. I'll lose two days' pay, but…' He shrugged. 'I just don't think you should be in the house on your own at the moment.'

'Oh. Thanks. I'm sorry about the money.' Merry closed the chemistry book; she wasn't taking any of it in, anyway.

'It's OK.' Leo was fiddling with a ten-pence piece one of them had left on the table, spinning it round and round between his thumb and forefinger. 'The witchcraft – you are being careful, aren't you, Merry? I mean, you're not actually summoning psychotic blond boys from the nether world?' He didn't look at her, just kept spinning the coin.

'Of course not, Leo. Honestly, I haven't done any magic recently.' Not intentionally, at any rate. 'I kind of decided to take a break. It's dangerous, especially if you're not properly trained. Gran and the rest of the coven can do some pretty impressive things, from what I've heard, but you know I had to pick up stuff for myself.'

Yeah, picked stuff up and ran with it. It might have been OK, if you'd stuck to the spell books, hadn't started experimenting…

Merry tried to remember what magic Leo might have seen her using.

'What do you think I can do, apart from giving cold sores to unfaithful boyfriends? You knew about that, right?'

'I did. Though I thought you were only supposed to use the craft to help people. Didn't Gran make a big thing a few years back about—'

'Yeah, well,' Merry interrupted, 'there's no need for Gran to know about the cold sores. Besides, since I'm not officially a witch, I haven't actually had to sign up to the whole good behaviour thing. But you mustn't tell Mum I used to, well, dabble. She'd go psycho. Probably lock me up in a tower for the rest of my life. So… promise?'

'Promise.' He smiled at her and squeezed her hand.

Merry smiled too. She and Leo were a team. Over the years they'd learnt to look out for one another, especially as their mother spent more and more time away at work, and became more and more distant. Things might have been different once, before their father left, but Merry had only been four when he took off. As far back as she could remember it had been her brother who watched her back and took care of her, despite his occasional grumbling. She knew Leo would love her no matter what she did. No matter what she'd done.

He will, won't he?

Course he will.

Course.

She dropped her gaze as she squeezed his hand back.

Leo tapped the trinket box with one finger.

'So… ready for our visit to Grandma's house?'

'Oh yeah. Got my red riding hood and everything. Let's hope we don't meet a wolf on the way.'

Leo laughed.

'A wolf messing with Gran? I'd like to see one try.'

Gran used to live in the house in which Leo and Merry lived now. She had been born there, grew up there, and stayed there on her own after Bronwen (her only child) moved out and after Grandpa died. But when Merry was born, Gran decided her daughter and son-in-law needed the space more than she did. She sold (or possibly gave – Merry wasn't quite clear) the old house to the young family, and moved nearer to the town centre. The house Gran lived in now was deeply ordinary: a 1930s semi-detached house pretty much identical to a million other 1930s semi-detached houses across the country. Mock Tudor, bay-windowed, laurel-hedged suburban.

Merry stared up at the house.

'Do you remember when we used to love coming here? All those weekends we stayed over? The stories she used to tell us, and the games we played?'

Leo nodded.

'I remember: it was magical. I mean, literally magical. Like all those times we'd sit around the fire with hot chocolate and marshmallows, and she'd make the flames take on the shapes of the characters in the story she was telling us?'

'Or the time she made it snow for us in the garden in July, so we could build snowmen? But none of the neighbours could see it. We must've looked off our heads, prancing around in her back garden, wearing winter coats in the middle of summer.' Merry smiled. 'That was a great day.'

'Yeah, it was.' Leo sighed. 'Not so much fun after Mum found out what was going on, and she and Gran had that argument though, was it.'

That argument. It really deserved capital letters: That Argument. In the whole of Leo and Merry's childhood, Mum had never practised the craft in front of them. She wouldn't even talk about it; she got cross once just because Merry wanted to dress as a witch for a fancy dress party. Halloween was a no-go area. So when, on Merry's twelfth birthday, Gran had asked if she wanted to be tested, to see if she was a witch, Merry had hesitated. But only for about two minutes. Sure, Mum would disapprove – if she found out – but to have the chance to learn some of the stuff she'd seen Gran doing... there wasn't really any question about it.

Merry knew she would remember the night of the test her whole life. Since she couldn't yet cast any spells, her ability had to be evaluated by seeing how well she could resist spells cast by other witches. Taken to a hidden spot up on the downs, blindfolded and left in the darkness, she had only heard the voices of the witches who were testing her. They didn't speak to her directly, and half the time they were using a language she didn't understand; it had taken every ounce of her courage not to tear off the blindfold and run, especially once the spells began to hurt. She emerged from the experience with a broken arm and what looked like sunburn all down one side of her body.

But apparently that was an excellent result: most of those tested didn't get off half as lightly. So Merry was delighted, even though she was stepping into the unknown, even though she knew nothing would ever be the same –

Too delighted: she forgot the secrecy Gran insisted on, and let something slip to her mother. Mum wasn't just disapproving. She went ballistic. The sleepovers at Gran's were banned, the proposed magical training was banned, and Merry was forced to promise that she would never, ever do magic. Gran was forced to promise that she wouldn't teach her anything, at the risk of all contact being severed. Even then, Mum started to limit the amount of time they spent with Gran. She said she wanted them to be normal children – which was totally hypocritical, since Merry was certain that Mum still did some spells herself – but four years on, Merry could sort of see her point. Messing about with a little bit of magic – casting spells so boys would like you, or so you'd get picked for the netball team – it was all well and good when it was just fun, when you were just using it to make life a little bit easier. But it could go bad so quickly. And bad, where magic was concerned, was really bad…

'Hey, Merry?' Leo was waving his hand in front of her face. 'Shall we?'

'Oh – sure. Let's get it over with.'

They got out of the car and walked up to the front door. As they stepped on to the porch, Merry glanced up, and raised her eyebrows: three horseshoes nailed up now, instead of just one. They had three at home too, though she had never thought to ask Mum why. Leo raised his hand to ring the doorbell, but the door swung open of its own accord. He shot Merry a look of exasperation as they trudged forwards into the hallway. The door slammed shut behind them.

They found Gran in the kitchen. She was smartly dressed as always: grey tailored trousers and a pale blue cashmere sweater, silver drop earrings, her grey hair cut into a fashionable, spiky bob. Not a wart in sight.

'Come here, the pair of you. Give me a kiss.'

Merry dropped a kiss on Gran's cheek and stepped back, but Gran took hold of her shoulders.

'I can't believe I haven't seen you since Christmas. Let me look at you…' She scanned Merry's face for a few seconds before pulling her into a tight hug. 'Well, you'll be fine. I'm certain of it.'

'What do you mean, Gran? Why wouldn't I be fine?'

Gran released Merry and shooed her towards the kitchen table.

'Sit down. We've got a lot to talk about.'

Once the kettle had boiled, Gran put three mugs and a teapot on the table. Merry poured out some tea and took a sip. It had the same strange taste she remembered; slightly bitter and grassy, though Gran had always sworn it was just regular PG Tips. True or not, somehow the tea was comforting.

'So. You found the trinket box?'

'Yes.' Merry glanced at Leo. 'It woke us up on Monday night. When I touched it I had a sort of... vision. A boy, on a throne. I've been having nightmares about him. And then on Tuesday night—'

'He broke into the house, Gran,' Leo interrupted. 'He was in Merry's bedroom. And the box is growing. What's going on?'

For a moment Gran covered her eyes with one blue-veined hand. Sometimes, Merry reflected, it was easy to forget how old her grandmother actually was.

'I didn't know this was going to happen, Leo. It was all so long ago, I had hoped...' She picked up her mug, staring into its depths as though she was trying to read the future. 'I begged your mother to talk to Merry about it. But, over the last couple of years, I almost convinced myself that Bronwen was right: the evil would never awaken, and

Merry would never need to be involved.' She sighed. 'I was wrong.'

Merry's breath caught in her throat.

'What – what evil? Mum knows? What does she know?'

'And what about the box?' Leo added. 'How do we get rid of it? It's following Merry around.'

'Do you have it here?' Gran asked.

Leo nodded and pulled the trinket box out of his bag. Gran touched it gently, running her fingers over the patterned lid in the same way Merry had done the night they found it.

'Fifteen centuries have been and gone since this box was created. Just like the key you used to open it.' There was a low whistle from Leo. 'It's made of willow wood and set with flint, for protection.'

'Protection from that boy, Gran? Or from something else?' Merry wasn't sure she wanted to know the answer. There was something in Gran's blue eyes that made the skin between her shoulder blades tingle. *Someone walking over my grave.*

'The box itself does not offer protection. It is merely the canary in the mine.'

Merry and Leo stared at each other blankly. Gran groaned.

'This is what comes of a modern education. It's like a – an air raid signal, or the countdown to a bomb going off.'

'You mean it's a warning?'

'Yes!'

'Well, you could have just said so,' muttered Leo. 'What's it supposed to be warning us about?'

'It is warning us that time is running out.'

Geez. Merry knew there was a time and a place for being cryptic and mysterious, probably, but this was definitely not it.

'Please, Gran, can you just, like, lay it out for us?'

Gran raised an eyebrow.

'Very well.' She sat up straighter in her chair. 'There is a powerful wizard, a master of dark magic, sleeping under the Black Lake. His servant – that boy – is already awake: he is responsible for the recent attacks. If the wizard himself awakes and escapes the lake, he will create an army of such servants: humans, possessed and controlled by dark magic drawn by him from the shadow realm. An army whose purpose is to destroy all love in the world.'

Merry swallowed.

'Controlled by dark magic from the shadow realm? What does that even mean?'

67

'The… things of the shadow realm are, as I understand it, more like… evil forces, powerless in themselves, until they are given a human body. Then they will obey the one who gives them human form, the one who gives them the chance to live out their desire to hurt, to destroy. No one will be safe. Your life, Merry…' Gran faltered. 'Your life is linked to an oath made by one of our ancestors. As a witch, you have already come of age, and you are currently the last of your bloodline. You will have to stop the wizard's servant. And… destroy the wizard.' She plucked a tissue from a nearby box and blew her nose. 'I'm so sorry, my darling. I know this must be terribly frightening, but we're all going to try to help you.'

Oaths – wizards – dark magic – Merry shook her head, trying to clear away the haze from her brain, the shreds of sleep. Because surely this was a dream? Surely her grandmother wasn't actually sitting there and telling her that she had somehow ended up being responsible for – for what? Stopping the attacks in Tillingham? Fighting a wizard? Killing him?

'But Gran, this is impossible. I'm not a witch, not a proper one. You know I'm untrained.' Another thought occurred. 'I can't afford to mess up my exams this year either. I haven't got time for this. I just—'

Leo stood, pulling Merry up with him.

'I'm sorry, Gran, but this is crazy. If this situation needs to be dealt with by a witch, then you can sort it out. Or one of your friends. We're leaving.'

'Will the two of you please sit down. Right now.' Gran didn't shout. She didn't raise her voice at all. But for some reason, both of them felt compelled to obey. Merry peeked at Leo's face – he was just as surprised as she was.

'I don't blame you for being angry, Leo, but anger isn't going to help your sister.' Gran paused for a moment, staring at the two of them. 'I think this would be easier if I told you a story. You've heard it before, though you probably won't remember. It's about the King of Hearts.'

Merry did remember, vaguely. It was a scary story: dark and sad. It had given her nightmares. She remembered Mum yelling at Gran about it. One of the many, many minor explosions in her mother's relationship with her grandmother even before they had That Argument.

'I remember a little bit – it was horrible. Wasn't there something about a wizard, and a prince? Or was it a princess? And—'

'And jars. Jars with hearts inside them,' Leo interjected. 'I remember it too. Mum got cross with you.'

'Your mother is always cross about something. The point

is, it's not a made-up fairy story. It's part of our family history. The most important part. The boy in your room…'
She paused to take a sip of tea. 'The boy is the prince. His name is Jack. In many ways, he is the victim of the story. He is also the monster.' Gran frowned. 'Stupid of me. I knew something was happening when the attacks started – you know we like to make sure Tillingham stays mostly free of violence. But I just didn't make the connection. You see, in the story, Jack didn't merely attack people. He killed them. He cut out their hearts.'

'Blimey.'

'Quite. Leo, be a dear and turn on all the lights. There's no sun today, and some things are better not talked about in the dark.'

Leo did as he was told and sat back down.

'Right. Are you sitting comfortably?'

'Not really,' Merry murmured, but Gran ignored her.

'Then I'll begin.' She cleared her throat.

'Once upon a time…'

Once upon a time – because that's how all the best stories start, even the ones that lead to death and darkness and unhappy ever after – there was a kingdom. For the most part it was a soft, green country, of rolling downs and rich fields and fine orchards.

To the south, where the land fell into the sea, the kingdom ended in tall white cliffs, with golden beaches at their feet. And the people of the land loved the sea, and built sturdy boats to fish and sail. But to the north lay steep, razor-backed hills, their lower slopes shrouded in sombre forests. Even in the springtime, none of the people went further into the forests than they had to.

All the land south of the forests was ruled from Helmswick, where the king lived in a great wooden hall built from mighty oak trees. King Wulfric was strong and ambitious, and kept the kingdom safe. He was wise too. Though not quite as wise as he might have been, if his queen had not died so young. But the king's law did not extend into the forests. And because this was the Dark Ages, before men had learnt to believe that magic does not exist, a sorceress lived in the dark heart of the wood. She was just as strong as the king, and just as ambitious, and no one had ever been able to defeat her.

At least, no one up until now...

THEN:

FIVE

THE KINGDOM OF THE SOUTH SAXONS, 498 AD

GWYDION RAN HIS finger under the collar of his tunic, and wished he could stop sweating. He could see the servants and guards looking at him sideways, smirking. He caught the subtle tone of mockery: 'A flagon of ale, *my lord*? Or perhaps some sweetmeats, *my lord*?' It was because he had grown up here. Many of the servants remembered him, and they knew him only as the son of the king's falconer, little more than a boy. To them, he was nobody.

Of course, he had almost been less than nobody. A slave

passed nearby, carrying a load of firewood for the kitchens, the permanent iron collar round his neck advertising his status. If King Wulfric had not freed Gwydion's father, that would have been his fate: a piece of property to be bought and sold, to live and die at the will of Wulfric and the rest of these filthy Saxon usurpers –

Gwydion mastered his anger and forced a smile at the woman who had approached to offer him some bread. After all, his fortunes were about to change.

In the meantime, however, he was sitting in the outer hall, kicking his heels while the king dealt with other matters. The son of an Irish chieftain had arrived earlier. Gwydion had caught a glimpse of him and his companions, sweeping into the palace courtyard: laughing carelessly, sunlight glinting off golden torcs and polished armour, their horses splashed with mud. The Celt was just as tall as Gwydion, strongly built, as blond as Gwydion was dark. Gwydion had disliked him the moment he had laid eyes on him. But he had been waiting so long now; waiting for the day when his worth would finally be acknowledged, when his life would really start. Waiting, and planning, and giving up so much. He could wait a little longer.

Finally, the door to the great hall opened.

Gwydion stood up, adjusted his sword belt and

straightened his shoulders. He walked through the long, vaulted room, past the assembled ranks of knights and captains, up to the dais where the king sat. There he stood stiffly, pulling his cloak forwards to hide the worn patches on his tunic.

The king cleared his throat.

'Gwydion, welcome. And forgive me for the delay in receiving you. But now the court is assembled, to do you honour for the great quest which you undertook and accomplished.' The King looked around at his courtiers, and gestured to a crystal jar that was displayed next to his chair. Inside the jar was a dark, shrivelled mass. 'Behold, my lords, the heart of the Sorceress, cut from her corrupt carcass by the hand of this young man. Truly, Gwydion, I know not how to reward you.'

Murmurs of surprise and disbelief ran around the room.

Gwydion bowed. 'Thank you, Sire. There is only one reward I desire: the hand of the princess I rescued. The reward promised to whomsoever should return her alive to Helmswick.' Gwydion heard the courtiers behind him muttering. He ignored them.

The king picked up the crystal jar, as though to examine its grisly contents more closely. 'To marry the heir to the kingdom – that was the stated reward, was it not?' Wulfric replaced the jar and stood, wincing as he straightened up. 'Come, walk with me a little.' The king, leaning on Gwydion's arm, passed out of the great hall into a smaller private room beyond. The room was dark apart from the bright squares of sunlight on the rush-covered floor, falling from the windows high up in one wall. 'Help me to that chair, Gwydion. Then sit.'

Gwydion fetched a stool from the side of the room and sat near the king, who beckoned to a servant hovering nearby.

'Here.' King Wulfric said, as the servant handed Gwydion a small, cloth-bound package. 'I have been waiting to give this to you.'

The package was surprisingly heavy. Gwydion balanced it on his knees and carefully opened the wrapping. A large gold brooch, fashioned in the shape of a wolf with garnets for eyes, glittered against the dark cloth.

Gwydion smiled. The wolf was the symbol of the royal house.

'Thank you, Sire.' He pinned the brooch to his cloak. 'May I see Edith now? I did not speak to her about our marriage on the journey back to Helmswick, but—'

'Gwydion,' Wulfric raised his hand, interrupting, 'I am afraid the matter is more… complicated than I anticipated.'

Gwydion frowned.

'I see no complication, Sire. I have completed the quest.'

'Yes, yes.' The king paused again. 'But you see, when I offered the reward, I did not expect...' He straightened up. 'The truth is, Gwydion, I did not expect the quest to be completed by one such as you.'

Gwydion felt the blood flame into his cheeks.

'The princes and lords you sent out failed, Sire. Most of them didn't even return.'

'I know. And I would give much to know the details of how you succeeded where they failed.' King Wulfric glanced up at Gwydion from under his brow: – a glance full of speculation – but Gwydion remained silent. 'Still, the ancient law is clear, as is the mood of the council. The heir to the throne must marry one of noble blood. Of noble, Saxon blood.' The King leant forwards awkwardly patted Gwydion on the hand. 'But you can still be a prince, Gwydion. You may marry Audrey. She is only fourteen, but in a year's time—'

'Audrey?' Gwydion clenched his fists. He could barely even remember Audrey. She had only ever been Edith's cousin, an annoying child Gwydion had always done his best to ignore. In Gwydion's universe Audrey was an insignificant, barely visible star. Edith was the sun. He had adored her since they were both children, and she had stopped the steward from beating him, had allowed him to join in her games on the lawns outside the great hall. By the time he was sixteen and Edith was fourteen, he knew he was in love with her. Since then, he had never thought about anyone else. And at some point, he did not remember when, he realised that loving Edith, gaining Edith, would bring him everything else he desired as well.

'I did not kill the Sorceress in order to become a prince. You and the council think me too lowly to take the throne. But I love Edith. I always have done. And she loves me.' He went down on one knee before the king. Wulfric, sick and weak as he was, would not willingly disinherit his only child. Councils could be dealt with. Laws could be amended. Gwydion took a deep breath, tried to steady the quickening of his pulse. Once he and Edith were actually married, everything else could be managed. 'I saved her life, Sire. I risked my own life to bring her back to you. Surely, if she wants to be with me, to give up her claim to the throne, you will not prevent it?'

Wulfric gazed down at him, and Gwydion wondered why the king's eyes were filled with pity.

'I think you had better talk to Edith,' Wulfric said. 'Let her be summoned.' A guard, who had been standing unobtrusively in the shadows, bowed and ran from the room. Gwydion saw two more guards, heavily armed, still waiting by the doorway. Did the king... fear him?

Edith soon appeared. She was pale and thin from her captivity, and Gwydion knew the long sleeves of her gown concealed scars that would never truly fade. The Sorceress had been bleeding her, stealing her life force to work dark magic. But she was still his Edith: her wavy chestnut hair was loose about her shoulders, and the copper colour of her gown brought out the golden flecks in her dark brown eyes. She smiled at him.

'Gwydion, I am so happy to see you.' She went up on tiptoes to throw her arms around his neck, hugging him tightly before stepping back. 'The healers would not let me out of bed until three days ago, and I was not allowed visitors.'

'I know. But now we can be together. And we won't ever be parted again.' Gwydion lifted Edith's hand to his lips and kissed it. 'You need only tell your father what you want.'

Edith's smile faded a little. 'What I want? What I want is for you to be honoured in this country, as you should be, and for you to live in Helmswick, and to be happy. And maybe in time, when Audrey is older...'

Gwydion shook his head, as the first cold tendrils of doubt crept into the dark corners of his mind.

'What does Audrey have to do with anything? You know how to make me happy, Edith. Tell the king you love me. Tell him you renounce the throne so we can be married.'

Edith stepped back, what little colour she had draining from her cheeks. 'But Gwydion, I don't understand. We've been friends for as long as I can remember; more than friends. I don't want to be parted from you. But I cannot – I cannot marry you.'

Friends?

'What did you say?'

'I said, I cannot marry you, Gwydion.'

Gwydion bit his tongue until he tasted blood in his mouth. This was supposed to be his moment of triumph – was the woman he loved about to snatch it away from him?

'Edith, if you still wish to be queen, I will try to understand. But I'm begging you, tell me we can at least still be to each other what we used to be. Tell me that I can live here with you, and we can walk together in the grounds each day, and I can teach you about the flight of birds and the uses of herbs and the movement of the stars. Tell me that you love me.'

Tears started into Edith's eyes.

King Wulfric stepped forwards. 'Gwydion, while you were—'

'No, father – I must tell him.' Edith took Gwydion's hands. 'Before you came to find me, you were away for three years, Gwydion. I was only fifteen when you left. Three years is a long time.'

'I went to seek my fortune. You were never going to marry me as I was.' Gwydion closed his eyes briefly. 'My father died while I was away. Did you know that?'

'I did; he was a good man. Gwydion, I understand why you left. But you did leave. And then, before the Sorceress—' She stopped, shuddering. 'Before I was taken, an Irish prince came to stay here. His name is Aidan. I love you Gwydion; I love you like a brother. But I am *in love* with him.'

Aidan. The image of the tall Celt Gwydion had seen that morning flashed into his mind.

'But I am in love with you, Edith. Did you never realise?'

'No. Because you never told me so, Gwydion.'

'How could I, until I had bettered myself?' Gwydion knew he was shouting, but he didn't care. 'And how did this Aidan have time to come here and – and make love to you, yet not have time to rescue you from the Sorceress?'

'He tried to. He nearly died.'

'I wish with all my heart he had.'

Edith snatched her hands away.

'If I could spare you this pain I would, Gwydion. You have to believe me. I would do almost anything. But I will not marry you.'

'But your father promised—'

'I should not have done so,' Wulfric interrupted. 'Aside from Edith's feelings, it is a good match. Edith has a responsibility to our people. We need allies, especially given the constant attacks of those Kentish thugs—'

'Father!' Edith shook her head, waving a hand to silence him. 'Gwydion, I will always be in your debt. You saved my life. But that does not give you the right to decide how the rest of my life should be lived, or to tell me who to love. I am going to marry Aidan.'

Gwydion stared at Edith; the sunlight from the high windows faded. The floor beneath him seemed to tilt, sending him sprawling against the wall. He covered his mouth with a shaking hand as his stomach churned.

'Gwydion!' Edith took a step towards him, but the king seized her wrist, holding her back.

Years passed in a matter of seconds. Gwydion realised he was shivering; he was cold to the very core of his body.

Slowly, he dragged himself to his feet. Something inside him was changed, suddenly and forever.

'The Sorceress warned me, before I slit her throat. She told me you would betray me.' Gwydion saw the guards draw their swords, but he ignored them. 'I vowed to love you, Edith, to protect you forever. I swore it over my mother's grave, sealed it by writing the runes in my blood, and the vow binds me. I cannot physically harm you. But your father, your—' Gwydion's mouth twisted as he spat out the word, '—lover, they are a different matter.'

'Guards, seize him!' Wulfric drew his own sword, but Gwydion waved a hand, drawing a complicated symbol, forming air into bright lines of fire that hung there for a moment before fading. The guards collapsed and the key turned in the door behind them.

Gwydion advanced on the king. 'Did you think I had merely been wandering the kingdom these past three years, wasting my time learning how to wield a sword or make songs about courtship? Did you think I could have defeated the Sorceress with nothing more than armour and courage?' Gwydion drew another symbol in the air, and the king bellowed and threw his sword away as the metal glowed red-hot. 'Fool. I have been using my time much more productively.'

'Gwydion,' began Wulfric, 'you must—'

'No. I don't want to hear the word "must" from you. I don't want to hear any more words from you.' Another symbol: the king dropped to his knees, clawing at his throat, his mouth opening and closing soundlessly.

Edith backed into the corner of the room, her eyes wide.

'Gwydion, what have you done to yourself?'

Gwydion didn't answer, but moved forwards until he was only separated from Edith by a hairsbreadth. He tilted her chin upwards.

'So beautiful. How was I to know that such a face could conceal such a heart? A heart just as black as the one now sealed in a jar next to your father's throne.'

'Are you—' Gwydion saw Edith's throat convulse as she swallowed hard, 'are you going to kill me?'

'I cannot. But I swear, that as you have snatched away everything I love, everything I hoped for, so I will take away what you love most.' Gwydion drew out the small dagger he carried at his waist and slashed down across the palm of his hand. He pressed his hand to Edith's chest, smearing the blood across her skin. 'You will not know the form of your punishment, you will not know the day or the hour, but eventually my retribution will find you,

Edith. And then you will suffer, just as I am suffering now. You will taste the bitterness of despair.'

He ran to a smaller door that let out into the courtyard behind the hall. There were horses stabled there, as he remembered. The guards and stable hands presented no difficulties, and soon he was outside the walls of the keep.

Gwydion rode without direction or thought for hours, without resting or trying to find food, hoping that bodily exhaustion would counteract the agony of his mind. When he finally realised that he needed some sort of plan, his initial instinct was to head south, to one of the coastal villages. From there he could make his way across the sea to the Kingdom of the Franks, or maybe to the Celtic tribal lands farther west. But as he rode away from the downs, the folds of the hills forced him east. A little before sunset he came to the marshes that formed the eastern border of the kingdom: a flat, treacherous landscape, carved by criss-crossing streams and dotted with stagnant swamps. On the edge of the marshes he dismounted. If he went any further this way, it would be easier to travel on foot.

Gwydion tied his horse to a tree and sat on the ground, trying to force himself to make a decision. The whole plan of his life, for as long as he'd had a plan, had been built around the idea that Edith loved him, and that she would be his if only he could find a way to show he was more than just the son of a servant. And with Edith would come status, wealth, power. Now his plans had proved no more than a fantasy, what was he to do with himself? He could still turn south and try to reach to the coast. Or he could go on into the marshes, and return to the only possible home that now remained to him: the hidden hall of his master, Ranulf, an old and powerful wizard who had taught him his magic. Gwydion had left with Ranulf's predictions of failure ringing in his ears, and without permission. It was possible Ranulf would try to kill him on sight.

The last shreds of Gwydion's pride pushed him to turn away and head for the sea. But the oath he had sworn to take vengeance on Edith – to fulfil that oath, he needed to complete his training.

He let the horse go free, and stumbled forwards into the marshes.

Gwydion reached the house just before dusk. It was a long, low building, built on stilts hammered into the boggy ground; Ranulf had placed a charm upon the wood to stop it rotting. Gwydion hesitated as he approached the door, but not for long; he had not eaten or drunk for nearly two days, and thirst drove him forwards. The door opened at his touch. He fell upon his knees.

'Well, boy?' Ranulf was standing in front of him, wheezing, even wider and more misshapen than Gwydion remembered. 'So you have returned to me, like the filthy dog you are?'

Gwydion risked looking up; if Ranulf had decided to kill him, he would not be bothering with questions. But there might be punishment. And that Gwydion would have to endure, if he wanted to learn the darkest of Ranulf's arts. He braced himself, expecting pain.

But to his surprise, Ranulf laughed.

'That princess of yours did indeed treat you like a dog, did she not? A fitting punishment for a disobedient apprentice. You look like you have suffered enough; for now, at least. Come.'

Ranulf led Gwydion into the house, set some wine and bread on the table and waved him to a chair.

'So, boy, it is eight months since you left me, so full of your own plans and abilities. What do you have to say for yourself?'

Gwydion looked down at his hands. 'You were right, Master. You were right about everything.'

'Tell us then. Tell us what happened.'

Gwydion cleared his throat, and began describing the weeks he had spent searching for the Sorceress in the great northern forest. Eventually he had found her, living in an ancient stone tower surrounded by a huge hedge of black holly trees: black bark, black berries, dark green leaves with thick, sharp, spines. He'd also found the bodies of some of the men who had already tried to break through the hedge. The branches had blunted their swords, and the spines scratched them and plunged them into a poisoned sleep, a perpetual night from which they never awoke. Inside the hedge, the tower was guarded by three enormous ravens, with beaks sharp enough to pierce chainmail and rend flesh. Gwydion had spent another two months practising the runes that would allow him to bend the holly trees and the ravens to his will, before he attempted the tower.

'I caused the hedge to open before me, and the ravens to become docile. After that, the Sorceress presented no difficulty: she was old and weak and had no other defence in place. Her magic was mostly that of potions and curses. She was attempting to work blood magic, to link the power of the shadow realm to a human body and thus create a dark servant, but she had not the skill.'

Ranulf grunted. 'The magic and entities of that realm

are evil and full of cunning. To summon such a one, and keep it housed within another's form, that requires more than blood magic. Great mastery and great sacrifice are needed. How did you kill her?'

'I cut out her heart, since I needed evidence of my deed. Then I searched for the princess. Edith was very...' Gwydion faltered for a moment. 'Very ill. We had to journey slowly on our return to Helmswick.'

'Hmm. Go on.'

'I don't wish to—'

'I told you to continue.' Ranulf lifted a hand, threatening.

'The king promised Edith's hand in marriage to whomever rescued her. But he is a cheat and a liar. And so is she. During our childhood, before I left to come here – she made me think she loved me. But it was all mockery. She is to marry another.'

Ranulf laughed, the same unpleasant cackle Gwydion remembered.

'What did I tell you, boy? Women are all the same: false and cunning. Their—' a fit of coughing shook him, forcing him to break off. Gwydion refilled Ranulf's ale mug and pushed it towards him. 'Their love is like a shallow pond, liable to dry up if they are not constantly showered with compliments and gifts.' He spat a gobbet of blood on to the floor. 'All love is but love of self, a woman's love doubly so. You should be thankful this Edith has found another fool to make miserable.'

Gwydion sat in silence. He didn't feel thankful.

Ranulf watched him for a while.

'And what would you now, boy?'

'I wish to complete my training. If you are willing, Master.'

'For what purpose? And do not tell me it is for love of me, or for the love of learning.' He sat back in his chair, waiting.

Gwydion thought a long time before he answered.

'I wish to complete my training not for love, but for hatred. I want to become powerful enough to take revenge upon the woman who spurned me. A revenge so complete that she will curse the day she was born. I want to make her suffer.'

'Very well.' Ranulf held out his hand, waiting for Gwydion to kiss the ornate gold and sapphire ring he wore on his middle finger. 'I will continue your training, boy. I will teach you the only true way to take and keep a woman's heart, or a man's: through blood and fire and dark magic. But there will be a price to pay.'

'Of course, Master.'

'Another six years, maybe five if you pay attention and work hard, and then, when the opportunity arises, you will be ready.'

'Ready for what?'

'Ready to create a monster that will serve your purpose. Ready to create a King of Hearts...'

For five years Gwydion studied with Ranulf. Every day he gained in knowledge; every day, lost something of that which had made him human.

King Wulfric, sick and frail as he was, did not long survive Edith's return, and she became queen.

Edith grieved for her father, and wondered often what had become of Gwydion. And yet, Aidan filled her heart with joy, and the kingdom prospered, and in the fullness of time the young king and queen were blessed with a child. A baby prince, who might one day become a king...

SIX

EDITH SLID AWAY from the warmth of her still-sleeping husband, threw a fur-lined mantle around her shoulders and crept into the room next door. It was not yet dawn; the sky outside was black. But by the firelight she could see the nurse, rocking the baby's cradle and singing softly. The woman jumped up as Edith entered.

'Your Highness. Did I wake you?'

'No. Is he asleep?'

'Just settled again, my lady.'

Edith leant over the cradle and gazed down at her son. Jack already seemed to have changed so much from the tiny baby she had held in her arms only six weeks ago. Edith loved to watch him while he slept, his mouth open in a tiny 'o', as if he were surprised, his little fingers clenching and unclenching as he dreamt. She had been so afraid throughout her pregnancy, so terrified that Gwydion would appear at any moment and do something to harm the baby. But Jack had arrived in the world unscathed and perfect. Edith's happiness would have been complete, if only her father were still alive.

Jack stirred, and the nurse went to pick him up.

'No,' Edith waved her away. 'I'll take him.' She wrapped a fold of her mantle around the baby and carried him back into her chamber. There was no point in trying to go back to sleep. She settled herself and Jack on one of the wide windowsills, opened the shutter a little, and waited for the sun to rise.

A while later, after the darkness of the eastern sky had faded to grey, Edith felt Aidan's hands on her shoulders. He wrapped another fur around her. 'You're going to catch cold.'

'No, I won't.' Edith glanced up at her husband. She could see the concern in his dark-grey eyes: he always looked at her as though she was somehow ethereal, something fragile and precious that might be snatched away from him at any moment. Sometimes Edith found it suffocating. But it was also one of the reasons she loved him. She put her hand on top of his and looked back out of the window. The land outside was swathed in mist. Helmswick felt shut in, sitting on its hill above the woodland and farmland of the Weald like an island cut off from the wider world.

'I don't like this weather.' She hugged Jack tighter.

'Sea mist, that's all. It will burn off soon enough.' Aidan dropped a kiss on the top of her head. 'I must speak with the steward before our guests arrive. Don't forget to eat something.' He paused. 'And do not sit there worrying. Today will be a good day, I'm sure of it.'

Edith nodded. But she could not escape the sensation that something was waiting for her, out there in the mist. As she watched from her window she could see the torches being lit on her father's burial mound, pale smudges of light flaring through the fog. And then she heard the summoning bell, muffled, calling all to the ceremony. Her servants came in to help her dress. It was time.

Hours later, the great hall was filled with noise and light, heat and colour. The rulers of the neighbouring kingdoms, as well as all the nobles of the land, had gathered to celebrate the naming of the Prince of the South Saxons. All were dressed in their finest costumes, vying to outdo one another in splendour. All except one woman, simply clothed yet sitting in a place of honour, three small children clustered around her. Mistress Anwen was a witch, and had been a devoted friend of Edith's mother. Until five years ago Anwen had lived at Helmswick, watching over Edith, guiding her as she grew. Aidan – whose people had embraced the new faith of the Christians – had not wanted to invite her. Edith had listened to all his arguments against witchcraft, and then invited her anyway.

Now, Edith caught the older woman's eye and smiled, but it was an effort; she felt herself flagging. The woollen overdress she wore was beautiful: elaborately embroidered with intricate designs in gold thread. But it was heavy, and her tightly-pinned hair was giving her a headache. She could not wait for the day to be over. Still, the christening ceremony had passed successfully. Jack had hardly cried at all, and now there was only the gift-giving to endure. As a new mother, she had decided she could leave presiding over the feast to Aidan. She glanced up at him and found he was watching her.

'You're pale, Edith,' he murmured. 'Do you feel unwell?'

'No. Only a little tired.'

He squeezed her hand. The steward continued with the presentation of gifts; already a table to one side was almost engulfed in a pile of gold jewellery, silver cups and bowls, fine cloths and barrels of Frankish wine.

'From the King of Northumbria: a gold torc in a casket of silver. From the Kingdom of Gwynedd: two drinking horns with silver rims.' And on, and on. Until, just when Edith thought she could not stand for another moment, the list ended. Aidan stepped forwards.

'We thank you all, friends and neighbours, for your generous gifts to our son. And now, as is customary, we hope you will honour our hall by joining us for—'

But the end of Aidan's sentence was drowned in an enormous crash that reverberated through the room. For a second Edith thought a thunderstorm had started, but then she looked at the opposite end of the hall: the huge, carved doors had been thrown open so violently they had broken from their hinges. A number of those standing nearest the doors had been struck down; there were screams and cries as people tried to free themselves from the wreckage. And standing there, in the middle of the devastation, was Gwydion.

'Edith, get behind me!' Aidan had jumped up and drawn

his sword. 'Defend the queen! Now!' The elite royal guards started to force a passage through the milling guests, forming a shield-wall in front of the dais where Aidan and Edith were standing. Edith snatched Jack from the nurse and clutched him to her tightly.

Silence fell as Gwydion walked through the hall.

For Edith, it was like looking at a ghost. He was in many ways the same young man she remembered; less gaunt, less wooden in his movements, but still with the same shock of thick, dark hair, the same slightly uneven gait. But he was not the same. For a start, he was dressed entirely in black. Edith remembered Gwydion as something of a peacock, taking a childlike delight in brightly-coloured dyes. The only ornament Edith could see now was a large gold ring, set with a sapphire, glinting on Gwydion's left hand. His mouth and eyes were marked with such lines of suffering and cruelty as to make his features almost unrecognisable to her.

'I pray forgiveness for my late arrival, your majesties. I had hoped to be here in time for the naming of the young prince.' Gwydion halted in front of the guards and held out his hands, palm up. 'Surely, you cannot think I mean to harm the child? See: I am unarmed.'

'What do you want, wizard's pupil?' Aidan shouted.

'Edith has told me what you are, what you threatened. You need no weapon to work evil upon us.'

'You know me, do you? That is good. For I know you too, Aidan Whiteblade, Aidan of the flashing sword. Who has not heard of your exploits? A prince of Ireland. And now king over the South Saxons, since you took from me the woman who was promised me, the woman who owes me her very life.'

'I do not choose to trade words with you. Leave my hall now, or die.'

Gwydion laughed. 'Oh, I think not. I am a pupil no longer.' He leapt back and with his hands made a complex movement in the air: sinuous arcs of ruby light. Everyone – apart from Edith, who had already seen his skill with fire runes – gasped in surprise; some screamed, and started to run from the hall. The royal guards collapsed, unconscious.

Edith saw Aidan raise his sword and begin to run at Gwydion, and she grabbed at his arm. 'No, Aidan. Stay away from him. You must look after Jack, keep him safe.' She kissed Jack, passed him to Aidan, and turned to face Gwydion.

'Here I am, Gwydion. Punish me. Kill me, if you wish. But I beg you, for the sake of the love we once bore each other, do not hurt my family.'

'Edith, do not be afraid.' Gwydion smiled at her, but Edith thought the smile a mockery of how he had once looked. 'I am not here to hurt your son. I am here to give him a gift.'

Edith stepped back, placing herself directly between Gwydion and Aidan.

'I want nothing from you, Gwydion. My only desire is that you should be whole again, free of this madness that has seized you.'

'But I have not told you what my gift is yet. And it is a great gift. When your son reaches his eighteenth year, I am going to take him for my apprentice.'

Edith's heart was hammering in her chest, so hard she thought it must surely smash through her ribcage. 'Gwydion, no. Please don't—'

'And that is not all.' He wrote another fire rune in the air, but this one was sharp and spiky and glowed white. It did not fade as the other runes had done, but hung like frozen lightening in the darkness of the hall. Gwydion stretched out his arm towards the baby. 'He will be an instrument of mercy. He will free your people from the pain and madness of love. He will be the King of Hearts, and all who love shall fear him.' The fire rune shone with blinding light then exploded into a hundred glowing embers that fell on to Jack's skin before melting away.

Edith screamed.

Gwydion disappeared.

Three hours later, the uproar had subsided a little. Many of the guests had fled as soon as their servants could be roused, anxious to escape a kingdom that had clearly fallen under a terrible curse. Some had stayed, either from friendship or because they thought it might be easier to negotiate some advantageous treaty while the South Saxons were under attack from within. Aidan had ordered the household knights to assemble their companies, but as yet no target had been found for them to attack. No one had seen Gwydion since he had laid the curse on Jack, and no one knew where he lived.

There was a knock at the door of Edith's chamber.

'May I come in, my lady?'

It was Mistress Anwen and her three daughters. Anwen put down the youngest, a pretty, green-eyed girl of about two, and pulled the queen into her arms.

'My unhappy Edith. To think that Gwydion should have become such a fiend.'

'Can you help me, Anwen?'

The older woman shook her head.

'I cannot break a curse such as this. My magic is protective, and Gwydion… It is many years since I have seen such power.'

Edith dashed a tear away from her cheek, as her last hope faded.

'Jack is lost then.'

Anwen guided Edith to the bed and made her sit down.

'Do not give up all hope. Three things I can offer you. First, advice. Send the child away somewhere secret, somewhere he can grow up hidden from Gwydion, and without fear of what is to come. Second, a blessing. Where is the baby?'

The nurse passed Jack to Anwen.

'Poor little one, to have such trouble thrust upon you.' Jack blinked up at her and smiled. 'I foresee suffering in your life, Jack. But there will also be love, and those who love you will never abandon you.' She traced her fingers across the baby's forehead and chest – as though marking him with invisible symbols – before putting him back into Edith's arms. 'The third thing I can offer, Edith, is a promise. If in time I see a way to help you, to break the curse or to defeat Gwydion, I swear that you will have my aid. I will bind my daughters to this promise also.'

Edith glanced at the three girls. They were sitting in the corner of the room; the eldest – a blonde child Edith judged to be no more than five – seemed to be telling a story to the other two.

'But they are so young, Anwen. It doesn't seem fair…'

'They will grow. And they will be powerful, I believe. Maybe they will be able to help you, even if I cannot.' Anwen stood and kissed Edith on the forehead. 'I owed your mother a great debt, which I never was able to repay. Let me—'

'Mother?'

The middle daughter was tugging at Anwen's skirt, her dark eyes wide and full of puzzlement. Anwen sighed.

'What ails you, Nia?'

'I can see a girl. She has a sword in one hand, and parchment in the other, but she is wearing hose. Why is she dressed as a boy?'

Edith looked around the room, but there was no one there apart from Anwen and the servants.

'Nia sees things the rest of us do not, my lady. Things far off, and things that have not yet come to pass.' Anwen shrugged and put her arm around the child. 'A gift, supposedly, though sometimes I wonder.'

Edith agreed. To know the misery that lay in store,

and not be able to avoid it – that wasn't a gift. It was a burden.

When Anwen left, Edith sent the last of the servants away and shut the door. She was too exhausted now to do anything other than lie on her bed, her baby asleep next to her.

'But we don't even know what Gwydion's curse means,' Aidan was saying. 'Perhaps he was just trying to frighten us?'

'No. He means to hurt me. He means, somehow, to take Jack away from us. When he turns eighteen, we will lose him.'

Aidan stood up again and picked up his sword, weighing it in his hand.

'I will not allow that to happen. There must be some way of defeating this – this monster.'

Edith closed her eyes, remembering Gwydion' face when she had told him she would not marry him. He looked as though his whole world had been ripped apart and stitched back together in a pattern he no longer recognised. 'Poor Gwydion. What have I done to him? What has he done to himself?'

'Do not pity him! He has free will, like all men. He

chose to become what he is now. We must send scouts to all corners of the kingdom; somewhere Gwydion is lurking, and I will find him. He is probably somewhere remote, maybe on one of the islands off the coast, or in the shadow of the hills...'

Edith's mind wandered. Somewhere remote, Aidan had said. Somewhere remote. She remembered Anwen's advice.

'That is what we must do with Jack,' she said.

'What?'

'We cannot protect him here. We have to send him away.'

'Well,' Aidan began, 'we could send him to Ireland, to my brother. Or to your cousin Audrey in Northumberland.'

'No. It has to be somewhere no one would expect him to be. Somewhere his identity can be hidden. And even he,' Edith paused, as the implications of Anwen's suggestion became clear to her, 'he cannot know who he is. It is the only way to stop Gwydion laying hands on him.'

'But Edith,' Aidan was frowning, 'that means he cannot know who we are, either. We will never be able to visit him, to talk to him...' He sat down heavily, covering his face with his hands. 'He will grow up without us.'

Edith stared at the hanging above the bed. It showed

the emblem of her family: a great wolf, silver and grey, its tawny eyes gazing back at her.

I will be like the wolf, and do what I must to protect my cub. Even though I can feel pieces of my heart freezing away.

'It will be hard, Aidan. Almost impossible. But if Jack is safe, and alive…'

She picked up the baby, put him in Aidan's arms and put her arms around both of them, trying to chisel this moment into her memory. All the tiny details: the translucent creaminess of Jack's skin, his tiny fingernails, the way he fit so perfectly in the crook of his father's elbow.

'He looks like you, Aidan.'

'But he has your eyes.'

The fire burned lower.

'But, if we do this – *if* – where can we send him?' Aidan asked.

'To Hilda. She used to be my nurse, and she cannot yet be forty. She and her husband live down by the coast.'

'And you trust her?'

'I would trust her with my life.' Edith looked down at her son, still sleeping peacefully in Aidan's arms. 'Jack will be happy there.'

'And if we can find Gwydion quickly, we may not need to send him away for long.'

'No. I will pray to your god, and to mine, that we will be able to bring him home again soon.'

And so Jack was sent away, to a village perched high on the white cliffs and a childless couple who quickly loved him as their own. King Aidan scoured the country for Gwydion, but the wizard had left no traces. Queen Edith had other children and Jack was not spoken of. Still, her people whispered about the sorrow that clung to the young queen like a shadow.

The years passed, harvest followed harvest, and Jack grew into a boy. Finally, his eighteenth birthday came and went, and Gwydion did not appear. The king and queen, believing the danger to have lifted, made preparations to bring their first-born home again...

SEVEN

'JACK? JACK! WHERE are you, lad?'

Jack sighed. He had just got comfortable, lying on the sand in the shade of the cliffs, and now he was going to have to climb back up to the farm at the top. The whole plan had been to work fast so he could have a sleep before the rest of the day's labour.

'Jack! If I have to come down there...'

There was no help for it.

'Coming, father.' He picked up the sacks of seaweed and carefully made his way up the steep track cut into the side of the cliff.

'Ah, good.' Edwin took the sacks from Jack's back. 'Rufus can spread this on the field, and we will have a fine harvest in the fall. Have you eaten?'

'Yes, father.'

'Then you can go and wash. Father Brendan is waiting in the house. I hope you've been practising your letters, and learning your history.'

'But Ned and I were going to go hunting this morning. If I catch a couple of rabbits, mother will be able make that pie you enjoy so much.'

For a moment Jack thought he was going to get away with it; he could see his father wavering.

'Well....' But Edwin shook his head. 'No. Hunting later. Learning first.'

'But why? None of my friends have to sit with Father Brendan and listen to him go on and on about—' Jack stopped. His father had that look in his eye, the look that meant: *If you don't do what you are told, I will tell your mother, and then we will see.* He sighed. 'As you wish, father.'

'You're a good lad, Jack. I know there's much you don't understand as yet, but one day soon it will all become clear. Off with you now.'

Jack hurried away. Recently, his father had often seemed

to come out with odd references to the future, to some revelation that would answer all Jack's questions. Given that Jack's questions were mostly along the lines of 'When will I be able to leave the village?' he suspected sometimes that the 'revelation' was just a delaying tactic – like their insistence that he still needed lessons. Jack could not see the point of reading, or learning about politics. What he really wanted was to go to Helmswick, fight for the king and win his own land. He'd listened to the heroic tales as a child: Beowulf defeating the monster and gaining renown and treasure from his lord. That was what he dreamt about. That, and winning the hand of a beautiful maiden.

Jack scowled and kicked at the rushes growing at the edge of the nearby stream. A cormorant squawked angrily and took off into the air. His dreams of glory were pointless; he was bound to end up a carpenter, just like his father. As for all the nonsense about a future revelation, maybe it was just a sign of old age. His parents were a good twenty years older than the parents of all his friends. An unlooked-for gift, his mother called him.

The house came into view. It was a low, comfortable building, with a separate area for the animals, and even two separate sleeping chambers. Jack sometimes wondered how his father had been able to afford to build such a house. Edwin was a good carpenter, but he made simple furniture for the other villagers, not expensive items for the king. Maybe this was another of the mysteries that would one day become clear.

Jack was just about to go into the house when he stopped, brought up short by the sight of a girl planting seeds in the garden of the house opposite.

'Good day, Winifred.'

A lot of the girls in the village liked Jack. He used to hear them as he walked around the narrow lanes, whispering about how strong and handsome he was, then he would wink at them and they would dissolve into giggles. He had to admit, he'd kissed quite a few of them too – when the elders weren't watching. But Winifred... Jack was never sure whether she liked him or not. She was the niece of the thane, besides being the prettiest girl in the village. She was so beautiful that Jack's brain seemed to seize up when he looked at her, all his usual wit and charm evaporating like rain on a summer's day. Jack had hardly ever tried to speak to Winifred, let alone kiss her.

'Good day, Jack.' She smiled at him as she stood up, and Jack could feel the hot blood turning his face red. 'Been on the beach, have you?'

'Yes.' Jack ran a hand through his blond hair and tried desperately to think of something else to say. 'We needed seaweed for the field, so I thought… the beach…'

Why? Why did I say that? Where else would I get seaweed? She's going to think I'm an idiot.

But Winifred just laughed, and put her hands on her hips, and looked Jack up and down. 'You've grown very tall, Jack.'

Jack stood up straighter.

'Maybe a bit too tall.'

Jack slouched again. 'Well, I am eighteen now. I mean, I probably won't grow any more.' He paused for a moment, chewing on his bottom lip, before taking a deep breath. 'Winifred, I was hoping—'

'Jack! Father Brendan is waiting.'

Jack could not believe it: his mother was leaning out of the window behind him. If Winifred had not been there, Jack would have sworn. As it was, he had to bite his tongue.

'I have to go.'

'Don't worry, Jack. I will still be here later. Probably.'

Jack went into the house and met his mother in the main room.

'Why did you shout at me in front of Winifred? I was

going to ask her…' he hesitated. 'Well, I suppose it doesn't matter.' He looked down at his hands for a moment; his palms and long fingers were covered with calluses from sawing and shaping wood. 'Mother, do you think Winifred would ever agree to marry someone like me?'

A fierce light came into Hilda's eyes. 'You are good enough for any woman, and I will stick a needle into any man who says otherwise. Winifred would be lucky to have you. You're the cleverest lad in the village.'

Jack smiled at his mother. He could never be cross with her for long. 'Well, that's true. And the most handsome. And the tallest.'

Hilda laughed and patted Jack on the cheek. 'Of course.' Her smile faded. 'As for Winifred, she is a girl who knows her own value. And you do not really know her at all. I think, Jack dear, you are in love with her face.'

'But it is such a face, Mother.' Jack sighed. 'You don't think the thane will allow her to pledge herself to the son of a carpenter?'

'I think perhaps there would be difficulties, though maybe not for the reasons you suspect.' She pulled Jack into a hug. 'Soon, the path you are meant to take will become clearer.'

Jack groaned. 'That's what father keeps saying.'

'And he is right. Now go, have your lessons before that troublesome priest eats me out of hearth and home.'

There was no time for rabbit hunting even after Jack had finished his lessons: his father had been summoned to repair one of the thane's barns, so Jack had to chop more wood, ready to be made into planks. He channelled his frustration into each stroke of the axe.

All this nonsense about things becoming clear – chop – *they are deliberately trying to hold me back* – chop – *to stop me from leaving* – chop – *Leofric is working on the lord's estate* – chop – *Ned is betrothed* – chop – *even Osric, who has a face full of spots, is getting married* – chop – *and my parents say I need more skills* – chop – *they just want to stop me ever being a man* –

'Ow!' The log had flown sideways and dropped on to Jack's foot. 'Ow, ow, ow!' He hopped over to a tree stump and sat down.

'Are you injured, lad?'

Jack glanced up. A mail-clad man on a horse – a nobleman – was looking down at him. The man was grinning, and Jack narrowed his eyes, but he still stood up: there were more knights, at least ten, waiting further down the lane.

'I am not hurt, my lord. If you are looking for the thane's house, it is further through the village, where the land rises.'

'No, I am seeking one Edwin, a carpenter. Do you know him?'

Jack frowned and picked up his axe. What did these men want?

'He is not here at present, but I am his son. Perhaps I can find him, if you will tell me your business with him.'

The grin fell from the man's face. He leapt down from the saddle and knelt in front of Jack. The other horsemen, seeing his action, did the same.

'My name is Harold Aethelson, and I lay my sword at your service. When all becomes clear, I hope you will forgive me, my lord.'

Jack thought: *Am I going mad?* 'When all becomes clear?' He shook his head. 'Have you been talking to my parents?'

'Jack, dear, did you finish—' His mother walked out of the house, and saw the knights. 'Oh. Already?'

Jack stared at her. Hilda looked as if she were about to cry, but she didn't seem surprised.

The knight got up. 'We are come, Mistress. And we must away again quickly. Tonight we lie at the king's hunting lodge, but it will take us at least three days to reach Helmswick.'

Jack put his arm around Hilda's shoulders. 'Mother, what's happening. Why are you going to Helmswick?'

'I'm not going, Jack. You must run to the thane's house and find your father.'

'But what shall I tell him?'

'Tell him—' Hilda's voice broke, and she threw her arms around Jack's neck. 'Tell him you are leaving us.'

Edwin had refused to answer any of Jack's questions about what was happening; he too seemed saddened but unsurprised by the arrival of the knights. When Jack and Edwin got back to the house they found the window shutters closed against the curious stares of the neighbours. Inside, Hilda was dashing about, finding clothes and other items and placing them in a small wooden chest. At the same time she was making some of Jack's favourite apple cakes.

'Hilda, leave the packing. I do not think Jack will need any of those clothes anyway, not where he is going,' Edwin said.

'But where am I going?' Jack plucked a pair of shoes

out of Hilda's hands. 'Will you please tell me what is happening?'

Hilda and Edwin looked at each other. Then Hilda burst into tears.

'Come now, sweetheart, we knew this day would arrive eventually.' Edwin put an arm round his wife. 'The truth is, Jack – in my heart, and in your mother's heart, you are our child. And I swear you always will be. But, by blood – by blood, you are not related to us.'

Jack shook his head. 'No. That's impossible.' He looked at his mother, but she said nothing; just dabbed at her eyes with a cloth.

There was a bracelet tied round Jack's wrist. His mother had woven the strap and his father had carved three wooden beads through which the strap was threaded: one bead for Hilda, one for Edwin, one for Jack. His family, or so he had thought.

Jack stepped backwards, away from his parents. 'Then all this is a lie.'

He ran out through the back door of the house, ignoring his father's voice, and climbed a tree that stood nearby. From here he could see the sea, taste the salt in the air, hear the gulls wheeling and calling above the cliffs. He could slip past the knights waiting in the road, go across country and be on a boat sailing to Frankia by tomorrow morning…

The wind shifted, and instead of the sea he could hear his mother weeping quietly. The sound shamed him. She and his father loved him. Jack knew that was the truth, whatever deceit they had been forced into.

And here am I, behaving like a child who cannot get his own way?

Jack went back into the house. His parents were sitting by the hearth. 'Who am I, father?'

Edwin glanced at Hilda; she nodded.

'Well, Jack… you are the son of the king and queen: John Aetheling, their firstborn. You are a prince. You will likely one day be king.'

Jack laughed, but the sound died in his throat as he realised his father was serious. Aetheling was the title given to potential heirs to the throne. Using that title – it wasn't something his father would do in jest.

'If I am their son, why did they send me away?'

'Your life was in danger,' Hilda replied, 'and now the danger has passed.' Hilda took Jack's hands in hers. 'Trust the queen, Jack. I was her majesty's nurse, many long years ago, and I love her almost as well as I love you.'

This comforted Jack a little; his mother would not love anybody unworthy of being loved. And now he thought of what this might mean: a chance to leave the village, to adventure...

A thought occurred, and Jack smiled a little. Winifred's uncle was bound to let her marry him now.

'You've grown into a man,' said his father. 'You must ride out to meet your destiny.'

A hour later, Jack was sitting astride a large grey horse, trying to understand his feelings as he waved goodbye to his parents and to Winifred, and trying to remember what he had learnt in the handful of riding lessons the thane's steward had given him. He did not feel very much like a man: surely a man should not feel this torn, excited about the future but also grieving for that left behind?

As soon as they'd ridden out of the village, Harold started talking to him about Helmswick, about the king and queen and his brothers, and what life would be like for him now. Jack knew the man meant well – he had a kind face – but the weight of so much instruction bore down on him like the sea. All he really wanted was to be left in peace, with his own thoughts.

Eventually, they came to a thick band of trees that grew across the top of the downs. Harold rode ahead; he said he had to make sure of the route, but Jack heard one of the other knights mutter something about outlaws. Jack looked around him with more interest, and surreptitiously tested the weight of the sword Harold had given him. It was still early in the year, and the trees were only just coming into leaf, but they were dense enough that only a few glimmers of sunlight breached the canopy, and the undergrowth on either side of the path was in deep shadow.

After a few minutes the party came to a halt. Jack nudged his horse forwards until he had caught up with Harold.

'What's the matter? Why have we stopped?'

'I'm uneasy, lad. I mean, my lord. I know these woods, and it's too quiet. There should be birdsong, animals – but there's nothing. Just this – silence.'

'Can we go back and find a way around?'

'We could, but it would take us far out of our way. We might take the road through the western Weald, but we would not reach the hunting lodge tonight.' Harold peered up and down the path. 'I think – I think we should go on. The lodge is just the other side of the trees. But be wary. There may be worse things than wolves in this forest.'

They rode on in silence with Jack now in the centre

of the company. After what seemed an age the rider at the front gave a shout of relief. Harold turned to Jack and smiled.

'See, we have nearly reached the end of the trees: just another half-mile or so. And from there it is an easy ride down to—'

There was a scream from behind them.

Jack swung round in his saddle.

A huge, brown-pelted wolf had dragged one of the knights from his horse; the beast had its jaws clamped round the man's shoulder and was shaking his body back and forth. More wolves – at least twenty, all different shades and sizes – were poised nearby, growling, teeth bared. And in the centre of them stood a man clothed in black, his thick, dark hair streaked with grey.

'It is the wizard,' cried Harold. 'Attack! Attack!'

The knights yelled and turned their horses, spurring them back towards the snarling wolves as the animals leapt forward to meet them. 'My lord, you must fly. Follow the path – it will bring you to the lodge.'

'But I can help,' Jack said. 'I can—'

'No! We cannot defeat him. We can only give you time to escape. Go!' Harold urged his horse forwards. The knights were hacking at the wolves with their swords, shouting at each other, trying to organise a defence, but they were outnumbered. Another horse was dragged to the ground, whinnying in terror, and Jack heard the scrape of claws on armour as its rider disappeared beneath a surge of fur and fangs.

Think, Jack, think.

These were not normal wolves. Jack could see the wizard moving his hands, as though he was directing their attack.

You cannot leave these men here to die.

He galloped towards the lodge, but at the last minute he turned off the path into the forest and rode back through the trees until he was close to where the knights were fighting. Abandoning his horse, he crept along as quietly as possible. Things were not going well: only Harold and two other knights were still standing, and they could not get past the wolves to get close to the wizard. The silent forest was now filled with the groans of dying men and animals.

Jack gasped. There was a wolf lying in front of him, but it seemed to be dead. Something glinted in the shadows, and Jack knelt down to get a closer look. The remains of a gold embroidered belt were fastened around the wolf's middle – the sort of belt a wealthy man might wear. But why in the name of all the gods would a wolf be wearing man's clothing?

A yell of pain reclaimed his attention. Whatever this evil was, the wizard was its source. That was where Jack had to strike.

Jack crept on past the battling knights and wolves, past the wizard, back in the direction they had come from. He drew his sword, wished he had brought his axe with him instead, and stepped out on to the path.

Two more knights were dragged to the ground, their screams cut short as blood sprayed across the clearing. Only Harold was left now, facing more than half a dozen wolves. He must have seen Jack, but he did not betray him, and the wizard still did not turn around. Jack crept closer and closer – raised his sword in both hands – sliced downwards –

Harold cried out and fell beneath the wolves. Jack's blow went wide, catching the wizard on the shoulder. The next moment his sword glowed red hot in his hands and he dropped it with a yell. The wizard spun around, pulled a knife out of his belt and held it to Jack's throat.

'Kill me then, you coward,' Jack panted. 'Or I will see you hanged for the deaths of these men.'

The man smiled.

'No. I don't think I will kill you today, Jack.'

The last thing Jack saw was the wizard writing in the air, lines of red fire pouring from his fingertips…

When he regained consciousness, Jack was somewhere dark and cold, his wrists and ankles tightly bound, propped up against a hard surface. He could not tell how much time had passed: hours, or days. Someone with a lantern was shaking his shoulder. Jack screwed up his eyes against the light as his memory returned.

'Who are you? What do you want?'

The owner of the lantern allowed the light to fall on his own face. It was a face that might once have been attractive, but now it was as cruel and hard as a talon: dark eyes glittering beneath arching brows, full lips twisted into a sneer, deep lines running from nose to mouth.

'My name is Gwydion,' said the man. 'I don't expect you have heard of me, but I know all about you, Jack. As for what I want – I used to want Edith, the queen, your mother. But since she decided she had no use for my love, for my heart, I am taking her son instead.' Gwydion laughed, a thin, shrill laugh that made Jack want to stuff his fingers in his ears.

'But – I don't understand—'

'Of course you don't. Your parents will not understand, either. I told them I would take you before your eighteenth birthday; I expect they thought you were safe.' Gwydion laughed again. 'But I lied.'

Jack strained against the bonds around his wrists, ignoring the pain as the rope cut into him. If only he could get his hands free –

The wizard shook his head.

'There is no escape, boy. You are too important for me to risk losing you.'

'What – what do you want of me?'

'Much. Oh, but my plans have grown in these eighteen years. You are to collect hearts for me, Jack – the still beating hearts of people foolish enough to believe they are in love – and from them I will gain power to create my dark servants, an army that will take away your mother's kingdom. And at the end, when she has nothing left, I will make her watch as I destroy that mewling Irishman she married. I think I'll cool his ardour by turning his blood to ice in his veins.' He smiled and glanced down at the ring on his left hand. 'I've done it before.'

'No! I will kill you before I let that happen. I'll—'

'Enough.' Gwydion waved his free hand in the air. Jack

saw orange shapes that hung in front of his eyes for a moment before fading. He tried to cry out, but his whole body was stiff and fixed; he could only watch.

The wizard walked away. But within a few minutes he returned, carrying a small bowl.

'Now, Jack, you will feel better once I have completed your initiation. Or to tell the truth, a lot of the time you will feel nothing.' Gwydion spooned something out of the bowl and brought it to Jack's lips. 'Open wide.'

Though every other part of his body remained immobile Jack's mouth opened and Gwydion tipped the contents of the spoon over his tongue. 'And chew.'

Jack's jaw and tongue started working. Whatever it was tasted foul: salty and metallic. But Jack could not stop himself eating and swallowing, even though he thought at any moment he was going to be sick, or pass out. The wizard fed him the whole bowlful. Then he dipped his finger in the juices at the bottom of the bowl and traced something on Jack's forehead. 'That girl in your village, Winifred. You loved her, did you not? You may answer.'

'Yes,' Jack croaked.

'And you wanted her to love you? You wanted her heart?'

'Yes.'

'Well, now you have it.' Gwydion held up his hands: they were covered in blood.

No. It's not possible. He can't have killed her. And I cannot have just – I can't have –

The wizard smiled.

'I'm sorry, Jack. But the curse is already taking hold, flowing through your veins, seeping into your bones. You will never be king at Helmswick. Instead, you will become my servant, and the King of Hearts...'

EIGHT

'**P**LEASE—' MERRY CLOSED her eyes, trying to shut out the images Gran's voice was conjuring in her head, '—please, just stop.'

She felt Leo nudge her. 'You OK?'

'No. I feel sick.' She clutched her stomach as it wrung out another surge of nausea. 'It's disgusting.'

Part of her brain was in denial.

It's just a story. It's not real. It can't be real.

Over and over.

But why would her grandmother make something like this up? She heard a sigh and the clatter of crockery as Gran started stacking up the mugs and plates.

'You're right, Merry,' Gran said. 'It is disgusting. But, unfortunately, it's the truth. The story I've just told you is part of your inheritance, just as much as the shape of your eyes, or the colour of your hair. And you are the one who has to give the story its ending.' She paused. 'It's up to you to… to kill Gwydion.'

Merry opened her eyes and stared down at the kitchen table, the plain pine surface marked with dents and scratches and water rings. She pressed her hands flat against it. The everyday solidity of the table was comforting: something real and believable in this nightmare of princes and wizards she'd somehow stumbled into.

'Gran,' Leo asked, 'I still don't understand why Merry has to be involved. Surely a properly-trained witch would have more chance of defeating this guy?'

Gran shook her head.

'The details that have been handed down are very specific. The braid that's in the trinket box will allow one witch to enter Gwydion's realm safely. When the first-born daughter of each generation comes of age in her fourteenth year the potential ability to defeat Gwydion will pass to her. We believe that ability grows with each generation.' Gran ran some water into the sink and started scrubbing the plates, as though she could wash away the family history at the same time as the cake crumbs. 'Your magic could be something very special, Merry; extraordinary, even. But now the wizard has awakened, the burden of confronting him passes to you, and to you alone. I'm so sorry darling, but this is the way it has to be.'

Merry couldn't believe what she was hearing. 'Why, Gran? Why didn't you or Mum tell me before now? I mean, you could at least have *tried* to warn me.'

Gran flushed.

'Because I hoped – I thought – why scare you, for something that almost certainly wasn't going to happen? And with you not being trained, and your mother—'

'I'm sixteen years old.' Merry slammed her hands down on the table top. 'I don't want to be *special*, Gran, not like this. And I don't want to die. But that's what's going to happen, isn't it?'

'Merry…' Leo put a hand on her shoulder, but Merry shrugged it off.

'Nobody's going to die!' Gran closed her eyes for a moment, frowning. 'It's going to be dangerous. But you – we – have to trust that the dangers have been planned for. That the three sisters, and those who have come after, knew what they were doing.'

'Three sisters?' Leo asked. 'What three sisters?'

Gran gave an exasperated sigh.

'Anwen's three daughters. I'll tell you the rest of what I know later. But I think first...' She peered at Merry. 'I think some fresh mint tea would make us all feel better. Merry, dear, there's some in the greenhouse at the bottom of the garden, if you wouldn't mind fetching a little.'

'Mint?' Merry frowned. *Really? At a time like this?*

'Yes, dear; you know what it looks like. And the fresh air will do you good.'

Fine, Merry thought. *Right now, I'd rather be anywhere else on the entire planet than in this kitchen.* She scowled at Gran, snatched the scissors Gran was holding out to her and slammed out through the back door.

Gran's garden was narrow but long. By the time Merry had walked past the neat flower beds down to the end of the lawn, the drizzle had cast a silver net of tiny raindrops across her jumper. She let herself into the greenhouse and cut ten slender stems of mint. There were other herbs here: rosemary, thyme, something lemony that Merry didn't know the name of. She skimmed her fingers across the leaves, breathing in the mix of fragrances, trying to calm herself. There were some vegetable seedlings and some winter lettuces too; for one insane moment Merry wondered whether she could just stay here, eat the herbs and the salad leaves, refuse to come out until all this nonsense with the trinket box and the mad Saxon boy had gone away, or been dealt with by someone else…

What if I could go back in time to last Monday, and not open the box? Or go back to when I was twelve, and not take the test?

But life couldn't be unravelled, and there really were no fairy godmothers to wave their sparkly wands and make everything better. The stuff with Alex had taught her that lesson. She picked up the mint and headed back to the house.

When she pushed open the door, Leo was sitting with his head in his hands, fingertips pressed against his eyes. Gran was talking, but she broke off and bit her lip as Merry entered.

Merry looked from one to the other.

'What's going on?'

'Nothing, dear.' Gran took the mint, rinsed it, dropped it into the teapot and poured boiling water on top of it. The scent filled the room. 'I was just saying to Leo that I can summarise the rest of the story, then you can go home and get some rest. The breakdown of the sleeping spell seems to be gradual – otherwise the King of Hearts would be out attacking people every night – so we can talk more later about preparation, training and so on. But you must both promise not to say a word about this to your mother. Her reaction would definitely be... unhelpful.'

Merry hesitated.

Leo straightened up and patted the chair next to him.

'Gran's promised to keep it brief. And sanitised.' He smiled at her, though there was something wrong with the smile –

It's his eyes. In his eyes, all I can see is panic.

But she didn't really have any option.

'OK.' She sat down.

I'm guessing no one's going to live happily ever after...

Merry remembered nothing about the drive home from Gran's, apart from the silence. Neither Leo nor she had spoken.

Now they were outside their house, still sitting in the car, listening to the rain as it plummeted from the sullen sky and thumped off the roof and windscreen.

Gran's summary had been brutally brief. As Gwydion's curse took hold, Jack spent more time transformed into the King of Hearts, and the wizard began sending him out to kill. He cut out the hearts of those in love with an enchanted sword and took the hearts back to Gwydion, so the wizard could use them to increase his mastery of dark magic. The murders, and the evil spells the wizard was using, began to blight the kingdom. Crops failed, the population dwindled, and the lives of Edith and Aiden were overshadowed by grief. Anwen's three daughters, bound by their mother's promise, wanted to find a way to free Jack from the curse and kill Gwydion. But they soon discovered that the wizard had protected his life and linked it to Jack's through a powerful enchantment: they could not destroy Gwydion without first overthrowing this enchantment. And they realised they didn't have the power to do it.

Still, Gwydion had to be stopped. So, the sisters bought time: they put both Jack and Gwydion into an enchanted sleep. One of the sisters, the youngest, vowed that she – or one of her descendants – would one day return to finally defeat the wizard.

Oh, and the name of the youngest witch was Meredith.

Because, obviously, if you want to protect your daughter from an Anglo-Saxon magical oath, the one thing you should definitely do is give her the same name as the person who swore the oath in the first place.

According to Gran, everyone else in the family thought the name was unlucky, but Mum had chosen it because 'she just wanted to be difficult.'

Way to go, Mum.

And that was it. Now Jack had woken up, and Gwydion could wake up at any minute, and the stuff in the box was supposed to help Merry kill the wizard – whatever that entailed.

The anger boiled up again inside Merry's chest.

'I don't want to have to deal with this, Leo! I know my life isn't perfect, or super-worthwhile or anything, but it's my life. I should have a say – I should get to choose whether I want to face some evil wizard or not. But instead, just because some – some insane relative of ours from hundreds of years ago decided to swear an oath – I'm stuck, I'm—'

She screamed and pounded her fists up and down on the dashboard.

'Merry, calm down.'

'I don't want to calm down! I don't see why this should all fall on me! You're just as much a descendent of Meredith as I am. And you're older, and way smarter. Its just totally sexist that men can't be witches, and – and…' She got out of the car and slammed the door as hard as she could. Leo followed her.

'Hey, watch it! There's no reason to try and smash up my car.'

'Do I look like I care about your stupid car?'

'None of this is my fault. All I want to do is help you.' Leo tried to wipe some of the rain off his face with his sleeve. 'Look, let's go inside. We're going to get soaked standing out here.'

'Stop being so bloody reasonable, Leo! You really don't get it, do you? What's the point in worrying about the rain when I'm probably going to – to—'

Pain seared Merry's fingers.

Oh God, no. Not now –

Merry dug her fingernails into her palms, trying to stop her anger in its tracks, but it was too late. She spun away from Leo, flung her hands out –

It was like someone had turned down the volume on the whole world. In that moment of stillness long tendrils, black and thorny, erupted from the ground in front of her. They rippled in the air, waving back and forth almost as if they were looking for something...

'What – the hell – is that?' Leo's voice was shaking. He edged closer to the tendrils, stretching out a hand.

'Get out of the way!'

Leo threw himself sideways as the tendrils lashed out. He wasn't quite quick enough: blood welled up from a long scratch on the side of his neck. Behind him, the tendrils fastened on to a big camellia bush right next to where he had been standing – ripped it out of the ground – dragged it back into the hole from which they had sprung. The earth collapsed back on itself and was still.

Merry stared at the broken ground.

I nearly killed him. I nearly –

What's wrong with me?

'Leo, I'm so sorry.'

Leo was still sitting on the ground, one hand pressed to the side of his neck.

'How did you do that, Merry? How? And why?'

'I didn't mean to! I don't know…'

'Because you told me you could only do small-scale stuff. That,' he stood up and pointed to where the bush used to stand, 'that was not small-scale. How did you do it?'

'Honestly, Leo, I don't know.' She stepped towards him. Leo backed away.

Merry flinched. It felt as though he'd just slapped her.

'Leo—'

He held up his hand to silence her.

'I just need a few minutes, Merry. I have to get my head round… whatever this is.'

'But you're hurt.'

'I'll be fine.' He walked away from her, towards the house.

Merry choked back a sob and pushed the wet hair out of her eyes. Leo opened the front door; she watched him slam it behind him, then she turned into the road that lead to Tillingham and started to run.

hundred years old, were young compared to the story Gran had told them earlier.

Nearly fifteen hundred years had passed since Merry's ancestor had – allegedly – uttered the oath that landed Merry in this mess. She couldn't take it in. When Gran had been talking, the people – Jack, Edith, Anwen – had all seemed so alive, so real. Merry felt she knew them, cared about them; it had been more like watching a film than just listening to a story. But apart from Jack – how had she known his name, in that nightmare? – they had all been dead for centuries.

Merry couldn't get inside the castle. It had a notice outside: *temporary closure*. Quite a few of the shops and restaurants along the high street were closed too; she'd noticed it last night. In the ten days since the attacks began, the situation in town had deteriorated; there had been minor protests outside the police station – people demanding more police presence, or maybe even the army – and the night before last a fight had broken out in one of the pubs. The tree-cloaked slopes of the North Downs frowned above the town, their tops disappearing into the fog that had become an almost permanent feature in the last few weeks. Merry shivered. The whole atmosphere of Tillingham was different. Now she understood: the protection the town had been under, that had kept it safe and unchanged all these years, was being overwhelmed, just as the swollen river was overwhelming the sandbags piled along its banks. And everybody seemed to feel it. A few people were around, heading out for the evening or finishing their shopping. But they walked hurriedly, heads down against the dank evening air, avoiding eye contact, clinging to the safety of the street lamps that were just flickering into life.

Merry wandered down to the station, ignoring the curious gaze of the police officers standing by the exit. From here, she could get a train to London, and from London she could get to Manchester, Edinburgh – even further if she went back and got her passport –

How far would she have to run, to escape this madness? How long would she have to keep running?

Merry looked at the bank of ticket machines, hesitated, and turned instead into the small waiting room. She needed to think, to work out what she should do.

The waiting room was warm, at least. She sat for a while, watching the trains come and go through the misted windows. The room was full of people sheltering from the rain. A babble of conversations swirled around her: who had been attacked – why – when would the attacker strike next?

Maybe you should run, said one part of her brain. *Sure, some people might die. But you probably won't be able to stop that anyway, and at least you won't be one of them. You're not trained for any of this. You most definitely did not sign up for it.*

'But what happened to him? Where is he?' A shrill-voiced woman nearby cut across her thoughts. Merry frowned in annoyance, and sank further down in her seat.

No, said the other part of her brain, *you didn't sign up for it. But how many lives is your life worth? What if fifty people die, or a hundred? What if he cuts the heart out of one of your friends? Look around you. What if Gwydion manages to create the army he wants? What if he destroys your home and everyone you love, and everything you've ever known?*

The thought of so much loss, on such a scale – Merry almost gasped with the pain of it.

But if I stay, I'm definitely going to die. The first voice was pleading now. *I may as well just jump in front of the next train and cut out the middleman. There's no way I'm going to be able to stop a wizard. Even if I knew what I was doing, I haven't successfully cast a spell for months. All I've done is break stuff and nearly kill Leo: I'm useless and dangerous all at the same time –*

'But you promised!' A small child sitting on the next

bench was pulling on her mother's sleeve; as Merry watched, the child began to cry. 'You said you would. You said…'

Merry got up and moved over to the window. The heat and noise in the room were starting to make her head ache. She put a hand out to steady herself on the windowsill. The voices got louder, making it impossible to think.

'—it's all my fault. I should have stopped him—'

'—don't blame yourself, you have lost so much—'

'—and my sisters, gone—'

'—for it to be truly over—'

And there she was, on the other side of the glass: the girl Merry had seen in the mirror at school, wearing the same clothes, her face only centimetres from Merry's. Merry gazed at her, barely breathing –

A non-stop express to London tore through the station, horn blaring, setting the glass in the window shuddering. Merry blinked – there was no one on the other side of the window now. She pushed her way out of the waiting room and scanned the platform as far as she was able to from behind the ticket gates, but the girl had vanished.

Maybe she got on a train.

Who am I kidding? There is no girl. She's a ghost. Or I'm going mad, and this whole thing is actually in my head –

Oh, God. What am I going to do?

She shivered, wound her scarf tighter around her neck and walked unsteadily back out of the station. The policemen stared at her again. No wonder – with the rain and the crying her face was probably streaked with mascara. Maybe she had a tissue in her bag –

'Merry?'

She jumped.

'Leo! What are you doing here?'

'Sorry. I've been looking for you.' He tilted his head. 'You OK?'

'Not really. I can't – I don't know how to deal with all this.'

'I know. And I went and made it worse. I'm really sorry, about earlier. I know you would never hurt me.'

'But I did, didn't I?'

'Not on purpose. Anyway – I'm sorry.' He took her elbow and steered her to a bench. 'Friends?'

Merry nodded, blinking away the tears that were threatening to spill on to her cheeks.

'I think I might be going mad, Leo. Either that, or I've acquired my own personal ghost.' She told him about the two visions she'd had of the dark-haired girl. 'Do you reckon it might be Meredith?'

Leo grimaced. 'Lord, I hope not. That's all we need:

another insane female relative trying to push us around. As if Mum and Gran weren't enough.'

'She probably wants to stop me doing a runner.'

'Maybe. But I wouldn't blame you, if you did.' He pulled his phone out and started tapping on the screen. 'Were you?' he added eventually. 'About to run away, I mean?'

'I was thinking about it.' Merry looked at the lights of the town, climbing up the hill. 'But I don't want to leave. This is my home. It's been our family's home for centuries. If Gran's right, and I am the only one who can stop Gwydion—' she swallowed, her mouth suddenly dry, '—I can't just walk away, can I? I have to try.' *Even if I'm almost certain to fail. Even if I'm terrified of dying, or of something worse.* 'What do you reckon?'

'That you're right. You should stay.'

Merry shifted so she could see Leo's face. He was obviously anxious: his jaw was tense and he was drumming his fingers on the edge of the bench.

'Really? Why?'

'Because – because of what you said, of course. Besides, remember what Gran told us, about the things in the box?' Merry did: they were the culmination of over a thousand years of preparation by generations of witches, all studying ways and means of destroying Gwydion if – when – the wizard reawakened. Or something along those lines. 'I don't see why you shouldn't beat Gwydion.'

Merry almost laughed.

'Apart from the fact that I've never been officially taught how to do any magic, I think Gran is seriously over-estimating my abilities, and I doubt they have *The Complete Guide to Killing Evil Wizards* in the school library...' She tried to breathe slowly. Getting hysterical again wasn't going to help. Gran seemed to think it didn't matter that Merry was untrained: her natural ability, plus the trinket box, would be enough. 'Maybe you should leave, Leo. Get away from Tillingham before anything kicks off. At least one of us would be safe.'

'Now you're being an idiot. We're in this together, OK? Even though most of the time you're a complete pain in the arse, you're still my sister.'

Another train clattered along the tracks behind them. Merry nudged Leo's arm.

'Hey – I'm sorry about the whole killer bush thing.'

'Yeah. About that—'

'I've never done anything like it before, honest. I was just angry. I wasn't thinking about – about hurting you, or anything like that. Even if I knew how I'd done it, I don't think I could repeat it.' She sighed. 'My magic's all over the place at the moment. I thought I was losing my powers, but maybe I've just lost control. I've literally no idea.'

'Don't worry – I'm sure Gran will sort it out. Too bad about the killer bush, though. It could have been a useful weapon against Gwydion.' Leo stood up. 'Well, maybe that box of magical junk will save the day. You want to go home and try to figure out how to use it?'

'No. I think Gran said that I have to wait for the parchment thing to "speak to me".' She'd have to check that later – there had been way too much information to process in one afternoon. 'But going home?' Merry rubbed the tight muscles in the back of her neck. 'Yeah, that sounds like a plan.'

Mum arrived back from France the next morning. Dark-haired and petite, she normally came across as completely self-controlled and self-confident. But today, Merry thought, her mother seemed awkward and twitchy, huddled inside her well-fitting clothes. And she definitely wasn't happy.

'But how could you not have called me, Leo? I left you in charge. If I'd known about the attacks I would have come home early.'

'Mum,' Leo shook his head, disbelief clear on his face,

'you've never come home early from a business trip, not even when Merry broke her leg.' That particular example of maternal indifference had bothered Leo, for some reason, though Merry hadn't been surprised. Mum had never exactly been super-affectionate, and for the last four years she'd worked abroad a lot. 'Anyway, the attacks have been all over the news. How could you have missed it?'

'I've been working eighteen-hour days, that's how: where do you think the money for your university fees is going to come from? The first I heard of the attacks was yesterday, when I called to book a taxi and gave them our address. And if you're trying to make a point about the amount of time I spend away from home, then you're being very childish.' Mum swung away and started unpacking the dishwasher.

Leo turned red.

'I'm being childish? I don't know why you're acting like this is all a big—'

'Leo!' Merry shot her brother a warning glance. 'Mum's tired. Why don't you give it a rest?' She knew what he had been going to say: *Why are you acting like this is a big surprise?* But she wanted to see what her mother would admit to on her own. Whether she'd tell the truth.

'What, Leo? A big what?' Mum asked.

Leo glanced uncertainly at Merry.

'A big… deal.' Mum was still putting dishes back into the cupboards; Merry risked a tiny, encouraging nod. 'I mean,' Leo continued, 'the people who were attacked, they probably knew whoever attacked them. We're not likely to be in any danger. It's going to be some kind of… gang warfare. Don't you think?'

Merry rolled her eyes. Gang warfare? In Tillingham? Sometimes, Leo didn't know when to stop.

But Mum didn't seem to notice the incongruity.

'Yes. Yes, I expect you're right. It's bound to be something like that.'

Merry couldn't quite believe it.

Who are you trying to convince, Mum? Us, or yourself?

Her mother sighed.

'I'm sorry I overreacted. I just – I have to keep you safe, that's all. I want you both at home as much as possible until this is all sorted out. Especially you, Merry. And – the woods are completely off-limits from now on.' She paused. 'They're lonely enough at the best of times. Understood?'

'Sure, Mum.' Leo nodded.

Merry said nothing.

Merry spent the next few days avoiding her mother and trying to not obsessively check the parchment from the

147

trinket box. The Manuscript, Gran had called it; she claimed it would provide guidance, but obviously no one had ever actually seen it working. So far there was no writing visible. Gran told her to be patient, that the breakdown of the sleeping spell and the activation of the oath was a process. But the waiting, the uncertainty, was like the barrel of a gun in her back. Even a couple of drop-in sessions at the local fencing club – suddenly, improved sword skills felt like a potential necessity – didn't help much. It was nearly two years since she'd last fought, and while she was there the mental discipline required cleared her mind. But the effect soon wore off, and her thoughts swung back into the same groove: endless worrying about what was going to happen next.

By Sunday of the next weekend the parchment was still blank. Merry spent the day in a flutter of suppressed excitement. She tried to ignore the whisper in the back of her mind – the hope – that somehow, Gran had got everything wrong. That the continuing attacks in Tillingham – another couple had been found, almost dead, just two days earlier – were really nothing to do with their family history. That the boy in her room had just been a coincidence, or a shared hallucination from the experimental vegetable stir-fry she'd made for dinner that evening. She tried to crush her growing optimism, but it was impossible.

On Sunday night she slept really well for the first time in ages: no visions or dreams, no strange noises, no fit but clearly dangerous boys barging into her bedroom. On Monday morning she hummed as she got ready for school, and began to at least contemplate making plans for the following weekend. There was a party on the Friday, then there was a new sci-fi film coming out she wanted to see. Ruby wouldn't be interested, but Jamie, a guy from her history class who had a ridiculously cute smile, might go with her — he'd asked her on a date once, before. She grabbed her school bag. Below it was one edge of the trinket box, sticking out from under her bed.

Maybe I should take another look, just to prove to myself that nothing has changed.

She picked up the box, lifted the lid and took a peek at the parchment.

The box slipped out of her hands and thudded on to the floor.

Merry went to school. She didn't know what else to do. But she felt like she was separated from everything going on around her by a thick sheet of bubble wrap: she could hear and see the students and teachers, but nothing they said to her made any sense. A low point came when she found she'd said yes to going on a date with Mark Taylor, a smug Year 13 muppet who didn't seem to be able to take no for an answer. But even after Ruby had finally made her understand what had happened, she didn't really care. None of it seemed important any more.

Leo picked her up as arranged. The smile slid off his face as she got into the passenger seat. 'What's happened?'

'I looked in the box again this morning.' Merry reached for it and realised her hands were shaking.

Leo leant over and pulled it out of her bag. 'Key?'

'Front pocket.'

He opened the box, took out the parchment and read it. 'This is it then.' He put his hands on the steering wheel, and Merry saw that his knuckles were white. 'It's started.'

TEN

THEY WERE IN the kitchen. Mum wasn't back from work yet. Merry was curled up on the old sofa, a crocheted patchwork blanket round her shoulders, holding the small glass of brandy Leo had poured for her. Leo was sitting at the big oak table, the parchment – manuscript – whatever it was, spread out in front of him.

'So, this word—' he tapped the manuscript.

Eala.

That was all it said. Four handwritten, angular letters, in dark brown ink.

Leo was looking at his laptop screen now.

'The top listings for "Eala" are EA Los Angeles, whatever that is, East African Legislative Assembly, and the European Air Law Association. I somehow doubt any of those are relevant, but—'

'It must be something in Anglo-Saxon.' Merry took another sip of brandy, grimacing as the fumes hit the back of her throat.

'Er, yeah. I was just about to say that.' Leo tapped on the keyboard a bit more. 'OK, here's an Old English translator. I'll just—'

Merry had a sudden vision: she was standing on a high peak, surrounded by the blackness of space, and if she took one more step forwards she would fall away from everything she had ever known –

'Leo – wait!'

Leo paused, his fingers poised above the keys.

'What? Why?'

'Because – I – I need more time.'

Leo sat back in his chair, his arms crossed.

'Merry... we don't know how much time you – we – have. Nobody's died yet, but,' he sighed, 'how long until things get even more dangerous? For you, I mean. Forget everyone else.'

'I—' Merry paused, trying to decide how to explain to

Leo; what to tell him. 'I'm just not ready for this. Like I said, I haven't cast any spells for nearly a year, apart from accidently, and to just launch into something this big...' She nodded at the manuscript. 'We don't know what's going to happen, once we figure out how to work that thing. I need more training.'

'No,' Leo was shaking his head, 'what you need is to start dealing with this. Now the manuscript's... working, you don't have any choice. Wizard Man and Psycho Boy aren't going to conveniently take a break while you have remedial witchcraft lessons. You said you were at least going to try—'

'I know what I said!' Merry stood up and went to pour the rest of the brandy down the sink. Last night she'd really thought this was all going to turn out to be a mistake, that somehow she was going to be let off the hook. But now...

'And I am going to try.' She grabbed the manuscript, folded it up and shoved it back into the box. 'Just not today.'

'Fine. Well, you let me know when you're feeling... up for it.' Leo shook his head again and shut the lid of the laptop. 'You'd better phone Gran, by the way. Let her know what's happened.'

'Yes, I know.' Merry picked up the box and marched out of the kitchen.

Right now, she needed to be alone.

Merry switched the light on and looked around her room, half-expecting to see the dark-haired girl standing in the corner, wagging her finger and tutting. But the room was empty. She dropped the trinket box on her desk and threw herself on to the bed. What was Leo's issue, anyway? Sure, she knew he was just trying to help her, would do anything he could to help her; but at the end of the day this was her problem. She was the one who was going to have to try to kill this Gwydion guy. She was the one who was going to have to try to break the curse...

Just thinking about it made her hands shake.

Of course, being frightened of what she was meant to do would have been easier to deal with if she wasn't also frightened – terrified – of the magic that was meant to help her do it.

Ha. Not going to tell Leo about that though, are you? Or why you're frightened of it. He doesn't know what you did...

Oh shut up. It's not like I actually killed anyone. Alex is still alive.

154

Maybe it had been a mistake: reacting the way she had done, swearing off witchcraft completely. What if she had a go at a spell now, when she wasn't under pressure, when there was no one else around to get hurt if things got out of hand? Her power might respond normally again. Merry took a deep breath, closed her eyes, and brought to mind the words of a charm for finding lost things. It was one of the first formal spells she'd learnt – on the quiet, by sneaking a book out of Gran's study – and it was easy. She'd used to find it easy, at any rate. You mentally pictured the lost thing, said the words and – abracadabra – you'd end up with a new mental picture of where the lost thing was. She tried it now, carefully, calmly, on an earring she'd dropped somewhere in the house about a month ago. Picturing the earring was simple enough: it was long and dangly, five little crystal-set snowflakes with two silver chain-links between each snowflake. And she remembered all the words of the charm: *O Sun by day and Moon by night, shine on the thing I seek, a light; guide my steps and light my mind until that missing thing I find…*

But her mind – apart from the image of the earring – remained stubbornly blank.

Oh, great. If I've managed to break my powers somehow, are

155

Gran and the coven still going to make me go out there, face Gwydion and his King of Hearts –

Something started rattling. Was the earring stuck at the back of a drawer somewhere? Merry had never had a physical indication of the whereabouts of a lost object before, but her magic had been so unpredictable lately… She jumped off the bed to investigate.

It was just the trinket box, twitching on the desk just like it had been doing the night she and Leo found it.

Merry swore at the box, slammed it up and down on the desktop a few times for good measure, wrapped it up in an old blanket and threw it in the bottom of her wardrobe.

No way was she phoning Gran now: she needed to get her head round what was happening, not be pushed into stuff by a *box*.

And I'm not going to look up what 'Eala' means, either.

So there.

But clearly, she was going to have to do *something* about that damn manuscript eventually.

The solution came to her overnight. She would ask one of the other witches in the coven – one of the official, properly-trained witches – to have a look at the manuscript for her. If another witch could get the manuscript to work, maybe Gran would change her mind, agree to the coven at least trying to deal with Gwydion without her.

But who to ask?

Not Gran, obviously. And she wasn't allowed to ask Mum. As she stood in the shower washing her hair, Merry ran through the other people she now knew were in the coven – thanks to the rune-casting episode outside the house the other week. Mrs Knox was another definite no. But the Zara girl… Merry turned up the temperature, letting the hot water ricochet off her tight shoulder muscles. Yes: Zara girl was the same age as her, more or less. She would understand. And it wasn't like Merry was going to use her as human shield or anything – she just wanted a bit of… help.

Merry had a plan – an achievable, concrete plan. For the first time in twenty-four hours, she smiled.

Unfortunately, it turned out not to be that much of a plan.

The Zara girl – whose name, when Merry tracked her down in the Year 13 common room, turned out to be Flo – had been happy to help. Almost enthusiastic. She said her mum wouldn't talk about Meredith's oath, or the curse: just dropped lots of dark hints that had driven her wild with curiosity. So Flo had led the way to a music practice room, chatting all the time, and waited while Merry got the manuscript out of her bag. But then…

Then Merry had pointed to the word, *Eala*. But Flo hadn't been able to see it. As far as she could tell, the manuscript was just a completely blank piece of paper. And she'd looked at Merry with such a mixture of doubt and pity in her eyes…

Now Merry was back in her bedroom. She'd spent the evening there, having told Mum and Leo – truthfully – that she had a headache. The failure of her plan, the realisation that Gran had been *absolutely literal* when she said that only a descendent could face Gwydion – made her just want to curl up under her duvet and hide. If she was asleep – even if she was dreaming – at least she didn't consciously have to think about what lay ahead of her.

Early the next morning, she was woken by the chimes of the grandfather clock on the landing striking seven. That meant it was actually only six-fifteen; the grandfather clock always ran fast, no matter what anybody did to it. She turned over and tried to get back to sleep.

But she couldn't settle. As well as the annoyingly loud

tick of the clock, there was a strange, pungent smell, almost like…

…burning. Something was on fire. Merry threw the bedclothes back and was halfway out of bed when she saw it.

A circle of flat stones – a hearth? – with a pile of logs burning brightly in the centre. In the middle of her bedroom carpet. As she watched, open-mouthed, the grandfather clock began to chime again, marking the half-hour. But the sound faded, as the room around her dissolved into a different place entirely. Almost entirely: Merry was still sitting on her bed, her hand still clutching the edge of the duvet. But the bed itself was now in the corner of – a cottage, she supposed it was. She could see a loom and a rough wooden cupboard against the far wall, just illuminated by the flames from the hearth. And around the hearth were three figures: the same girl Merry had seen at the station and in the mirror – Meredith? – and two others. One, with black hair and a thin, tear-stained face, was perched next to possibly-Meredith on the edge of a wooden bench. The other, tall and blonde, was standing with her hands on her hips, frowning at the weeping girl. None of them seemed to have noticed the sudden appearance of a stranger and a piece of furniture in their midst.

'…and it's as well for you we found you before the wolves did,' the blonde girl was saying. 'Wandering off like that, without a word to either of us—'

'Carys, enough.' Possibly-Meredith put her arm around the black-haired girl. 'Nia does not mean to do these things; she does not wish to be… troublesome. You know how it is with those who have the Sight.'

'I'm sorry, Meredith, I really am,' Nia murmured.

Merry thought: *I was right then. That is Meredith. And those must be her sisters.*

'Well…' Carys sighed and sat down in an empty chair opposite the other two. 'We need the truth now, Nia. We all of us know something is wrong, out in the wide world, though we haven't yet spoken of it. What did you see that drove you up into the woods?'

Nia stared into the flames and the woodsmoke, while the logs crackled and spat. Merry could feel the heat on her face.

'Two nights ago,' Nia said, 'I had a dream. There was a woman, a noble woman, I think, rocking a baby in her arms. I knew her, from somewhere. She looked happy, but there was a shadow over the child, and on his forehead the word *king*, written in blood.'

'What did the woman look like?' Carys asked.

'The woman had brown hair, almost the colour of hazelnuts, and brown eyes, flecked with gold. And then the woman and the baby disappeared, and I saw a man. He was young and handsome, but he was marked with the same word, and he was holding—' Nia shut her eyes tight, '—no – no, I can't say—'

'Nia, dear one,' Meredith took Nia's hands in hers. 'We must know what you saw.'

Nia nodded slowly.

'The man's hand was red with blood, so much blood that it ran down his arm and soaked the sleeve of his tunic. He opened his fingers, to show me what he held. It was a heart, Meredith. A human heart. And it was still beating.'

Merry blinked as the scene bled and shifted around her.

She was still sitting on her bed, jammed incongruously into the corner of the cottage. The fire still burnt brightly in the hearth. But now Nia was sitting in the chair, strumming idly on a small wooden lyre. Meredith was crouching over a cooking pot that was hanging from an iron tripod above the fire. The cottage door opened and Carys walked in.

Nia's fingers stumbled over the strings. Meredith dropped the spoon she was holding and stood up. 'What have you done to yourself?'

Carys's hair was in tangles, there were cuts on her hands and a long, bloody welt down the side of her face and neck. 'You must clean those scratches right away. Nia, where is the chickweed ointment? Did we not—'

Nia was still staring at Carys.

'It is begun, then?'

Carys nodded.

'What's begun?' Meredith was glancing from Nia to Carys. 'Carys? What's begun?'

'Our preparations, Meredith. For dealing with Gwydion. I have been able to find out where he conceals himself.'

'No...' Meredith grasped Carys by the shoulders. 'What have you done? What did you promise, to gain such knowledge?'

Carys held up a hand, silencing her.

'Do not ask me, Meredith. I was willing to pay the price that was demanded. We promised we would help, if we could.'

'She's right, Meredith.' Nia came and stood next to

Carys. 'We promised. And who will stop Gwydion, if we do nothing?'

The sisters all turned towards Merry, staring at her as if they were noticing her presence for the first time. But they didn't seem to be surprised.

'Who will stop Gwydion, if you do nothing, Merry?' Meredith asked.

'Yes,' Carys was nodding and pointing at her. 'You must act, Merry.'

Nia stepped forwards.

'Please, Merry. You are running out of time...'

Merry opened her mouth to reply, to explain – *I was going to try, but I'm scared, I'm so scared* – but before she could speak a soft chiming started up behind her. She turned away from the three girls, trying to work out where in the cottage the noise was coming from...

...and as she turned, she was back in her bedroom. The cottage, the round hearth with its bright fire – everything had disappeared. The grandfather clock finished chiming the half-hour and fell silent.

No time had passed at all.

Merry collapsed back on to her bed and lay there, shaking. She couldn't fight it any more. Any of it.

OK, Meredith. You win. I'll work out how to use the manuscript, fight Jack, kill Gwydion, do whatever you want. Or at least I'll try.

I promise.

Merry didn't go to school that day. After Bronwen and Leo had left for work the silence in the house was horrible.

It's like everything around me is holding its breath, waiting for me to...

She rang Gran.

Gran, thanks to Leo, already knew the manuscript had become active. Merry filled her in on the episode with Flo – there didn't seem any point in trying to keep it secret. Gran was sympathetic, though she seemed a little hurt by Merry's decision to ask Flo for help instead of her.

'I'm not going to force you into anything, darling. And I understand that you're scared. You've a right to be. But if you don't do something, things are only going to get worse. Have you seen the news this morning?'

'No. Has there been another attack?'

'Yes, just the same as before. They'd been stabbed, though once again the hearts weren't removed; I wish I knew why not. But unfortunately, it was an elderly couple this time. The husband didn't survive...'

Merry swallowed.

'OK.' That was it: people were actually dying now. 'So, do you want to come over and see the manuscript? So far it just says one word: e – a – l – a.'

'Eala. Old English for hello. But I won't be able to read it, darling. Only you, the last of the bloodline, can see what's written on it.'

'That's not true. Leo can see the word too.'

There was a moment of silence on the other end of the phone line.

'Are you absolutely sure? That doesn't sound right.' Another silence. 'Well… let's just focus on one thing at a time. I'll email you some ideas I've had about how the manuscript might work, but it may just respond to you automatically.'

'OK.' Merry hesitated. She didn't want the phone call to end: that would mean she had nothing left to do but get on with her 'destiny'. Gran must have sensed her anxiety.

'Sweetheart, the manuscript isn't dangerous, not to you. Work out how to use it, and it will guide you. Now, I've been talking to the other coven members about your training—'

'But what if I can't do it Gran? What if, when the time comes to face Gwydion, I literally can't cast a single spell—'

'Merry, you're a witch: it's in your blood. I am certain the magic will be at your disposal, and you'll know how to use it whether you've been trained or not. Think about it. Your ancestors spent hundreds of years preparing for this moment. You just have to take the first step.'

Merry remembered the image that had flashed into her head two days ago.

The first step, off the precipice and into darkness...

ELEVEN

LEO WAS HOME by early afternoon. The terrible weather – gale force winds now, as well as torrential rain and flooding – meant there wasn't as much for him to do on the farm as usual. Now he and Merry were sitting at the kitchen table, the manuscript spread out in front of them. There were two words on the page now:

Eala, Merry.

Obviously, the damn thing was making a point.

'So…' Leo cleared his throat. 'What's the plan?'

'Gran emailed me a few suggestions. Work through them, I suppose.' Merry lifted her hands, held them above the manuscript; at least they weren't trembling too noticeably.

Just get on with it. What's the worst that can happen?

Er...

She slapped her palms down on the open pages, rushing the words out before she could change her mind: 'Reveal. Speak. Show.'

Nothing happened.

'Huh...' Grabbing the carrier bag from the floor next to her, she tipped the contents out on to the manuscript.

'What's that? It looks like—' Leo poked at the bits and pieces with one finger, '—bits of plant, and jewellery.'

Merry held up a spray of dark green needles.

'Yew – I cut it off the hedge, earlier. It's for divination and communication; Gran's idea. This one is sage, for wisdom. That,' she said, pointing at an earring she'd pinched from Mum's jewellery box, 'is turquoise, for psychic abilities. And this,' she picked up a silver chain with a small purple crystal hanging from it, 'is amethyst. For intelligence.'

'I've never seen you wear it.'

'It was a sixteenth birthday present from our so-called father. Why would I want to wear it?' The necklace, its chain so tarnished it left black marks on her fingers, was the first gift their father had sent her since he left them. Merry remembered the letter that he'd sent with it. A pathetic letter, full of excuses and evasions. She dropped the necklace on to the parchment. 'I don't even know why I kept it.'

She arranged the objects in a rough circle around the pages of the manuscript and tried again.

'Reveal. Speak. Show.'

The yew and the sage burst into flames.

'Damn—' Leo put out the fire by throwing his tea over the plants. The manuscript was unharmed, but it was also still blank apart from the greeting. 'Maybe you need to say the same words, but in Old English? Or – could you just try saying *hello* back?'

'Um, I suppose.' Merry picked up the parchment, held it like a book in front of her, and took a deep breath. 'Hello, er, manuscript. Do – you – speak – English?' She caught sight of Leo's raised eyebrow and flushed. 'I mean, modern English?'

For a moment there was no response. Then more letters bloomed on the page.

Yes.

Merry glanced at Leo. His eyes were wide.

'Put it down. See if you have to be touching it. Ask it – ask it something it must know.'

She replaced the parchment on the table.

'OK. Where is Gwydion?'

The parchment didn't reply, so Merry picked it up again and repeated the question.

'Where is Gwydion?'

The wizard Gwydion sleeps still, under the Black Lake.

'Right. Great. So, what's next?' Merry asked.

No response. Again. Merry threw the manuscript back on to the table and leant back in her chair.

'Any more suggestions?'

Leo pulled the parchment towards him, traced his fingertips over the letters.

'Dunno. Maybe,' he wrinkled his forehead, 'maybe the answers it can give are already set, so you have to know the right question. Try something else.' He pushed the parchment back to Merry.

She sighed and rolled her eyes, but picked the manuscript up again.

'OK. Manuscript... how do we stop the King of Hearts stabbing people?'

The servant acts for his master. To end the danger, both must die.

Leo gave her a thumbs up.

'Right. And what do we need to do, for them to end up dead?'

The puppet hearts must be destroyed.

That didn't sound so difficult.

'What are the puppet hearts? Oh – are they the same as the jars of hearts that are in the story?'

No. The puppet hearts are a dark magic, conceived by Gwydion. One heart for the master, and one for the servant. While the puppet hearts exist, Gwydion and his King of Hearts cannot be harmed.

'Now we're getting somewhere,' Leo said. 'Sounds like the first thing to do is find these hearts.'

Merry nodded.

'Manuscript, where are the puppet hearts?'

The hearts are hidden, under the lake.

That didn't sound good. She'd used to swim a lot; for fun and competitively. But her relationship with water, apart from showers and baths, had gone sour since dragging Alex out of the river.

'OK. So how do we get at the hearts?'

You must go to the lake.

'Yeah, I think we get the lake part,' Leo muttered.

Merry was about to ask another question, but more words appeared of their own accord:

This night, the servant will walk abroad after the Moon has risen.

Go to the lake.

★ ★ ★

When Mum came home from the gym, Merry retreated to her bedroom. There, she tried asking the manuscript for details of what she was going to have to do at the lake, how she was supposed to retrieve the puppet hearts, whether she was meant to try to kill the King of Hearts as soon as she saw him. But it just kept repeating itself: *Go to the lake.*

Leo knocked on the door and came in. 'You OK?'

She shrugged.

'Well,' he sat on her bed and picked up the ancient, misshapen teddy bear that still lived on her pillow, 'at least we have a plan now. Hopefully, once we get to the lake, the manuscript will give us more instructions. We'll be able to finish this thing tonight and everything will go back to normal.'

'Yeah. Maybe.' Merry paused. 'What do you mean, we?'

'There's no way you're doing this alone. I'm coming with you.'

'But Gran said only one witch could enter Gwydion's evil lair, or whatever he's calling it. You heard her.'

'Screw what Gran said. You're going to be in charge, but every hero needs an assistant, a – a – '

'Sidekick?'

Leo scowled.

172

'I was thinking more like a second-in-command, a wingman, actually. Besides, we don't know yet whether this is going to involve any actual lair-entering. And if it does I'm not a witch, am I? I won't even register on Gwydion's magic meter.'

Merry hesitated. It was so tempting, but –

'No, Leo, it's too dangerous. I won't let you.'

Leo stretched his legs out and clasped his hands behind his head.

'But you don't understand, little sister. Either you agree that we're doing this together, or I tell Mum everything that's happened so far. Then Mum will probably go nuts, you'll be grounded, and Gwydion will end up killing us all anyway.' He smiled. 'Your choice, of course. I'll just pop downstairs and tell her now, shall I?'

'Are you completely insane?' Merry bit her lip. He was bluffing. Probably. 'When this is all over, you're dead.' She made an exaggerated throat-cutting gesture with her forefinger. 'So dead.'

'If we're both still alive when this is over, I'm willing to bet you'll forgive me.' He winked and grinned at her.

Merry couldn't help laughing.

'OK. You make a good point, my lovely assistant.' She tilted her head and gazed at him appraisingly. 'I wonder how you'd look in a sparkly leotard? Maybe with, like, an artistically-positioned feather boa...'

'That's something neither of us will ever know.' Leo got up to leave. 'You should call Gran. I'll try to figure out how to get out of the house without making Mum suspicious.'

The conversation with Gran was surreal. Gran was happy that the manuscript was responding, and reassured Merry again that all she had to do – *all* – was follow the instructions; everything was bound to turn out fine. Then she said she would alert the rest of the coven so they could make sure the area around the lake was clear of 'civilians', by which she meant non-witches. Initially, Merry assumed this communication would be done by magic, possibly involving owls or bats, but no: Gran was going to text everyone and put a message up on the coven's Facebook page.

Dinner was stressful. Mum was irritable; she picked at her food and looked like she hadn't slept properly in days. According to Leo's cover story, he had a pool competition at a pub in town and Merry needed to go to Ruby's house to work on an art project. Leo would take her and pick her up on the way back; how late they got home would depend on how far he made it through the competition. Pretty good, Merry thought. Still, Mum immediately said no, at the same time as pointing out that it was a school night and that Leo had work in the morning. It took a while to persuade her that Ruby's house was safe, and that the project wasn't something Merry and Ruby could work on over Skype. Eventually, Mum gave in. But she was obviously suspicious.

Merry forced down the last spoonful of her spaghetti carbonara and went upstairs to get ready. As she shrugged herself into her coat – it was raining again – she had to resist pinching her arm. She knew the events of the last couple of weeks had really happened, but right now she felt like she was moving in a dream. Or a nightmare. She tried to quickly memorise her room: the pink Union Jack duvet cover, the *Sherlock* poster on the wall, the dressing table, strung with lights and overflowing with make-up and hair accessories. Maybe she should have written a note for Mum, explaining, just in case she didn't get to come home –

Leo knocked on her door.

'Where's the box?'

'Under the bed.' The key and the box were now both at least twice as big as they had been, and Merry had taken to wearing the key on a chain round her neck. She handed the chain to her brother; Leo retrieved the box and unlocked it.

'You want to take all of this?'

'May as well. Just in case.'

'OK. So... let's put the instruction book in this pocket.' Leo lifted Merry's arm and shoved the parchment into a large side pocket. 'And the sword hilt, which would probably be much more useful if it had an actual blade attached to it, can go in this pocket.' He lifted Merry's other arm. 'And finally the hair extension can go...' He paused, then tied the braid of hair around Merry's left wrist. 'There. All set. You can put your arms down now.'

'Great. Have you got a torch?'

'Yep. Torches, a flask of coffee, and some chocolate bars.'

Merry hesitated. 'OK. But I think you should bring the big carving knife from the kitchen too.'

Leo raised his eyebrows.

Merry shrugged. 'Like I said – just in case.' She glanced around her room one last time. 'Let's go.'

It didn't take long to get to the Black Lake. There was a tiny gravelled parking area with a faded information board, but compared to the other open spaces nearby, the woods here were dense and sombre; the area never seemed to attract many visitors. Merry was surprised to see a silver saloon parked by the path into the trees.

'Great start,' Leo muttered, switching on his torch. 'Let's hope whoever it is goes home soon.'

Hoods up against the rain, they were walking past the car when a figure got out and stepped into the torchlight.

'Merry? It's me, Mrs Galantini. Your grandmother, she sent a message.'

Mrs Galantini, owner of the Italian deli on the high street, her accent still strong after forty years living in English suburbs. And also, apparently, a witch.

'Er... hi, Mrs Galantini. Terrible weather, isn't it?'

Great, I'm talking about the weather. I'm only sixteen and I'm already turning into my mother.

Mrs Galantini shrugged. 'It's England. It rains. Now, you are not to worry. I make sure nobody else gets through here. Your grandmother and others are in the woods, casting shielding spells.' Her eyes narrowed as she glanced at Leo.

'Leo's just here to – keep an eye on me. He's not going to get involved.'

Mrs Galantini made a dismissive sound – the sort of sound that clearly meant 'Men – what's the use of them, really?' – and turned back to Merry. 'Good luck, *brava ragazza*. I pray for you.'

That, Merry reflected as Mrs Galantini climbed back into the warmth of her car, was not very comforting.

They plodded along the path through the dripping trees, following the signposts to the lake. Eventually the trees gave way to open heathland, and the lake lay before them.

'It's bigger than I remember,' Leo said eventually.

Merry shivered. The lake stretched away from them, its farthest shore lost in the darkness. The near shore was flat, apart from one section where the land rose into a hill. A cliff, really; it dropped away sharply into the water. The restless surface of the lake, rippled by raindrops, mirrored her own disquiet. She turned to Leo.

'I think you should wait here, at least until we've got more of a handle on what's going on. The King of Hearts – Jack, or whatever – is only interested in attacking couples. We don't want him to find out too late that he's made a mistake.'

Leo pulled a face, but he nodded. 'Alright. Here: you should take the supplies.' He pushed the backpack into her arms and patted her awkwardly on the shoulder. 'I'll just be hanging around in the bushes then. Lurking. And watching.'

'Thanks. Feel free to intervene if it looks like I'm about to get murdered.'

Walking away from Leo and from the shelter of the trees was so difficult. Merry forced herself to keep going, until she was about six metres from the lake edge. She put a plastic bin liner on the sodden ground, pulled her hood as far as it would go over her face, and sat down to wait.

The first hour went slowly. The rain stopped. A couple of times Merry nearly fell asleep, catching herself as her head nodded forwards. She read her Twitter feed. She drank some coffee and watched the moon rise higher and higher above the treetops, washing the landscape silver. Around ten, fingers numb from the cold, she pulled the manuscript out of her pocket.

'Hey, manuscript. So, where is the King of Hearts?'

Still beneath the waters of the lake.

'Still under the lake? I wish he'd get a move on.'

The manuscript didn't comment. Merry's wrist itched, and she remembered the braid Leo had tied there: her entry ticket to Gwydion's realm.

'How does the braid of hair work?'

The braid provides protection.

Vague, but good to have confirmation.

'Is it our ancestor's hair? Did she put the protection in place?'

No. The protection was devised by Gwydion.

Gwydion? That couldn't be right. Her phone beeped:

Leo checking in. Pushing the manuscript back into her pocket, she picked up the phone to text him back.

This is weird. The

She stopped and looked up at the lake, straining her eyes to see into the darkness.

There was nothing there. The gently shifting surface of the water glimmered silently in the cold air. Yet Merry could feel goose pimples rising on the skin between her shoulder blades, despite the warm clothes she was wearing. She pulled the zip on the coat up higher, bent over her phone again. But it was no good. Dread grew like a lengthening shadow in her mind.

Something was coming.

The breeze sprang up again, tumbling last year's dead leaves across the ground and blowing Merry's hood back from her face. She stood and hastily stuffed the bin liner into the backpack before it blew away.

I should definitely get further away from this damn lake.

But she couldn't move. Her limbs felt as though the blood pumping through her veins had been replaced with lead. And she could not tear her gaze away from the lake.

The wind strengthened, ruffling the water into waves.

As she watched, a disturbance grew at the edge of the lake: the wind seemed almost to be forcing the water into a spiral, carving out a depression in the lake's surface.

The water started to spin, faster and faster, filling the air with flying spray, forcing Merry to fling her arms over her face until –

– until Jack leapt gracefully on to the shore, the vortex behind him collapsing instantly back into the lake.

The wind whipped Jack's hair away from his face. His cloak billowed out, and Merry saw a sword belt slung low around his hips, the jewelled surface catching and reflecting the moonlight. For a moment he stood, scanning the landscape in front of him. Then he turned away from Merry and began walking in the direction of the town.

Merry gasped as whatever had been pinning her in place – terror, or magic – vanished.

'Damn—'

She dropped her phone and fumbled for the parchment. There was a new line of writing, an instruction.

The monster is intent on sin. Name his name to draw him in.

There was a single sentence underneath:

Ætstand, heortena cyning

Was she supposed to translate it? Right now?

'Seriously?' Merry yelled at the manuscript. But Jack was getting further away. Merry swore again, and ran after him. 'Hey, you! Jack!'

There was no response.

'OK. Um... eye-t-stenday... sinning – or maybe kinning, – hay-or-tan...'

Jack stopped walking, turned around and stared at her. 'Er...'

He started moving towards her. Merry backed away, holding one hand out in front of her, fingers spread wide. There was a shielding spell she'd learnt ages ago – had used successfully a couple of times – but as she chanted the words under her breath, over and over, nothing seemed to be happening –

Oh, God – where's an insane burst of magic when I need it?

She heard Leo screaming at her to run, but that would mean turning her back on Jack, not knowing whether he was about to catch her. Better to keep walking backwards, faster and faster, hoping not to stumble, not to fall.

Jack grinned, and drew his sword. The blade was snapped off about a third of the way down. The broken edge was jagged and uneven.

But probably still sharp enough to kill me.

Merry had always thought of herself as strong. Tough,

even, given all her sporting activities. But the shock of the King of Hearts' appearance, of the brutality and bloodlust written so clearly across his beautiful face, made her feel weak and exposed, like she might just shatter at his slightest touch –

'Leo – help!'

Leo was pounding towards her across the grass, but he was going to be too late, she knew he was going to be too late –

The ground dipped, twisting her ankle, throwing her sprawling on to the grass.

Jack stood above her, silhouetted against the stars.

He raised the blade above his head –

TWELVE

HE WASN'T GOING to make it.

Leo was already running when he saw Jack stop, turn around and focus on Merry. He'd sped up when Jack started walking towards her – had screamed at her to run, with every spare bit of breath he had. But instead she'd tripped over, and Jack was only metres away from her, and she was throwing up her arm for protection, but Jack was running at her now with a sword in his hand and Leo was going to be too late, he was too late –

In Leo's memory, what happened next was almost in slow motion.

Jack brought the blade down, aiming for Merry's upflung arm. But it didn't connect.

Instead, Jack flew backwards, as if he'd run into some solid barrier. He flew backwards through the air and landed on his side some distance away.

And then the world sped up again and Leo was on his knees next to Merry, trying to check for blood and hug her at the same time.

'Are you OK? What happened – what did you do?'

'I don't know – I—' she stopped and pointed. Leo noticed her hand was shaking. Then he spotted Jack; Jack, pushing himself back to his feet, lunging for his sword. He looked at Leo and snarled.

'Oh, no…'

Leo dragged Merry upright and got in front of her.

'Run!'

But Merry didn't run. Instead, she was fumbling with the manuscript.

'Merry – get away from here! Now!'

Jack raised his sword again and Leo realised the blade was broken. But it still looked sharp. He pulled the kitchen knife out of his belt – wondered whether he would be able to buy his sister enough time to escape –

'Ga to reste, đu eart werig, ga to reste…'

Merry's voice was faint and wobbly and she stumbled over the words, but that didn't seem to matter. As she finished speaking Jack's eyes rolled back in his head, the broken sword slipped from his fingers, and he fell inert upon the grass.

I'm still alive. I'm alive, and he's – he's –

'Is he dead? Leo?'

'Um, hold on—' Holding the kitchen knife out in front of him, Leo inched forwards until he could touch Jack's neck. 'No. Not dead. But he's out cold.'

'Oh, thank God…' Merry collapsed, wincing and clutching at her ankle. Leo sank down next to her and covered his face with his hands. For a few minutes neither of them spoke.

'That… that was not what I expected. I thought he was going to – to—' Leo gave up. Merry didn't blame him – there were really no words for what had just happened.

Leo loosened the scarf around her neck.

'You're hyperventilating: try to calm down. I don't want you passing out.'

'OK.' She took a few slow, deep breaths. 'Tell me what happened. When I fell over, and he was about to—'

Leo frowned.

186

'You cast a spell on him, didn't you? He just sort of… bounced off.'

'I tried to cast one. It didn't work.'

'Well, it must have worked eventually; looks like it just kicked in a bit late.' Leo picked up the manuscript from where she had dropped it and shone his torch on the page of writing. 'Nothing here about what we're meant to do next. D'you reckon we should have a go at—' He coughed and tried again. 'Should we try killing him?'

'We can't. Remember what it said earlier?'

Leo flicked back a page.

While the puppet hearts exist, Gwydion and his King of Hearts are both immortal.

'Well – just ask it anyway. It would be better to get it over and done with.'

Merry sighed, but she took the manuscript from Leo's hands.

'Manuscript, can we kill the King of Hearts now?'

The answer materialised in front of their eyes.

No. While the puppet hearts exist, neither the wizard nor the servant can die.

'See?'

'So what's the plan? Just hang around until Jack wakes up and has another go at stabbing us?'

'I don't know, Leo. I have no idea what the plan is. OK?'

Leo muttered something under his breath, but Merry decided to ignore it. He was probably feeling exactly as she was: that if she had to just sit here, with nothing to do but contemplate this terrifying, insane situation, she might just lose it. They were sitting some distance from the lake now, but the sound of the dark water lapping at the shore was still clear. She got up and stamped some feeling back into her feet.

'I'm going to check out the lake. I won't be long.'

Leo nodded, so Merry jogged away from him towards the water. The night had become cloudy again and the lake was almost indistinguishable in the darkness; just a smudge of dark grey against the black of the sky. When she reached the water's edge she shone her torch down into it, probed it with a dead branch lying nearby, but she couldn't see or feel the bottom of the lake. There were no handy steps she could use to get underneath the lake and collect the puppet hearts, either. And there was no sign of any hiding place. It was completely impossible that Jack should have sprung out of the freezing water dressed in those heavy clothes and completely dry. But then, he was an Anglo-Saxon prince who had been asleep for the last millennium and a half. It was kind of ridiculous to expect him to obey the laws of physics.

Merry made her way back to Leo and sat down again. Her brother had obviously found the backpack: he was pouring coffee, and handed her a cup.

'Thanks. Has he moved?'

'Uh-uh.' Leo shook his head. Merry picked up the manuscript.

'Can you tell us what to do now?'

There was no response.

Well, this is great.

Leo stood up.

'What are you doing?'

'I'm going to chuck it in the lake.'

'Chuck what in the lake?'

'That.' He directed the beam of his torch on to the hilt of the broken sword, still lying where Jack had dropped it. 'If he wants it back, he can swim for it.'

'No, that's not a good—' Merry began, but Leo ignored her. She shook her head and followed him.

The blade of the sword was of some dark metal, its broken edge corroded away, but the hilt was similar to the hilt they had found in the trinket box. It had the same type of gold filigree work around the pommel and guard. Leo leant down, brushed his fingers across the gilded surface –

'Ow – damn it!' He snatched his fingers back. The tips were blistered. 'It's red-hot. I don't understand.'

Merry knelt down closer to the sword, frowning. She stretched out her hand –

'Merry,' Leo whispered, 'look—'

Merry shone the torch in the direction he was pointing. Jack was awake.

Ten minutes had passed. They knew that because Leo had looked at his watch. A mistake, it turned out: Jack brought his knife up again when he saw the watch light up on Leo's wrist.

'You lie: you are a wizard!'

It would almost have been funny. If they hadn't been standing in the dark, frozen and exhausted. And if the knife Jack carried – he'd made no move to pick up the broken sword – hadn't been considerably longer and more dangerous-looking than Leo's kitchen knife. At least Jack, rather than the dark creature that had attacked them earlier, seemed to be back in charge of his body. For now anyway.

Merry groaned and rubbed her sore eyes.

'Look, Jack, please try to understand. I know you think you know me, but the first time I met you was the other night, in my bedroom. My name's Merry. And this is Leo – he's not a wizard. He doesn't know how to use magic, not even a little bit. The torch, and the lantern, and the watch – it's all electricity…'

Jack kept his knife pointing firmly at Leo, but he turned towards Merry.

'I would have the truth. I remember you, from before, I am sure of it. Why do you deny it?'

'I just – I don't know what to tell you…'

Jack lowered the knife.

'I remember you, and I remember that I am bound somehow to the evil wizard Gwydion, through the curse that taints my blood. I remember my name, and your face – but that is all I remember. Do you understand?' The pain in Jack's voice caught in Merry's guts like thorns. 'I know nothing of my life, or who I am, or why I am in this place. Why will you not help me?'

Without thinking, Merry moved closer to Jack. Leo grabbed her wrist and pulled her back.

Jack hesitated, then pushed his knife back into his belt.

'Have you brought this wizard here to kill me?'

'Jack—'

'Very well. I will not oppose him.'

He sat down with his back to them.

And that was it, for the next half-hour. Leo asking questions that Jack wouldn't answer, Merry trying to get the manuscript to tell them what the hell they were supposed to do next.

'How long have we got until you turn evil again?' Leo demanded. 'Can you at least tell us that?'

Jack ignored him.

'Oh, for—' He turned to Merry and jabbed a finger at the manuscript. 'Are you sure that thing doesn't say anything about killing him?'

'Leo...' Merry made a shushing motion. 'There are things we need to know, Jack. It's important. We have to stop the wizard. We have to get under the lake, to wherever it is you came from. And you know about this... curse, that takes you over...'

Jack turned his head slightly towards them. 'I feel it, even now: it struggles to regain mastery. But what it desires, or what I have done while under its command...' He shook his head. 'I cannot remember. Though I fear – I fear I am damned.'

Merry winced. The idea of telling Jack that he'd been forced to cut people's hearts out was deeply unappealing.

Jack shifted position so he was facing them again, and stared at Merry, his brows drawn together. For a few moments she met his gaze, hoping to somehow get through to him. But he was studying her so intensely that eventually she had to look away.

'I am completely alone, am I not?' Jack asked. He sounded exhausted. 'There was someone... but whoever she was, she has left me.'

'I'm sorry,' Merry replied. 'She must have. It's been such a long time.'

Jack's eyes widened and he gasped, a spasm of pain crossing his face. 'The monster returns—' Jack dug his nails into the earth, as if he were trying to stop himself getting up. 'You must... fly...'

Leo scrambled to his feet.

'What do we do?'

Merry seized the manuscript in both hands. 'Help us! The – the King of Hearts, he's come back—'

Jack was back over by the broken sword; he seized the hilt – no sign of pain – swung the blade out in a wide arc and stalked back towards them. Leo jumped in front of Merry.

'Well?' he asked over his shoulder.

'Hold on—'

'Merry!'

'OK, got it: "Awende on – on sinnihte, scea – sceadugenga."'

As though a switch had been flipped, Jack's face went from rage-filled to completely blank, all trace of personality wiped away. He shoved the sword back into the sheath hanging at his waist and started walking back towards the lake. Through the darkness Merry heard the ripple of water, gradually getting louder: the vortex, rising up out of the lake to receive the King of Hearts back again.

A fierce gust ripped the clouds away from the Moon. Merry squinted, raised her hand to shield her eyes from the wind – but when she looked towards the lake, Jack had disappeared. It was over.

For now.

Mrs Galantini had gone by the time Leo and Merry had walked back to the parking area. Gran was waiting there instead, but once she'd checked that they were both in one piece (and given Leo some ointment for his hand) she didn't delay them, just told Merry to get some sleep and that she'd call her the next day. In the car, Leo drove too fast and talked too much; he knew he was in shock. Clearly, some part of his brain had decided that if he kept moving, then maybe, somehow, the stuff that had happened at the lake wouldn't catch up with him. Maybe wouldn't have even happened at all. Every so often he glanced over at Merry, waiting for her reaction: tears, or shaking, or uncontrollable hysteria. Something tangible. But she just sat there, staring out of the windscreen, her face almost as blank as Jack's had been just before he turned away from them.

They got back home just after midnight, that was one mercy: just early enough for Mum to accept Leo's story that he had won the pool competition, left the pub at 11.30 and picked Merry up from Ruby's on the way back. Merry still seemed completely calm. Leo followed her upstairs and stopped her just before she went into her room.

'Merry – are you sure you're OK?'

'Yes. I'm fine. 'Night Leo.'

'G'night then. Give me a shout if—'

But she had already shut the door behind her.

Merry stretched under the duvet, wiggling her toes and gently flexing her sore ankle, trying to relax into the warmth and softness of the bed. Her wrist was itchy; she ran a finger under the braid of hair, loosening it a little. The manuscript and the sword hilt were locked back inside the trinket box, but the braid... Whatever Leo said, Merry knew it hadn't been her own magic that sent the King of Hearts flying when he ran at her. That had failed her, again.

Still, she was alive, and so was Leo. Both of them had survived their first encounter with the King of Hearts. That should make her happy, right? Or something – surely, she should be feeling something, after what they'd just been through. But no amount of probing, rerunning the evening's events over and over in her head, produced any response. She'd been anaesthetised. Or had left her capacity to feel somewhere back there in the darkness, at the edge of the Black Lake.

Alex told me once I had a lump of ice for a heart. Maybe now it's true...

The next few days were the same. Leo kept watching her, as if she were a suspicious package that might suddenly start to tick. The manuscript summoned them three more times to the lake, but Merry gave Jack no opportunity to attack them. As soon as he emerged from the water, she read out the words that knocked him unconscious and returned him to himself. When the curse regained control, she said the words that sent him back to the water. Inbetween, she and Leo tried to get information out of Jack or searched for ways to get under the lake. Merry went back there one morning on her own, hoping daylight would reveal something they had missed, but so far no secret entrance had materialised. At least their presence at the lake meant that no one in Tillingham was being attacked, or bleeding to death; the atmosphere in town eased a little. But the manuscript didn't give Merry any idea what was to come next, or for how many nights she was going to have to keep sneaking out of the house in the dark. Gran, and Ruby (although she didn't know it), were both helping keep Merry's activities secret from Mum, but it wasn't easy. Worse, her magic still wasn't cooperating. There hadn't been any more dramatic outbursts, but the few basic spells that Gran had asked her to try – healing cuts and grazes, making a sleeping potion, creating a globe of witch fire – none of them had worked at all.

Jack was still refusing to talk to them most of the time. He did become a little more communicative on the third night, though, when Leo offered him some cold roast chicken that had been left over from dinner. Jack ate the chicken rapidly, watching them the whole time.

'I know you don't trust us,' Merry tried again, 'and I know you don't remember much. I know you don't believe anyone can defeat Gwydion. But surely there must be some questions you want to ask, even if you won't answer ours?'

Jack ate the last piece of chicken and licked his fingers. 'Very well. Why is it that I seem to recognise you?'

Merry had been thinking about this one. 'I reckon that you're confusing me with Meredith. She was a witch, and I'm... related to her. She tried to stop Gwydion. She put you to sleep.'

'And is this man your betrothed?' Jack gestured towards Leo.

'Leo? Ew – no. I told you last time: he's my brother. And before you ask again, he's not a wizard. But I'm a witch. Well... sort of a witch, anyway. My turn to ask you a question now. Do you recognise this place?'

Jack shook his head. 'I remember someone putting something on my eyelids – this Meredith you speak of, perhaps – and I remember falling asleep. We were in Gwydion's underground hall, one of the rooms he built beneath his tower.' He closed his eyes, frowning. 'The tower was hidden by a dark, thorny hedge, that was—' he opened his eyes, again shaking his head. 'Somewhere in the kingdom. I've forgotten. The hall is still there, under the lake, but where the lake came from, or where the kingdom has gone...' He gestured at the surrounding countryside. 'There should be forests of trees, high hills. But instead, almost everything I see is wrong: the garments you wear, the buildings, the sounds.'

'Well...' Merry trailed off, unsure how to begin to explain the twenty-first century. 'How come you know how to speak modern English? I mean, how come you can understand us?'

Jack sighed.

'I do not know, any more than I know the wizard's purposes, or how you are able to hold me here against his will, and the will of the curse that is upon me. Can you explain it to me?'

'No. I don't understand how the magic works either.'

'Then, even if you are what you claim to be, how will you help me?'

Merry didn't reply.

Help you? I think I'm supposed to kill you. And I don't even know how to do that.

Jack turned his back, and spoke no more to them that night.

★   ★   ★

'Meredith Cooper! Is there any hope that you might actually pay attention, given it's your future we're discussing?'

Merry flinched and dropped her pencil. It was late Thursday afternoon, just over a week since she and Leo had first gone down to the lake and watched Jack leap out of the surging waters. The stress – and the lack of sleep – were getting to her.

'Um…'

What was she talking about? University choices? Or… degree subjects?

She glanced down at the paper in front of her. No help there: she'd been writing a list of possible ways under the lake ('ask Gran re water spells') and sketching pictures of Jack's face.

'Well, really.' Miss Riley – art teacher, careers adviser and all-round supervillain – rolled her eyes for good measure. 'Your careers assessment form, Meredith. It was meant to be completed three weeks ago.' She smiled maliciously at the rest of the class. 'Ever since you rescued that boy from the river, you seem to have decided that deadlines don't apply to you. I can assure you that is not the case. Surely you have some aims?'

Merry bit back a retort. Her List of Possible Things To

Do With My Life had been completely blank for months. And now it was worse: when she tried to imagine her future all she saw was a tunnel, completely dark, with no light at the end.

I'm not sure it even is a tunnel. Maybe it's just a cave. A dead end. Literally.

Filling in a stupid spreadsheet wasn't going to change anything. But she didn't have the energy to argue. 'Sorry, Miss Riley. I'll bring it in tomorrow.'

Finally, the bell rang and she could go home. Merry avoided Ruby. She knew her friend was going to ask her to go shopping, but Merry just wanted to wallow in the bath – and in self-pity – and hope the manuscript didn't summon her to the lake. Unfortunately, she didn't manage to avoid Gran: her bright red Mini was parked right outside the school. Merry got in.

Gran didn't waste any time. 'How are the spells going?'

'Not… great. I gave myself a paper cut and couldn't fix it. The sleeping potion I concocted just made me feel sick.'

'And the witch fire? It's such a useful spell. Show me how far you've got.'

'What, right now? In the car? While you're driving?' Merry clutched at her seatbelt as Gran sped round a corner, apparently oblivious to the rain and the general lack of visibility. 'What if it goes wrong?'

'What's the worst that can happen?'

Merry sighed.

Creating a massive fireball that consumes the car and everything within a ten-metre radius? Would that be the worst?

But – on the basis that nothing had happened the first ten times she'd tried this spell – she brought her palms close together, closed her eyes and concentrated, murmuring the incantation, listing all the different types of fire, but imagining the violet flames too...

Her hands felt warm. Between her fingers hovered a small, very faint, globe of blue-purple light. Merry shrieked and the globe disappeared.

Gran smiled as she pulled up in front of Merry's house. 'Don't look so surprised, darling. You're a witch. But I do think it would be a good idea if you come to a meeting of the coven. We can assess your skills properly, get a training schedule in place—'

Merry was already out of the car, house keys in hand. 'Um, sure, Gran. I'll give you a call later. But I have to go check the manuscript now.'

'But Merry—'

'Thanks for the lift!' Merry walked quickly into the

house and shut the front door behind her. She knew she wouldn't be able to put Gran off indefinitely, but she needed to figure out what had just happened.

So, I obviously haven't lost my powers.

She tried the witch fire spell again. Nothing.

Great. Not magical enough to be a proper witch, too magical to be an ordinary person. Dangerous. But not dangerous enough to stop a wizard's curse.

Still, she couldn't deny it had felt good, even for that brief moment in the car: using her power, controlling it. The desire tugged at her...

No. I can't give in to it. Not again.

But – if I'm powerless...

She took a couple of deep breaths, and the craving faded. Was that really her choice: risk becoming a monster, or die at the hands of somebody who already was one?

Merry kicked her school bag across the floor, then forced herself to go upstairs and pull the manuscript out from the bottom of her wardrobe. Before she even asked the question, two lines of text bloomed on the page:

This night the servant walks abroad.

The wizard wakes.

Fantastic. Merry threw the manuscript on to the bed and went and knocked on Leo's door. He was standing in front of his mirror, a towel wrapped round his waist, working wax through his hair.

'Hey, do you have plans this evening?'

'Yeah – I'm going out with Dan.'

She shook her head.

'You *were* going out with Dan. I'm sorry…'

Three hours later they were back at the lake. Jack came out of the water and Merry said the words that knocked him out, just like the other nights. There was no sign of Gwydion. But as soon as Jack regained consciousness, it was obvious something was different. He knelt before Merry, drew the knife he carried at his waist and offered her the handle.

'I have remembered. Not everything, but I remember what I have done.' There was such a depth of anguish in his eyes that she shrank away from him. 'I beg you, if you have the skill, end it now. Kill me.'

THIRTEEN

IT TOOK A while for Jack to calm down sufficiently for Merry and Leo to make any sense of what he was saying. One minute he was talking about the recent attacks in Tillingham – attacks he now knew he had carried out – the next he was reliving the past, mentioning names and places neither of them had ever heard of. But one thing was clear: the manuscript was right. Gwydion had woken from the enchanted sleep. As far as Jack knew the wizard had only been awake for a few minutes. But that had been enough to trigger the recovery of Jack's memory, at least partially.

'This is all Gwydion's fault, not yours,' Leo offered. 'You know that, right? It's not really you attacking people.'

Jack shook his head.

'My hands wield the blade. My hands are red with their blood.' He looked at Merry, his eyes glittering in the moonlight, and Merry thought how different his face was really from that of the King of Hearts: still beautiful, but kind and sad too. 'Did I not try to kill you?'

Merry nodded. 'Yes. Though you didn't get to, in the end. I mean, something stopped you, or stopped whatever was controlling you.' She didn't know what else to say. But, as Jack dropped his head into his hands, she felt a twinge of pity for this strange boy, fifteen hundred years away from his home, more alone than any of the other seven billion people on the planet. 'I'm sorry, Jack. I wish we could help you. I wish—' She caught herself, and stopped. Because she wasn't supposed to help him, not really. She had to keep reminding herself: if she was reading the manuscript right, she was supposed to kill him.

'There is one thing you can do.' Jack started ripping blades of grass out of the ground next to him. 'You can tell me truthfully how long I have been asleep.'

★ ★ ★

All things considered, Merry reflected, Jack was taking it pretty well. He accepted Merry's outline of what had happened – there was a lot of stuff he still couldn't recall – and her explanation that a new plan for dealing with Gwydion had been constructed while he was asleep. But when she finally told him, after using as many delaying tactics as she could think of, exactly how many years had passed since he had last seen the sun, she thought he might freak out. After all, he had just learnt that all the people he had ever loved were dead. And not just dead: *so* dead that nothing was likely left of them but dust. Not even dust.

If it were me, thought Merry, *I would be completely freaking out right about now.*

But Jack didn't. He clenched his jaw, and for a moment Merry could see his hands, balled up into tight fists, shaking. But that was it.

'Um, are you OK? I mean, it must be a terrible shock for you. Do you—' *I'm sitting here in the dark with a fifteen-hundred-year-old boy who tried to stick a sword in me eight days ago, and I'm about to ask him if he wants to talk about it. Seriously?*

Merry cleared her throat. 'Do you believe us now? That we are who we say we are? Because we really need your help.'

'I believe you. And I will do anything I can to stop the wizard.'

'OK.' Leo leant forwards. 'Do you know what Gwydion's current plan is? I mean, is he trying to get out from under the lake himself, or is he just going to keep sending you out? And aren't you meant to be cutting people's hearts out?'

Jack groaned and dropped his head into his hands.

'Oh,' Leo murmured, 'I'm sorry.'

They waited while Jack recovered himself. After a few moments he looked up again.

'I cannot answer you at the moment. Perhaps the knowledge will return to me. But Gwydion must not escape the lake. Before, he would take people from their homes, practise his magic on them – I used to hear them screaming...'

Leo blanched. 'We can't let that happen here. And we're not going to. We've got various, you know, magical artefacts that have been passed down to us.'

'May I see them?'

Leo went to get the parchment out of Merry's pocket, but she put out her hand to stop him. 'I think – I think maybe that's not a good idea. We don't know whether the – whatever it is, that takes you over, whether it gets to know the things you know.' She frowned. 'Or whether it tells Gwydion what it knows. Do you understand what I'm saying?'

'Yes. You are right, of course. I am not—' Jack's mouth twisted into a parody of a smile, '—safe. When the curse controls me, I am trapped inside my body. I see what it does as it follows the wizard's orders, hear it speaking with my voice, but I have no knowledge of Gwydion's deeper strategies. Perhaps it is reversed when I am myself.'

'Vengeance,' Merry whispered, almost to herself. Jack's eyebrows raised. 'Um, in the story our gran told us, Gwydion wanted revenge, on your mother. Because she wouldn't marry him?'

'My mother?' Jack shook his head. 'I have no memory of her. But you may be right.' He hunched over, wrapping his arms around his knees. The movement revealed thick white scars around his wrists.

Merry wondered briefly what had caused them, before deciding she would much rather not know. Instead, she asked: 'What's it like, under the lake? How do you get in and out?'

Jack glanced over at the water. 'There is a staircase, up to the lake bed. The shadow within me speaks to the rock

– at least, that is how it seems to me. And somehow a passageway opens… But I can never remember the words it uses. There is no other way in or out of the ruins.' He waved a hand towards the lake. 'The tower is gone. All was drowned.'

Silence fell. Merry poured herself some more coffee from the flask. It was even colder tonight, almost as if the seasons were running backwards; Leo was looking at his phone, and she could see his breath condensing in the air.

She thought of the braid, the thing that had protected her from Gwydion's own servant – if the manuscript was right. Was it Gwydion's hair she had tied round her wrist? The idea turned her stomach.

'Jack, when you were about to, you know, hit me with the sword last Sunday, something stopped you. Leo said it was like you'd run into a brick wall.' Merry hesitated. 'A brick is a sort of—'

'I know what a brick is.' Jack said.

'Of course you do. Sorry.'

'The giants left them.'

'Er…'

'That is what the stories say, at any rate, though Father Brendan said they were untrue.'

'OK… Well, do you remember whether anything like that has happened before? Have you – I mean, has the thing possessing you ever tried to kill someone, but not been able to?'

The sky had clouded over again, and in the darkness Merry could no longer see Jack's face clearly. He was silent for so long she wondered whether he was slipping back into some kind of magical trance; at her side, Leo shifted and raised his knife again. Eventually, Jack lifted a hand and brushed something away from his cheek. 'The King of Hearts is without mercy. I remember clearly the first evening Gwydion sent him – me – out to kill, to collect hearts; from then on, I believed none would escape him. But I am certain, one night, some mishap sent the wizard's plans awry.'

'What happened? What was different?'

'I cannot recall… I see myself holding the sword, plunging it downwards, but then – the blade – I—' He slammed his palm against the ground. 'Why can I not remember?'

Merry leant closer to him. 'Hopefully it will come back to you, like you said. Maybe next time.'

Jack gasped and cried out. Leo swore.

'Quick – get back. He's losing control.'

They backed away from Jack as he fought to stop his hand moving towards the broken blade. Merry pulled the manuscript out of her pocket. There was the line of words that would force Jack – or the monster now inhabiting his body – back into the lake. But underneath was a fresh instruction.

Jack finally pulled the broken sword from its scabbard and stood up. He weighed it in his hand a moment, looked at them and smiled.

'Merry?' Leo murmured, 'Say the words.'

'But Leo, the manuscript, it—'

Jack – but not Jack – started walking slowly towards them, the blade weaving back and forth as though he was trying to choose who to attack first. Leo spread his arms wide in front of Merry.

'Say the damn words!'

Merry shouted the unfamiliar syllables as quickly as she could. Jack's face became expressionless and she shuddered, even though she had seen this transformation several times now. He sheathed the sword, turned away from them and walked back towards the lake.

'What the hell happened?' Leo was at her side now, breathing hard, his knife still gripped tight in his fist.

'Look.' Merry held the manuscript out to him,

pointing to the new line of instruction. It was just two
words.

Follow him.

Leo stared at the manuscript, glanced up at Merry and
shook his head.

'No. No, we can't just...'

'But Leo, I have to try.

*I can't believe I said that. I can't believe I'm even thinking
about getting into that lake.*

Oh, God.

Leo shook his head again, but he grabbed Merry's hand
and they both threw themselves after Jack.

Within a few moments they were approaching the water's
edge. But Jack was too far ahead of them. He veered off,
began running up the slope where the land rose to form
a cliff, leapt – and for a second they saw him outlined
against the stars, before he dropped feet-first into the
seething waters and disappeared. Leo hesitated, turned away
from the hill and plunged down towards the lower edge
of the lake, tugging Merry with him.

'Kick off your shoes. We'll have to swim.'

They waded out deeper, the lake bed fell away from
beneath their feet and Leo let go of Merry's hand. She

tried to push herself forwards, to make her arms and legs move together, to regulate her breathing as she'd been taught, but already the frigid water was in her eyes and soaking through her clothes, taking her breath away –

– cold, that's what she remembered, the river was so cold and black, the weight of it crushing her, dragging her downwards as she tried to pull him back to the bank, the water getting into her throat, choking her –

Merry sank.

'I'm sorry, Leo.'

'Don't be ridiculous. You could have drowned. You nearly did.'

They were sitting in Leo's car. Flo's mum, Denise, had been the witch on duty at the little car park. She'd called Gran and then asked Merry if *she* wanted to have a go at drying their clothes, managing to look simultaneously amazed and unsurprised when Merry declined. The spell Denise used seemed to suck the moisture out of the fabric: Merry had watched, trembling with cold, too numb to be envious, as streamers of water vapour spiralled away into the night air. When Gran arrived she brought a large flask of a fiery liquid that tasted strangely of thyme. Metheglin, she'd called it. While Merry was sipping it, her insides thawing,

Leo shared what they'd learnt from Jack. Gran was particularly interested in the idea of a word that would open the passageway under the lake. Now, she'd gone off to do some research – Gran didn't seem to keep normal hours – and Leo was waiting for his hands to warm up so he could drive Merry home. At least there was no urgency: at Gran's (magical) prompting, a work colleague had invited Mum to see a musical in London. The coast was clear for once.

'But I am sorry,' Merry said again. 'We – we might have been under the lake by now…'

'No. We'd be dead. I was stupid, to think—' Leo took his hands away from the hot air vent, flexed his fingers. 'I don't understand it. There's no way he should be able to swim down through all that water. Though even if the lake was shallower, even if we'd been better prepared, I'm not sure you…' He glanced at Merry, shrugged. 'I thought you loved swimming… but… you didn't seem to be dealing with the water that well.'

Merry rubbed the tears away from her face. Her chest ached, partly from choking and coughing up water, partly from the effort of not weeping uncontrollably. All the emotions she hadn't been feeling for the last week – all the shock and terror and disbelief – were beating down on her like hammers on an anvil.

'I can't do it, Leo. I don't think it would make any difference if the weather wasn't so cold, or if I had a wetsuit on – I can't do what Jack did. We're going to run out of time. Gwydion has already won.'

'No, he hasn't. There must be another way under the lake. Or maybe we can get Jack to bring the hearts to us. We'll figure it out.'

Merry wasn't so sure.

Not for the first time, Merry wished that Bronwen was the kind of mother who kept stashes of prescription drugs in the house rather than relying on herbs, yoga and willpower. Then, she might have been able to swallow a sleeping pill, instead of lying in bed, wide awake, nearly two hours after they'd got back from the lake. Every time she dozed off, some night-time noise in the house jerked her awake, setting her heart thumping, forcing her to switch on the lamp to make sure no one else was in the room with her. Every time she switched the lamp off again she saw faces in the darkness: Jack; Meredith; Alex, his skin blue with cold as she dragged him out of the water. All the people she had failed. Eventually she gave up, and left the light on. The parchment and the sword hilt were in the top drawer of her bedside table, but the plait of hair was still tied around her wrist; she hadn't taken it off since that first night, when Jack – the King of Hearts, rather – had almost got close enough to kill her. She examined it now – a light nut-brown, with a few strands of grey – and wondered what it was that Jack had been trying to remember.

The recollection of the conversation they'd had with him, the agony in his voice as he told them what he'd done – Merry pulled her knees up to her chest, wanting to shut out the sudden stab of compassion and remorse. It would have been so much easier if he had just kept glowering at them.

She looked at the braid again, trying to think dispassionately about what she might have to do. After they'd destroyed the hearts – whatever they turned out to be – she would say the words to knock Jack unconscious, and then –

What? Kill him magically? Stab him? Cover his mouth and nose with a pillow until –

Merry squeezed her eyes shut against the pictures in her head. Even though the image of Jack standing over her with the broken blade was fresh in her mind – still made her breath short with terror – she couldn't hate him. After talking to him this evening, she pitied him. More than that: she almost (kind of) trusted him. It didn't make any sense. But somehow, he felt... familiar.

Poor Jack. She tried to imagine him dressed in modern clothes and with a different haircut, and the thought made her smile a little. Jack would make a pretty cute twenty-first century teenager. If things had been different, maybe they could have been friends.

In the dream, Merry wasn't wearing pyjamas. She was wearing a gown of thick, red-brown wool that fell in heavy folds from below the belt around her waist. Glancing down, she saw objects hanging from the belt: a leather pouch, a knife, a stone with a hole through its centre. Nearby stood a pair of enormous wooden doors, dark-coloured, scarred with runes and symbols.

There was a touch on her shoulder. Jack was standing behind her. He cupped her face in his hands, gazing down at her as though he was trying to memorise every detail of her skin, her eyes, her lips.

'Jack...' Merry's eyes closed. Jack's lips were firm and cool as they moved against hers; he put his arms around her and pulled her close. For one infinitesimal, infinite moment, Merry was burning, and liquid gold was running through her veins.

Jack drew away, and Merry realised the wooden doors had swung open to reveal –

Trees. Crowded up against the doorway, blocking out the light. Huge holly trees with thick black branches, dark green leaves the size of her hand, long spines, like talons tipped with silver, curving out from their edges. Jack was whispering in her ear.

'You left me. You poisoned me with the black holly and you left me there, buried alive, as the centuries passed.' Slowly, his hands tightened around her wrists; he began pushing her forwards, towards the trees. 'You shouldn't have left me.'

'Jack, what are you doing? You're hurting me.' Merry struggled to break his grip, to force him back from the doorway, but his hands were like iron manacles on her arms. 'Jack, stop!'

They passed the door posts and Jack did stop, holding Merry a few centimetres in front of the wall of holly.

'It's time for you to sleep, Meredith.' Jack shoved her forwards.

Merry closed her eyes as the spines pierced her skin...

Jack woke up in the darkness of his room under the lake.

He remembered things, now. He remembered sitting

with Merry and Leo next to the lake, confessing the terrible things he had done or been made to do. And all the time his memories of the past were getting clearer. It was hard to believe that Merry was right, that such a weight of years had passed since the witch sisters had left him and Gwydion sleeping under the lake. And yet, the world was so very different. He could recall his childhood: playing among the wood shavings while his father worked, or listening to the clatter of the loom as his mother wove cloth.

His foster-mother, not his actual mother. Because he had only seen his birth mother once.

Once, in – Helmswick. That was the place. Jack closed his eyes, trying to inch his way into the past, to that particular evening. To the night he had been sent out to kill his own brother, to cut out his heart –

The memory flooded back. That was what he had been trying to describe to Merry: the only other time he – the King of Hearts – had failed…

In his mind's eye Jack could see the room clearly, the bunches of mistletoe and scarlet hangings: it was near Yuletide. His brother was lying on the bed with his eyes closed, a smile on his lips. Dreaming about the girl he loved, no doubt: the very thing that made him vulnerable to the King of Hearts' malice.

The smile faded when he opened his eyes, and saw Jack.

The boy stared at him, and somehow – was it the wolf's-head brooch Gwydion made him wear, or some family resemblance? – recognised him.

'Jack.'

'Yes,' the King of Hearts replied. '*And you must be Edmund. There's no need to be afraid. I am here to help you. To save you.*'

The boy talked to him. Imagined he could, somehow, save himself '*Please, Jack – you are still my brother. Let me help you. Surely there is some part of you that is still – human?*'

And Jack fought for control of his body, felt the shadow within him waver, weaken – but only for a minute. '*No, Edmund. I do not desire your help. I desire only to serve my master. And his desire is to set you free.*'

Edmund leapt towards the door then, but the King of Hearts shouted out the words that rendered his victims powerless and the younger boy fell as though someone had swept his legs out from under him.

Jack went to stand over him, drew his sword, raised the blade point-down above his head –

'*Jack!*'

A woman, standing on the threshold, eyes wide, burning against her pale skin. His mother. The next moment she threw herself across Edmund's body, shielding him. But the curse inside Jack did not hesitate. Jack watched, horror-struck, as his own arms plunged the blade downwards towards Edith's back, as Edmund screamed –

The blade shattered.

Jack gasped and opened his eyes. And there was Gwydion, standing before him, unchanged by the centuries that had passed: the same dark hair, touched with grey; the same scarred, narrow face; the same contemptuous expression. Jack felt for his knife.

'It is not there. Neither is the sword. My King of Hearts put them somewhere safe on his return from the world above.'

Jack did not reply. Gwydion watched him for a while.

'How many years has it been, Jack, since we last stood together under the open sky?'

Still Jack remained silent. How much had the dark shadow that inhabited his body already revealed to Gwydion, that was the question.

'Oh, I know what has been happening at the lake: when the King of Hearts loses control of you he is deaf, but he is not blind. But who is she, this girl who has thwarted my servant, turned him aside from his purpose?'

'I do not know,' Jack burst out. 'I only understand a little of what she says, and I do not know how she is able to – to prevent me from…' He stopped. Gwydion would surely realise that he was lying, at least in part.

And then what? Torture. Or Gwydion would use some spell to break open Jack's mind like an oyster shell – Somehow, he would have to resist.

Gwydion was speaking again. '… that is the question. What is it about this girl that defeats us?' Gwydion paused, his eyes narrowed, studying Jack's face. 'Soon I must rest, but first I think… I think it is time to renew the curse.'

'No!' Jack backed away.

Gwydion raised his eyebrows. 'No? But the magic has to be fed, until I can make the effect of the curse permanent. Come now.' Gwydion beckoned to Jack. 'You know you cannot resist me.'

Jack stared into Gwydion' dark eyes, but found no mercy there. 'I know it.'

He followed Gwydion along corridors, up and down stairs, until they reached a cavernous room lit only by a fire burning in a trench in the floor. There was a chair set facing the fire; a huge chair, made out of some dark wood, carved all over with swirling patterns that seemed to form leering faces when Jack looked too closely. Narrow leather cords were attached to the frame of the chair.

Jack murmured a prayer, took a deep breath, and sat down on it. The cords came to life like so many snakes, wrapping themselves around Jack's body, his head, his face, holding him fast.

'Good, good.' Gwydion bared his teeth, the closest he came to a smile. 'I enjoy hurting you, but it does save time when you do as you are bid. Now, let me select the sacrifice.' He went to a wall at the far end of the room, entirely covered with long shelves. Three of the shelves were filled with glass jars.

Jars of hearts.

The hearts that Jack – the King of Hearts – had cut out of the bodies of his victims. Jack tried to remember: how many months had passed between Gwydion capturing him, and the three witches putting him into an enchanted sleep? How many people had he killed?

Gwydion picked up one of the jars and brought it over to the fire. 'The body is dead, so now I sacrifice the soul.' Gwydion raised his hands and started to draw the fire runes in the air, chanting in a language Jack did not understand. The runes were a dull red-brown, the colour of old blood. They burned themselves directly into Jack's brain until he gasped and sweated with the pain of it, but the cords on his face still held his eyelids open. Gwydion pulled the stopper out of the jar and tipped the contents into the fire.

The heart screamed.

As the sound faded, Jack felt himself fading too, until he was sealed somewhere inside his own head, a spectator without any free will. Someone else, or something else, took control of his body.

The leather cords fell away, lifeless. Jack found himself kneeling before the wizard.

Gwydion put one hand on Jack's head, as if he were blessing him, then raised him to his feet.

'Welcome again, my King of Hearts.'

FOURTEEN

SOMETIMES, THE DREAMS were different.

They all started off OK, with her and Jack kissing. Kissing so intensely it made her dizzy. But the good bit never lasted long.

Mostly, the dreams ended with Jack killing her in various inventively gruesome ways. On the worst nights – the nights she woke up gasping for breath, heart pounding, bed-sheets twisted and damp with sweat – he drowned her, holding her down as her lungs filled with water.

Those nights were bad.

But just occasionally, the dreams ended with her killing Jack. Like tonight. She was sitting astride him, her knees

226

either side of his hips, her hair curtaining his face as they kissed. But behind her back she held a sword. With a curious sense of serenity, she pulled away from Jack, brought the sword round and thrust the blade underneath his rib cage. Jack's eyes widened as the blood began to flow.

Nights like this were pretty bad too.

There was a strange, high-pitched ringing sound, and Merry wondered whether Jack was screaming. But the light had gone out of his eyes: he was already dead. Maybe she was screaming?

The sound kept getting louder, more insistent. Merry pushed herself away from Jack, got her legs tangled in something –

– and fell off the bed.

'Ow!' She rubbed her eyes and kicked the duvet away from her feet. The sound was alarm clocks: three of them, all ringing at once. It had been six days since Leo had dragged her out of the water. Six days that had included two visits to the lake (each time ignoring the continued insistence of the manuscript that she should 'follow him'); a trip to the local swimming pool (an unsuccessful attempt at aversion therapy); more nightmares than she cared to remember. Multiple alarm clocks were now the only way she could get herself out of bed.

Merry picked up a nearby shoe and hurled it at one of the clocks, but the damn thing just kept on ringing. It was clearly going to be one of those days.

She started getting ready for school, trying to figure out exactly what story she could spin her athletics teacher about why she'd missed javelin practice again. Ruby was going to be angry with her too: it was Ruby's birthday, and instead of going out for coffee and cake at lunchtime, Merry was going to be in the library trying to do a week's history homework in forty-five minutes. She was about to text Ruby to suggest coffee after school when she remembered the worst thing about today. Gran had finally forced her to commit to a meeting with the coven. As soon as school finished, provided the manuscript didn't summon her to the lake, Merry had to go and be tested.

Merry left it to the last minute, but Jack wasn't obliging enough to come out of the lake and give her an excuse. The meeting took place in Mrs Knox's house: the full coven was too big to fit into Gran's sitting room. When Merry arrived, Mrs Knox lead her through to a cavernous room at the back of the house.

'Used to be a ballroom, back in my grandfather's day. No call for such things now, but it serves our purposes.'

She glanced at Merry over her shoulder and smiled. 'No need to be nervous. We're not going to eat you.'

It took a few minutes for Merry's eyes to adjust to the dimness: the curtains were closed and the only light came from a variety of candlesticks positioned round the edges of the room. There seemed to be about twenty women waiting for her; she hadn't been expecting so many.

Gran emerged from the throng. 'Hello, darling. You look tired.' She hugged Merry tightly. 'Well, you can relax now. We won't be doing anything too demanding.'

Merry nodded, but she wondered what Gran's definition of demanding included.

Gran quickly ran through the names of the coven members Merry hadn't met before – Merry was glad to see Flo there, despite the unfortunate episode with the manuscript – and then pointed Merry to a chair on its own, facing the semicircle of fully trained witches.

'So, let's get down to it. I know you've been having problems with the spells I asked you to try. But what magic can you do?'

Merry looked around the ring of expectant faces. 'Er...'

'It's alright, Merry, I know you must have experimented. No one will blame you in the circumstances.'

'Quite a good thing, actually.' Mrs Knox's loud

interruption – she didn't seem to know about indoor voices – made Merry jump. 'Magic with no outlet is liable to go wild. That's where stories of poltergeists come from. Usually just some poor, untrained girl who doesn't know her own power, and then—'

'Yes, thank you, Sophia.' Gran, in contrast to Mrs Knox, spoke quietly, but her voice commanded instant attention from the other witches. 'Merry, it's been over four years since we tested you. Tell us what's been happening, magically speaking.'

Merry's insides squirmed.

'Well, I did try some stuff out on my own. I… I borrowed a book from your house and, you know, just had a go.'

'And?'

'Um, some of the spells seemed to work.' Merry thought back to the first couple of years of her 'experimenting'. She was definitely going to have to be selective. 'I learnt a spell to get rid of spots. A memory charm, to help me study for tests. Um, and a deflection spell, which seemed to stop teachers asking me questions in class…' A couple of the witches were frowning and peering at her searchingly. She could feel her face flushing and looked away. 'A few other small things.'

'OK.' Gran, at least, didn't seem to be judging her. 'Have you progressed at all since then?'

'Well… no. I stopped, last summer.' Gran's eyebrow lifted, so Merry ploughed on. 'I got scared that something would go wrong, with nobody to correct me.'

'That's the whole reason?'

Merry nodded, grateful for the dim lighting.

'And how has your magic behaved?'

'Nothing happened for a while. I thought—'

Hoped? Or feared?

'—I thought maybe I was losing my powers. Like you said, I've been struggling with casting spells. But I've also had these kind of… random episodes. Magic exploding out of me.' She looked down at her finger nails. 'I've broken a couple of things.'

'Like what, dear?'

'I broke a mirror at school, a big one. It shattered.'

'Perfectly normal.' Gran smiled. 'What else?'

'Well, this thorny bush thing shot out of the ground and basically murdered another plant. Dragged it back under the soil.'

And nearly killed my brother. But I don't think I'm going to mention that.

'Oh. Well, that is a bit more unusual. But, as we start training you, those sort of magical outbursts—'

'And I'm seeing things.'

231

There was some subdued muttering from the coven. Gran shushed them.

'What did you say, Merry?'

'Er...' Merry paused.

Damn. They really didn't need to know that. Flo probably thinks I'm nuts. Maybe I could pretend I meant dreaming...

But the way Gran was looking at her, she couldn't lie.

'I've been seeing Meredith. Our ancestor. At least, I'm pretty certain it's her. Last time, she told me I had to get on with it. More or less.'

'Well.' Gran drummed her fingers on the arms of her chair and stared at Merry. Lots of the witches were staring. Merry started trying to pick a bit of old varnish off her thumbnail. 'Well. I suppose we are all dealing with something completely new here. Just... keep us informed, Merry. If anything else abnormal happens.'

Yeah, right, Merry thought. *My entire life is abnormal at the moment. How long have you got?*

But she just nodded.

Gran looked round at the other witches.

'Any more questions, ladies?'

Most shook their heads, but one woman raised her hand.

'Yes, Roshni?

'I would like to ask, Merry, what you think the aim of

your training is? What do you think you should become?'
The woman was smiling, but her appearance – dark hair
pulled up into a bun, a dark skirt-suit – made Merry think
of her headmistress from junior school. She could feel her
palms getting damp.

'Um…'

What are my aims?

Not to die.

*Not to hurt anyone. I mean, apart from the bad guys, I
guess.*

Not to mess up.

The silence around her was solidifying.

'Um… I suppose… to be a good witch?'

Roshni glanced at Gran, who pursed her lips.

'You sound uncertain, Merry.' Roshni's smile had faded.
'Also, you're wrong.'

'But, I—'

'Your aim, at this stage, in this state of emergency, is to
be a powerful witch. There is no room for doubt.'

Gran was nodding.

'Roshni is right. Confidence is key. Shall we begin?'

Two hours later, Merry was on the verge of tears.

Gran sighed.

'Let's just try one more time. This is a basic shielding spell, Merry. I thought you'd done something like this before.'

'I have, and it used to work.' Merry coughed and took a sip of water, wincing as she swallowed. 'I didn't know I was supposed to sing it.'

'Music enhances the power of the words. It should make it easier. Try again.'

Merry cleared her throat and began to sing the spell once more. Her voice sounded croaky.

'Hard as bronze, hard as iron, strong as a shield-wall round the stone tower...'

Flo, who was her opponent in this exercise – and who looked as miserable as Merry felt – raised her hands and began to sing another spell: a stinging hex. Flo was so good at the spell that she actually only had to sing one line to set it going.

Merry – envious – tried to sing louder. Her shielding spell seemed to be holding: the hex (like a nettle sting crossed with an electric shock) wasn't getting through.

Is it working? Please, let it work this time –

Her left cheek burned. She gasped – clapped her hand to her face – stopped singing – and her arms and neck began to throb with pain too.

'Stop!' Gran was next to her, singing softly, and the pain faded.

'I'm so sorry!' Flo was hovering nearby. 'I didn't mean to come on that strong, but you seemed to be doing better—'

'Merry dear, it's not about singing louder, it's about – about getting inside the real meaning of the spell, focusing on what you want to achieve—' Gran sighed. 'I think we should stop for today. But I had hoped you would be more... advanced. You're going to need regular lessons from now on.'

'I thought you said the stuff in the trinket box would be enough? That it didn't matter about me being untrained?' Merry could hear the pitch of her voice rising as the panic and shame bubbled up inside her.

Gran didn't answer immediately.

'I think it will be enough,' she said eventually. 'I have confidence in all the witches – your ancestors – who have planned for this moment, even if you don't. But, it's only sensible to be as fully prepared as possible, especially since you haven't yet been able to find a way under the lake. Have a rest now. I'm going to talk to the others, see if we can organise some kind of schedule.'

Carefully avoiding eye contact with any of the other

witches, Merry went to sit in one of the armchairs in front of the huge, empty fireplace. There was a table next to it, and on that were glasses and a few jugs of iced water – Mrs Knox's idea of refreshments.

What did you expect? This isn't the Women's Institute.

Shutting her eyes, Merry leant back in the chair.

A cup of tea, that's what I could do with right now. Or a really strong coffee.

Ruby's dad had one of those posh Italian coffee-making things, the type you put on the stove to boil. The last time she'd been there at the weekend he'd made coffee for her in it; she remembered the sound of the bubbling water, and the scent of coffee filling the kitchen…

'Merry, what on earth are you doing?' Merry opened her eyes. Mrs Knox was standing over her, pointing at the jugs of water. The iced water was… boiling. Steam was rising up to the ceiling.

'But – I didn't do anything!' Merry sat up straighter. 'I mean, I was thinking about coffee, and boiling water, but I don't know any spells for that. How could it be me?'

Silence. Followed by a buzz of conversation around the room. Gran appeared.

'Merry, I need you to be totally honest with me. Did you try another spell? Sing or say anything in particular?'

'No, Gran, I was just thinking about having a hot drink. Really.'

Gran held her gaze for a moment.

'OK.' She raised her voice. 'Ladies, if you please…' Gran swept off to the far end of the room again, followed by the other witches. Merry couldn't really hear what they were saying, but she caught the word 'dangerous' a couple of times. And then Flo looked over her shoulder, back at where Merry was sitting, and Merry recognised the expression on her face.

She's frightened.

She's frightened of me.

The fear Merry had felt when she realised what she'd done to Alex – that terrifying sense of her own potential for evil – rose up inside her again as strong as ever. What if she was really dangerous? What if they decided she was just as bad as Gwydion? Would they turn on her?

'Merry,' Gran was beckoning to her, 'come here.'

Merry hesitated.

This is ridiculous. That's your grandmother over there. She's not about to transform you into a frog.

She walked over to the coven, head held high.

'Well?'

'We've decided,' Gran stared around the ring of women,

as though daring anyone to challenge her, 'that your training may need a – a different approach. Usually the whole coven would be involved in training a witch, but for the time being you'll work mostly with me, and occasionally with Roshni and Sophia. Your abilities are clearly very unusual: virtually non-existent in some areas, highly developed in others. To be honest, it's not something any of us have come across before.'

'If anyone was to ask me,' began Flo's mum, 'I'd say what she's done is – well, it's not natural. Not at all how any true witch would go about things.' She backed away a little as Gran turned to glare at her.

'Oh, for heaven's sake, Denise, do stop being ridiculous! Merry's abilities are most likely to do with who she is. What she is.' Gran paused, but Denise didn't seem inclined to argue. 'Well, we're done for today, ladies.' The witches separated. Some stayed and chatted, but Merry noticed Denise hustling Flo straight out of the room.

Merry pressed her fingers to her forehead, trying to push away the headache building behind her eyes. Gran hugged her.

'You can go too, Merry; I'll call you later. Unless there's anything you want to ask me now?'

Merry shook her and turned away. She'd remembered

what Leo said, the night they found the trinket box. That she would be the kind of witch who eats children.

So I'm not going to ask Gran who I am, or what I am. Somehow, I don't think I'd like the answer.

It was the next day, and Merry was sitting in the garden shed. The shed was full of spiders, but that meant Mum wouldn't expect her to be in there. Merry was pretty certain her mother had put some kind of eavesdropping spell on the main house.

She settled herself on an old bag of potting compost and thought about practising her witch fire spell, before deciding she was too tired and pulling out the manuscript instead.

'Hello, manuscript.'

Eala, Merry.

'So… can we get into Gwydion's fortress through a tunnel system that runs under the lake?'

No.

Merry sighed and crossed 'tunnel' off the list in her notebook. Other suggestions the manuscript had rejected included a secret entrance, a magic portal and a rip in the space-time continuum (Leo's idea). Gran had tried putting charms on Merry to remove her fear of the water, but so far none of them had stuck. Merry wasn't surprised, given she couldn't even force herself to get into the local swimming pool.

Maybe there's something I can do to the water, instead of something being done to me?

She thought back to the incident at Mrs Knox's house.

Maybe I can make the lake boil away? If I can figure out what the hell I did to the water in those jugs. Although, people might notice an entire lake disappearing...

The whole magic thing was so confusing. She was frightened of being a witch, but she needed to be a witch. She had to try to be good at spells, but she felt sure she shouldn't *want* to be good at spells. Why could she work some magic easily and some not at all? And were there going to be any more killer plants or other dangerous outbursts?

Just a lot of questions. No answers.

Shaking her head, she made a note to consider the boiling lake idea further, then went back to the list she'd already made.

'OK. Is there a spell we can use to destroy the puppet hearts from a distance?'

No.

Another line through another list; they'd already run

through variations on the idea of getting Jack to bring the hearts out of the lake (without, of course, revealing to him – and potentially the King of Hearts – exactly what they were attempting). Nothing doing there either, apparently.

'Is Jack going to leave the lake tonight?'

Yes. Follow him into the water.

'But – I can't swim down through the damn lake! I can't—' Merry threw the manuscript to the floor. Every other night now, the answer to that last question was 'yes'. There was no point in crying about it. But she was just so very tired.

Merry barely noticed when they arrived at the little car park in the woods that evening. Leo turned off the engine and twisted round in his seat to look at her.

'You were very quiet during dinner. Try to talk a bit more. Mum's going to get suspicious, given it's normally impossible to get you to shut up.'

'She's already suspicious. You saw the way she was watching me.'

'I guess it's not surprising; you look terrible.'

'Gee, thanks.'

Leo drummed his fingers on the steering wheel. 'School OK?'

Merry shrugged. *Not really. Currently I have no social life, no time to study and I'm probably about to get dumped from all my sports teams.*

But she just said: 'Same as usual.'

'Right… Well, is there anything you do want to talk about, while we're on our own?'

'What, other than the fact I'm turning out to be the most rubbish witch in history, and Gwydion is probably going to catch me and – and turn me into a pumpkin, or something?'

'Wrong fairy tale. But yeah – anything other than that?'

Merry considered. There was something else on her mind: Jack. Even when she wasn't having nightmares about him, she couldn't seem to stop thinking about him. It was disturbing. And wrong, surely: to start looking forwards to spending time with somebody you were supposed to kill. Definitely wrong to be dreaming about kissing him.

'Well?' Leo nudged her.

Better to say nothing, maybe. But there was so much she was keeping hidden at the moment. And this was Leo she was talking to…

'Do you think Jack's hot?'

Leo's eyebrows shot up, but he pursed his lips, musing.

'Course. If you like that whole tall, blond, ripped, murderous thing. I definitely fancy him. I mean, who wouldn't?'

Merry laughed. 'I suppose. You're obviously going to think he looks good, because you're tall, blond and ripped yourself. Not quite as tall or blond, and definitely not—'

'Yeah, yeah, I get the picture. But Merry—' the smile faded from Leo's eyes, '—you what know Jack is, what he is capable of. Or at least, what that thing that takes over his body is capable of. You're not falling for him, are you?' He looked so serious.

Merry shook her head as she opened the car door. 'Don't be an idiot, Leo. Let's get this over with, shall we?'

A little while later they were sitting with Jack near the edge of the lake, huddled close to the small portable heater Leo had started bringing with him. Gradually, some of the missing fragments of Jack's memory seemed to be returning. He told them about the impenetrable hedge of black holly that had grown around the tower, and how the witch sisters had used it in the spell to cause enchanted sleep.

'I remember them now. They were all beautiful. Carys, the eldest, was tall, with hair the colour of primroses. Nia, the middle sister, was pale and dark. There was something… unusual about her.' He described them exactly as Merry had last seen them, standing with Meredith in their fire-lit cottage, asking – commanding? – her to deal with Gwydion. She took a deep breath, trying to control the sudden swirl of anxiety in the pit of her stomach. How was it possible for her to have been talked to by people who'd been dead for almost fifteen hundred years?

'What about Meredith? Did she seem really powerful? Did you know she was a witch as soon as you met her?'

Jack shrugged and plucked a daisy out of the grass. Its petals were closed up against the night. 'None of the sisters were as I imagined witches to be.'

In the darkness, she tried to make out Jack's expression. He obviously didn't want to talk about Meredith. Maybe he hated her. After all, she hadn't freed him from Gwydion, and she hadn't killed him; she'd just left him buried alive under the lake for fifteen hundred years. *I can kind of understand it, if he hates her. I'm not exactly a big fan either.*

'I'm sorry. You must've been really lonely.'

All at once, Jack covered his face with his hands.

'Jack—' Merry started to scramble to her feet, thinking only of what Jack was suffering; of whether he was OK. But Leo grabbed her arm and pulled her back down, frowning and shaking his head. Merry muttered under her breath, but she didn't disobey.

'We will find a way to stop Gwydion,' Leo said gently. 'Meredith must have believed he could be defeated. And at least while we're here the King of Hearts isn't hurting anyone else.'

'That's right.' Merry cast around for reasons to be cheerful. 'And hopefully, that means Gwydion isn't getting any stronger, that he's no closer to escaping from the lake.' She looked at Jack for confirmation, but he shook his head.

'I do not know. The wizard still struggles to shake off the effects of the black holly, but he sleeps less than he did.'

'Oh. Well…' But Merry couldn't think of any other comforting suggestions to make; she just didn't know enough, that was the trouble. She didn't know how much of Gwydion's strength was drawn from the King of Hearts. And she didn't know why the King of Hearts was – so far – sticking his sword into people but not cutting out their hearts.

Maybe he just hadn't got his mojo back before we got in the way…

Merry shuddered a little and shook the thought away.

'So, you really were completely alone until the witches showed up?'

'Not exactly.' Jack looked at her strangely for a moment.

'There was a… a kitchen maid. She came in the autumn after I'd been captured. Gwydion made her cook for us, and she would come to sweep the floor and lay fresh rushes. We became friends. I – I liked her. A lot.'

'Oh. Did she like you too?'

'I believe she looked upon me with favour.'

Merry felt herself straighten up and pull away from Jack a little. *Seriously? I'm jealous of a dead Anglo-Saxon maidservant?* She forced herself to smile. 'I'm glad you had someone to talk to. What was she like?'

'Both fair and fearless. When the wizard – when he tortured me, whether for sport, or because I tried to resist him, she would come afterwards and take care of me, even though she knew he would hurt her if he caught her. I remember one day…'

And Merry was no longer sitting in the dark by the lake. She was in a small room, faint light coming from a deep-cut window high up in one wall, and next to her was –

– Jack, lying on the floor of his cell, barely breathing, his skin torn and discoloured with bruises. So pale, she'd feared he was dead when she first knelt on the rushes next to him. But he was frowning now, flinching as she washed the blood away from the welts on his back and arms. When she was finished, he opened his eyes a little and murmured her name.

'Oh, my poor Jack, what has he done to you?' She lifted his head and pressed a cup to his lips. 'Drink a little, then I will look to your wounds.'

'No – don't...'

'Please, Jack, try the medicine.'

Jack swallowed a little of the liquid. She dipped one finger into a pot of sweetly-scented cream and gently smoothed it across a graze on his cheekbone. He caught hold of her hand.

'Don't help me. I should suffer. I deserve to suffer. I nearly killed – I nearly—'

'Shh, don't talk now. Rest, and I will put poultices on the rest of these cuts. Then we will talk...'

Merry blinked and coughed as a gust of cold air blew across the lake. Leo was shining his torch in her face.

'Leo, what the—' She squinted, pushing the torch away.

'Why didn't you answer me? Are you OK?'

'I don't know, I—' She stopped.

Was she now daydreaming about Jack, too? It had been so vivid: the sensation of his bare skin beneath her fingertips...

She felt her face grow hot.

'Merry?' Leo shook her gently by the shoulder. 'What's the matter?'

'Nothing. I'm just tired, that's all.' She'd pretend nothing

had happened. Act normal. 'Um, Jack, do you remember—'
But there was no time for more questions. Jack had gone,
the King of Hearts had taken his place, and Merry had to
say the words that would send him back into the lake…

FIFTEEN

STANDING IN FRONT of the sink, doing the washing-up, Merry yawned. She couldn't help it. Since her meeting with the coven just over a week ago she'd spent four evenings at the lake. The three free evenings she'd spent at Gran's, having several hours of 'remedial witchcraft' lessons. A few of the spells were going OK: she could now produce a globe of witch fire fairly reliably. Most were not: she'd failed to perform any kind of healing spell to Gran's satisfaction, and her shielding charm consistently collapsed less than two minutes into an attack. The manuscript was still telling her to follow Jack under the lake, and so far she was still ignoring it.

But she was – slowly – forming some sort of a plan.

The idea of boiling the lake away seemed too insane to contemplate, regardless of what she'd managed to (inexplicably) do at Mrs Knox's house. But maybe she did have some special, unexpected skill with water. And maybe there was some other way she could use that skill to get past the barrier of the lake.

The house was empty – no one else around to get hurt if things went wrong – so Merry took the last pan out of the sink and stared down at the water.

Supposing I just… push the water out of the way?

She concentrated, trying – as Gran had told her – to focus on what she wanted to achieve.

Nothing happened.

She tried harder, gripping the edge of the sink, glaring at the water until the muscles around her eyes and her jaw started to ache.

Slowly, almost imperceptibly, the water in the centre of the sink started to dip.

The dip became a hollow, which became a deep conical depression, the displaced water spreading up the sides of the sink. Her fingernails began to tingle, just like when she'd conjured up the killer plant, but now the sensation spread up through her hands and her arms, crawling across her skin. She could almost touch the plug without getting her fingers wet – almost –

The water collapsed back on itself, spraying Merry and the whole sink area with soapy suds.

'Damn it.' She grabbed a tea towel and started drying herself off.

If this is going to work, I'm going to have to get a lot better at it. Really fast.

Sure, she was stopping the King of Hearts from attacking people. But despite that, Jack was now emerging from the lake so frequently that she had to assume the wizard was still, somehow, getting stronger. The manuscript didn't seem to know. Gwydion escaping the lake, Gwydion confronting her when she still had nothing which to fight him – no puppet hearts, no real magical skill – these were the fears that increasingly haunted her dreams.

She shivered and switched the kitchen lights on. Mum wouldn't be home this evening – luckily, her workaholic tendencies had got the better of her maternal concern again, and she was staying in London overnight for a conference – but Leo would be back soon. Then once more they would probably have to traipse over to the lake. She yawned again. At least she'd get to see Jack.

★ ★ ★

The manuscript had sent them out at sunset, this time – the first time, apart from in her dreams, that Merry had seen Jack in anything approaching daylight. She was sitting under an umbrella with her folder balanced on her knees, supposedly revising Henry VII's foreign policy, but actually just staring at Jack's face. At rest, the frown lines between Jack's eyes disappeared. He looked peaceful, and young: Merry realised with a shock that he couldn't be much older than Leo, even though he had already been through so much. She stretched out her fingers, planning to brush away a smudge of dirt from Jack's cheekbone, when he opened his eyes and smiled at her. Merry snatched her hand back. 'Oh. You're awake.'

'*Eala*, Merry.'

Leo handed Jack another umbrella and started rummaging in his backpack. D'you want something to eat?'

'Yes, if it please you.'

'Here. I brought some of our mother's so-called chocolate cake.'

Jack peered into the plastic food container. 'What is so-called chocolate cake?'

'Well, it's got beetroot in it, and virtually no sugar.' Leo pulled a face. 'But I've poured half a bottle of syrup over it so it should still taste OK. Plus, I'm not entirely sure how your body would handle exposure to some of the preservatives and food colouring they use nowadays…' He went off into a long, involved, pre-med school student rant about the food industry. Merry – who had heard it all before – pulled the hood of her coat over her head and got up to stretch her legs.

She wandered down to the edge of the lake. It didn't look quite so forbidding at dusk, even though there was no glimmer of sunset through the thick rain clouds. She tried to remember when she had last seen a sunset, and eventually gave up. But there was a way to make it a little lighter. Quietly singing the words Gran had taught her, Merry conjured a flickering ball of witch fire. Her own personal supernova, it blazed into life on her left palm; stuck there, strangely heavy, as she turned her hand back and forth. The shifting surface warmed her skin without burning it, and when she held the ball close to her ear it crackled like a distant log fire. The violet flames cast strange, twisted shadows across the water; the rain, still pelting down, was falling, through the flames, not extinguishing them, but slicing them into tiny fragments of light. Merry frowned. Not thinking about what she was doing, she imagined an invisible shield around the witch fire, something to protect her little bit of magic from the unnatural winter that Gwydion's dark sorcery was spreading.

There was that prickling feeling again, starting in her nails. And, in the circle of space immediately above her globe of light, the rain stopped falling.

I've done it, I've done something against Gwydion. It's only small, but —

The mutterings of Flo's mother came back to her. Not natural, she'd said; not what a true witch would do. Merry knew what spells were supposed to be: ancient words, in different languages, learnt by heart and passed down from generation to generation. Doing magic as she had just done it, by thought only, without words or ritual... What if it was wrong? Bad?

She snatched her hand back. The witch fire was extinguished, and the rain carried on falling, as if there had never been any interruption in its journey into the lake.

I shouldn't be messing around anyway — we're running out of time. First thing tomorrow I'm going to tell Gran about what I did earlier, with the water. See if she can teach me a spell I can use to do the same thing. A proper witch's spell.

Merry turned away from the lake and walked back to where Jack and Leo were still sitting under umbrellas next to the heater. They seemed to be talking about family. Merry caught the end of Leo's sentence:

'…even when she's actually at home. But, you know, she's still our mum. What about your parents?'

'If you mean my blood mother, I only saw her once. I never met my father. But my parents, the people who raised me, were good people. They worked so hard to make sure that I was prepared for my future life, even though it would mean I had to leave them…' There was a faint catch in Jack's voice, and he trailed off.

Merry didn't know what to say. She had never had to face the death of even one person she loved. Jack had lost everyone: his real parents, his foster-parents, the girl in the village that Gwydion had killed, the kitchen maid who had befriended him… Sitting down next to him she hesitated for a moment – realised that the deepening twilight would at least prevent Jack from seeing her blush – then reached out and slipped her fingers into his, squeezing his hand hard. Jack glanced up at her, his lips parted in mild surprise. Merry's heartbeat accelerated.

The portable heater burst into flames.

All three of them scrambled away from the blaze. Luckily, the rain put the fire out quickly.

Merry noticed Leo staring at her. She opened her mouth

to say: *It wasn't my fault, or if it was, at least there was no killer plant this time…*

But something in his expression stopped her. She knew he would end up lecturing her when they got home: about staying focused on the mission, and how she was supposed to be trying to kill Jack, not date him. But, as she sat down and took Jack's hand again, she decided she didn't care.

The school library, it turned out, was a pretty good place to take a nap. There was one dusty, remote corner of the Classics section where it was possible to rest quite comfortably between the end of the bookcase and a small window, with virtually zero likelihood of being disturbed. After the previous evening's drama, Merry had needed to catch up on some sleep; now she was sitting, eyes still closed, thinking about the phone call she'd had with Gran that morning.

Merry had explained about the stuff she seemed to be able to do with water – in addition to making it boil really quickly – and her plan for moving the lake water out of the way. When she'd mentioned stopping the rain, Gran had been… somewhat concerned.

'And you're not using any words as part of this spell? Nothing verbal at all?'

'No. I'm just thinking about what I want. Really hard. Isn't that what we're supposed to do? It's not... bad, is it? Dangerous?'

'Oh, no. Not dangerous.' There had been a pause on the other end of the phone line. 'Just not encouraged. But don't worry about that now. If it's working for you, stick with it.'

'OK.'

And that was the end of the conversation, more or less. Merry couldn't help feeling depressed afterwards: Gran just hadn't seemed that excited about her plan. Maybe she didn't think it would ever work. And what had she meant by 'not encouraged'? It was almost like she was starting to agree with Flo's mum...

Somebody nudged her in the ankle.

Merry looked up. 'Ruby! What are you doing here?'

Ruby narrowed her eyes. 'I could ask you the same question. I thought you had English this period. And you never come to the library.'

'I do now. I needed a book for history.' She tapped a book lying next to her on the floor, and hoped Ruby wouldn't notice it was actually a collection of spells, bound in old leather with gilded runes on the front cover.

'Yeah, right.' Ruby shook her head. 'I don't get what's happening, Merry. You're missing classes. You're about to be kicked off the athletics team, which used to be like, your *life*.' She paused and examined her fingernails. 'You never seem to want to hang out any more.'

'That's not true. It's just—'

Ruby carried on talking, ignoring Merry's protest. 'And have you looked at yourself in a mirror lately? You're a mess. You look like you're on drugs, or something—' She broke off and crouched down next to Merry. 'You're not on drugs, are you?'

'No! Course not.'

'Well… I don't know what you've got going on with this Jack bloke, but he sounds like bad news to me. I thought we were best mates. But I'm not going to keep covering for you if you don't start acting more… normal.'

Merry had found herself an unsuitable boyfriend: that's what Ruby had assumed. When Merry asked if she could use her as an excuse to get out of the house, Ruby thought that Merry was hooking up with someone she needed to keep hidden from her mother. Merry had gone along with it; there was no way she was going to attempt to explain to Ruby what was really going on.

But Gran needed help distracting Mum from Merry's frequent absences, so Merry needed Ruby to keep covering for her.

'OK, look – I promise you I am not in an abusive relationship.' Strictly true. 'Jack's older than me, that's all.' Also true. 'And all the other stuff – I'm just really stressed about the exams, and what I'm going to do after school.' Ruby didn't look that convinced. 'Honestly, I'm going to sort myself out, but I just need to get through the next few weeks. Jack's leaving soon, and I won't see him again.' And that was true too: if the manuscript was right, either Jack would be dead at the end of all this, or she would be.

Ruby was still watching her, her eyes full of doubt.

Merry pressed her knuckles hard against her breastbone, pushing the panic and fear and anger back under the surface, praying that Ruby would believe her. 'Hey, I'm not doing anything at lunch. Why don't we go to the cafe in the park? See if that fit waiter's working this week?'

Ruby smiled slightly, but shook her head. 'Can't. I said I'd go into town with Ciara. She wants me to look at shoes with her.' She stood up. 'Maybe next week, yeah?'

'Sure.'

Merry watched her go. *She's really angry with me. Or she's just going off me. Not surprising, since I've stopped…* She dropped her head into her hands. *I guess she's finally realising that, deep down, I'm not a very nice person…*

She'd lost Alex, now she was losing Ruby. Soon, her brother would be the only friend she had left.

Leo was leaning forwards, explaining. It was Sunday evening, three days after Merry had blown up the portable heater. But Leo had gone straight out and bought a new one: they were nearly halfway through March now, but the evenings were no warmer. Colder, if anything: the ground beneath them frozen solid.

'So that's when I first thought, yeah, I'd really like to be a doctor.'

Merry laughed, despite the now-constant sick feeling in the pit of her stomach, the anxiety that lay like chainmail across her shoulders.

'All because you stole my toy doctor's kit and kept pretending I was dying of the Black Death?'

Jack – who'd looked pretty blank during most of Leo's explanation – reached forwards to take a biscuit from the packet Merry had brought with her, revealing a fresh red welt across his forearm.

Leo sighed.

'I guess it doesn't seem so funny when you've seen real bloodshed…'

Jack dropped the biscuit and sat back, tugging the sleeves of his tunic down.

Merry didn't comment. She and Leo had guessed at what was happening: that Gwydion was punishing Jack for his failure to do whatever it was he was supposed to be doing, whether that was cut people's hearts out or just stick his sword into them. But Jack wouldn't talk about it, let alone allow Leo to use modern medicine to help him… She blinked hard. Pity wouldn't help Jack. 'And what about you, Jack?' she asked. 'What did you want to do with your life? I mean, before Gwydion?'

Jack's shoulders relaxed again. 'I did not want to be a carpenter like my father, for all I loved helping him fell the trees and shape the wood. It all seems so distant now, almost like – like somebody else's life, that I heard of in a story. I had great plans, of course. I wanted to leave the village, to see the world.' He sighed and smiled briefly. 'That was before I found out I was the son of the king. I only spent one day as an aetheling, and during the first part of that day, at least, my wishes were mainly to do with not falling off my horse.'

'I'm sure you would've been a really good king, Jack,' Leo offered.

'I am less certain. However, it is kind of you to say so.'

He shook his head, as though shaking away memories. 'And what of you, Merry? What do you wish your life to be?'

Merry had a sudden vision of her – still uncompleted – careers questionnaire.

'Really, I have no clue. I guess you've always been much more focused than me, haven't you?' She looked over at her brother, who shrugged. 'But—'

Leo's phone buzzed. He glanced at it, drew in his breath sharply and jabbed his fingers at the phone to unlock it. Watching his face by the glow of the screen, Merry thought he was about to be sick.

'Oh, no…'

'Leo? What's happened?'

Silence for a moment. And then –

'It's a text from Mum.' Grabbing his bag, Leo started trying to drag the picnic blanket out from underneath Merry, tipping her back on to her elbows. 'Get up! We have to go.'

'But – but we can't both leave! I mean, what about—' Merry waved a hand at Jack. 'He'll come back, and if we're not here—'

'God – I guess—' Leo groaned and squatted back down on the blanket next to her. 'Mum bumped into Ruby's mum at the train station. She's found out you're not with

Ruby, at least not this evening. Now she's on her way to The Swan.'

'The Swan?'

Leo threw his hands in the air.

'The pub, Merry – the place I'm supposed to be working this evening? I told her I was covering for Dan.'

'Oh, God.'

'Exactly.' They both turned to look at Jack, who sat looking down at his feet. 'Er – OK – you stay here with Jack. If I leave now I might just make it before she does. If you can find anything out from Ruby – like how much damage has been done – text me.' Leo stood up again and fished the car keys out of his pocket. 'I'll get back as soon as I can. You going to be alright?'

'I'll be fine, just go.' Merry pulled her phone out of her bag and messaged Ruby.

What's happened? How much does mum know?

She waited a couple of minutes.

R u there?

Please, what's happening?

Still nothing. Merry swore and threw the phone down on to the blanket, trying to think: what would Ruby tell her mum? Was she going to drop her in it, after their conversation on Friday?

Oh, damn...

'Merry?'

She had almost forgotten Jack was there.

'Sorry, Jack. A bit of a crisis. Our mum's not supposed to know about any of this. She definitely would not approve.'

'I wish – I wish I was able to help you.'

'Don't worry. Leo will sort it out somehow.'

She stared back towards the trees, willing Leo to get to the pub in time, willing him to come up with a plan.

'Um... what were we talking about? Before?'

'You were going to tell me your plans for the future. What you want your life to be.'

Merry let out a shout of laughter. She couldn't help it: it was all so – ridiculous.

'Not this.' She waved her hands around, indicating the lake, the darkness, the whole insane situation. 'I don't want this.'

'I understand. It would have been better if Meredith and her sisters had killed me.' Jack drew out the long, angular knife he wore at his waist and stabbed it into the ground next to him. 'Better still if I had never been born.'

'Don't say that, Jack. I don't mean—' Merry bit her lip, unsure of what exactly she did mean. 'It's not just this – this nightmare that we're going through now, anyway. Even before that, my life was going nowhere. I barely scraped through my last set of exams. And now…' She glanced at Jack. 'You don't really understand most of what I'm saying, do you?'

Jack took Merry's hand, turned it over and began tracing patterns on her palm with the tip of one finger. That was new, she reflected, as her blood tingled just under her skin; their fingers had brushed against each other many times, Jack had once swept a stray strand of hair away from her face, but – apart from the night he broke into her room – he had never touched her so openly before.

'I understand you are frightened. You have no hope for the future. I have little hope or desire to survive what is to come. But you are a good person, Merry. God willing, you will survive, and you will find your path.'

Merry could feel the calluses on Jack's hands, the legacy of years of manual work. He was such an odd mixture of child and adult. Jack could barely read and write, but Merry knew he had far more practical skills than Leo. And he seemed so… transparent. Most people, Merry thought, really needed to come with a label, the sort they put on toys and cigarettes. Ones like: 'Warning: borrows money and never pays it back, may seriously damage your bank account.' Or: 'Only after one thing: not suitable for under-sixteens, beware of small parts'. But Jack seemed to be completely straightforward; there was no act, no angle.

She made a decision: she would tell him the truth.

'I'm not. I'm not a good person, Jack. Not really. You know I told you I don't do much magic, that I haven't been properly trained?' Jack nodded. 'Well, the training bit is true.' Merry picked up a nearby pebble and threw it into the lake. 'But for some reason, that doesn't seem to have mattered. Not long after I passed the test Gran gave me, I found there was some stuff I just seemed to know how to do. I've no idea why. But I've not – I've not used it to help people. I've just helped myself.'

'There is no shame in wishing to make a better life for yourself.'

'But I don't mean working hard to get a better job, or something like that. I'm popular at school – well, not so much recently, but I was – and I liked being that way. Sometimes, I used magic to... nudge people's reaction to me in the right direction.' Merry lay back on the blanket and looked up at the stars. This would be easier if she couldn't see Jack's face. 'Apart from Leo, I've only had two really close friends in my life: Ruby, and a boy called Alex. And I've used magic to control both of them.'

'What did you do?' Jack's voice wasn't shocked, or critical – yet. It would be once she told him.

Merry took a deep breath.

'I've kept Ruby to myself. Any time she seemed to be getting too friendly with another girl, I used magic to stop it. I don't know if you know much about girls, but sometimes we can get a bit... cliquey. Bitchy.' She remembered her encounter with Esther Perkins a few weeks back. 'Some people in town talk about our family, spread nasty rumours about the witchcraft. No one knows anything for sure, the coven are too careful, but... I didn't want to end up being the one on the outside. I didn't want Ruby to end up liking someone else better than me. And I always thought she would, if I didn't use magic to stop her.'

Merry paused, squinting up at the distant glimmer of the Milky Way, and wondered why she felt that way. Not that it mattered. Because she was right: she'd lifted her spells, and Ruby was already drifting away. 'I haven't done Ruby any permanent damage, I hope, but I've... messed with her head. Alex—'

267

She swallowed. She didn't want to say any more, not really, but the words seemed to be burning their way out of her, unstoppable as a lava flow. 'Alex, he said he was in love with me. I definitely wasn't in love with him, but I did love him following me around and – and *worshipping* me. So I kept him dangling, and every time another girl showed interest in him I used magic to drive her away, and every time he began to like another girl I used magic to make her laugh at him. To make her treat him like he was some kind of – pathetic loser.' Merry dug her nails into her palms as hard as she could. 'Well, let's just say that I got a bit carried away. I couldn't control what I was doing. The spells I cast were too dark, they had too many side effects that I hadn't anticipated. Alex started to hallucinate. He became… paranoid, I guess. He decided that everyone hated him. Even his family. I did my best to reverse the damage I'd done, to undo the spells, but it was too late. So one night, he jumped off a bridge. He almost drowned. I went in after him, managed to pull him to safety, but it was all my fault he was in there in the first place.'

The words dried up. Merry rubbed her eyes, forcing back the tears. She had no right to cry. Really, if Jack managed to kill her one of these nights, it would be no more than she deserved.

'What happened to this boy?'

'His parents took him away from school. I did talk to him, try to explain, but… it didn't go so well. That was about seven months ago now; I haven't had any contact with him since. And I tried to stop using magic, I really did. That's why my last exams went so badly; I'd used magic before, to help me remember stuff. I've forgotten how to study without it. Then, recently, I couldn't make any spells work, and the power just started discharging from my fingertips, destroying things – I even injured Leo a few weeks back, I—' She stopped, took a couple of long, slow breaths. 'It's a bit better, since I started training with Gran. But I'm scared, Jack. Never mind what I have to do: I'm more scared of what I might become.'

There was silence, for a while. Eventually Merry couldn't bear it any longer. She sat up; Jack, sitting next to her, was frowning down at the ground.

'Please, say something. Tell me how wicked I am. Tell me I'm going to end up in hell. You won't be saying anything I haven't already said to myself.'

'How can I say such things to you, Merry? How can I judge you, knowing what I am? What I have done?' He pulled his dagger back out of the grass and ran one finger gently along the edge. His hands were trembling. 'Do you know how many people I have killed?'

'But that's not the same. You can't help what you've done.'

Jack shook his head.

'Someone... someone clever once told me something about magic. She said there's more than one kind of magic in this world. There's wild magic and tamed magic. There's magic of the elements: of root and stone, of river and wind. There's the magic of light: of sun or moon or star, of fire or candle. And then there is the dark magic, that of the shadow realm. But apart from that last, magic in itself isn't good or bad. It is only made so by the person using it.' He moved closer to her, and there was such warmth and understanding and *certainty* in his eyes that she had to look away. It was almost as if he knew her – knew what was deep down inside of her – better than she did herself. 'You're brave, Merry, and strong. And I know that you will always choose to do the right thing, in the end. You do not desire to hurt people. That is the difference between you and a monster like Gwydion.' He sighed. 'That is the difference, I hope, between Gwydion and me.'

'Maybe. Or maybe Gwydion started off just like me.' Merry giggled. 'Maybe that's my future: "Don't worry about my careers assessment, Miss Riley. I'm going to take a degree course in black magic and get a job as a murderous psychopath!"' She laughed again; she didn't seem to be able to stop. 'Maybe I can open a posh shop selling poisonous herbs, and – and manacles, and cursed swords—'

'Merry! Stop this!'

Jack was shaking her, holding her by her shoulders, and Merry realised her face was wet with tears.

'But what if I can't stop it, Jack? What if—'

And then she stopped, because Jack's arms were around her, and his mouth was pressed against hers.

The shock of his touch blew all other thoughts out of her mind. The way he had touched her in her dreams – she realised now what a pale imitation of reality her imagination had come up with. She responded to him automatically, lips returning the force of his kiss, hands twisting into his long hair, body curving backwards until they fell together on to the blanket. Until her fingers, drifting down on to his shoulder, found the golden wolf's- head brooch. She remembered, and pulled away. 'Jack, wait—'

He stared down at her, breathing hard, his brown eyes almost black in the darkness. 'I'm sorry. I should not have—' He sat up. 'I ask your forgiveness, Merry. I wished only to help you, as you have helped me, but then—'

271

Merry sat up too, and touched his cheek lightly with her fingertips.

'It's OK, Jack. I'm not angry.'

'You are too good. But I cannot… given what I am, and that…' he trailed off, his face flushed.

He was shy. And he was trying to protect her. Merry watched him for a moment, her heart thudding in her chest. They hardly knew each other, and Jack wasn't exactly someone she could take home to meet her mum. Oh, and she was pretty sure she was supposed to be figuring out how to kill him, and he had already tried to kill her.

But since they might both be dead soon, did any of that really matter?

She put her arms round his neck and drew him back down on to the blanket. As he returned her embrace, the rain started falling once more. Merry waved her hand, and within the space that they were lying, the rain stopped.

Jack kissed her again, and time seemed to stop too.

SIXTEEN

'**A**RE YOU SURE you're not taking something?' Ruby asked the next day while they were standing in front of their lockers. ''Cos if not, you're doing a really good impression of someone who's high.'

'No, honestly, I'm just—'

But Ruby was already walking away, shaking her head.

'—happy. That's all.' Merry sighed. But right now, even the Ruby problem didn't seem insurmountable. At least Ruby hadn't told Mum where Merry really was last night. She grinned to herself and went to her next class.

Maybe, Merry reflected later, she should have thought about what Ruby said, and toned it down a bit.

After school, the evening turned out to be unusually pleasant. Merry didn't have to go to the lake and Gran had a coven meeting, so there was no training. That meant Merry could fit in a drop-in session at the fencing club. Thinking positively, at least the increased ability to defend herself would be handy, given the still-sporadic success of her spell casting. Best of all, Mum appeared to have swallowed the line Leo had spun her about a mistake: Merry was never meant to have been at Ruby's yesterday – he himself had dropped her off at another friend's house – Mum had just got confused. The other friend he named was the daughter of the local vicar; a piece of genius, since Mum had fallen out with the family years ago, and would never pick up the phone to check Leo's story. For once, dinner was quite lively: Mum made Merry laugh by describing a couple of recent near disasters at work, and only Leo seemed a bit subdued.

Later, Merry was lying on her bed, half-heartedly reading one of her English set books, when Leo started texting her.

What happened last night?

What? Why you texting me?

In case mum's listening.

What happened after I left?

Merry hesitated. There was absolutely no way she was going to tell Leo about her and Jack.

Nothing happened.
We talked. Sent him back to lake. You turned up.
Same as always.

There was a pause. Then Leo texted back:

Liar.
I know something happened.
When I got in from work, you were humming.
Why are you happy?

Merry frowned.

Why shouldn't I be happy?

She hit send, then realised what she'd done.

Not happy. Just pretending for mum.
Like you said.

275

Yeah right. I'm coming in.

Leo pushed the door open a few moments later. He put his finger to his lips – Merry saw he still had his phone in his hand – and sat down next to her on the bed.

I'm not stupid. You were dancing round kitchen!

He mimed her dancing, flapping his arms around. Merry scowled.

Point is...

Leo hunched his shoulders over, blushed.

Did you and Jack...???

Merry threw her hands in the air.

Did we what???

She raised her eyebrows, but Leo just looked even more flustered. He tapped his forefinger on the edge of the phone for a few seconds, staring at her.

I don't want you to get hurt.

Remember plan is to kill him. Probably.

You can't fall in love.

Merry shook her head.

I know what I'm doing.

Stop killing my buzz.

Leo rolled his eyes and stood up.

Whatever. Don't say I didn't warn you.

He left her room without looking back.

Merry sighed and turned off her phone. Leo was so ridiculously uptight sometimes. What was the point in having a cool, older brother if he was going to act like a Victorian father? Coming into her room, making her feel guilty...

But she wasn't going to feel guilty – why shouldn't she have some fun? Besides, the stupid manuscript might be wrong, or they might be... misinterpreting it. Maybe she could find a way around it, and they wouldn't have to kill Jack after all. Maybe she could save him. Maybe.

★ ★ ★

There was no opportunity for fun on the next two trips to the lake. Instead of being able to talk to Jack, Merry spent most of the time trying to manipulate the water, determined to force it aside so she could simply walk to the bottom of the lake. She was getting better at it. But the magic was mentally exhausting, and she just wasn't improving quickly enough, given the manuscript's constant demand that she should follow Jack under the lake. The furthest she got was maybe a metre into the water, before it rushed back over her feet, soaking her. Plus, she had no idea exactly where on the lake bed the entrance to Gwydion's lair might be, or whether it would even be visible. Whenever she took a break, it was just awkward. Leo stuck to her like glue. He wasn't horrible, or anything; he was just as pleasant to Jack, just as chatty. But he made sure he sat between Jack and Merry the whole time. All she and Jack could do was exchange glances and smile at each other when Leo wasn't looking.

At least Merry's training sessions were going better. She didn't know whether it was her good mood, her new resolve to fight Gwydion and (if she could) save Jack, or just that something in her brain had finally clicked. But for whatever reason, the spells Gran had been struggling to teach her no longer seemed quite so difficult – even though she was carefully sticking to the official, coven-approved method of doing magic. One afternoon everything went so well that Merry decided to try to recreate what she'd done for Leo. They'd gone for a run at the local gym together – the endless rain (and hail, and sleet) meant that the footpaths Merry used to use were now impassable. As Merry finished her five miles, Leo was standing, leaning on the next treadmill along, gasping.

'You are so unfit.' Merry rubbed a towel over the back of her neck.

Leo just glared at her.

'I s'pose at least you eat fairly healthily. Fancy an apple?'

'Huh?' Leo raised his eyebrows. 'I guess, but—'

'Here you go.' Merry reached into her bag and pulled out an apple. A small, withered apple, with a spot of mould on one side.

'Grim. I'm not eating that.' Leo backed away.

'No? OK then.' Merry looked around to make sure they were still alone. 'What about this?' She held the apple out, repeated the words Gran had drummed into her – Gaelic words, she thought, but she had no idea what they meant – and waited.

Like one of those accelerated nature films in reverse, the fruit began to rejuvenate. The mould disappeared, the wrinkled skin grew smooth and plump again, and within two minutes Merry was holding a glossy, red apple. She offered it to Leo.

'Fancy a bite?'

Leo tapped the apple with his fore finger.

'What the – that is just – it's amazing, I can't—' He picked the apple up, smelt it, opened his mouth and—'Is it poisoned?'

'What?' Merry shook her head. 'No, of course not. Why would it be poisoned?'

'Well, apples in fairy tales… you might have turned into the wicked queen.'

Merry laughed. 'I think that would make you Snow White. Too bad I'm fresh out of magic corsets. But you do see what this means, don't you?'

Leo crinkled his forehead.

'Er…'

'The spells must be working better because I'm happy, Leo. And I'm happy because… because I got to spend a bit of time with Jack. On my own.' She felt the blood rush into her cheeks and looked away. 'I admit it. We… had fun together, the other evening. So maybe—'

'Oh, no. I see where this is going.' Leo gave the apple back to her. 'I'm sorry, Merry, but it's too dangerous.'

'But Leo…'

'You're not spending any more time on your own with Jack.' Leo put a hand on her shoulder. 'Trust me, it's for the best.'

But the day after next fate intervened, in the shape of Leo's best friend, Dan. Dan had turned eighteen about seven months ago, but he was only now having a party – a joint twenty-first with his elder brother. Their parents were really pushing the boat out; hiring a local hall, a band, caterers, the works. Leo had said yes to the invitation ages ago. Still, when he realised, on the afternoon of the party, that Merry was going to have to go to the lake without him, he nearly changed his mind.

'I'm just not comfortable with this, Merry. Perhaps I should stay. Or – or maybe we could go to the lake first, then if the King of Hearts turns up quickly I could get to the party later. Or—'

'Leo, relax. You can't miss any of the party – Dan will be really upset. Besides, it's going to be fine. I'm probably just going to keep working on the magic I'm trying to do with the lake. Jack can watch a film on my laptop, or something. And I've got so much studying to do...'

Leo hesitated, but he didn't want to let Dan down. So now Merry was standing in the car park by the woods, and Leo was about to drive away. He lowered the car window.

'I'm really not happy about this.'

'I know. But it's only for this one time.'

'Huh. Will you promise me you're not going to do anything stupid?'

Merry sighed. 'Leo, you're not my dad. I know how to look after myself.' She pointed at her chest. 'Witch, remember?'

'Yeah. Trainee witch, prone to random magical… outbursts—'

'It's been over a week—'

'—dealing with something completely out of her league.'

'Gee, thanks for the vote of confidence.' Merry turned and began to walk into the woods, but Leo called after her.

'I'm just trying to take care of you. So do me a favour, and remember what Jack sometimes is. You're not on a date.'

'I know. I *know*.'

'Really? Did you look at yourself before you left the house?'

And with that Leo drove off, churning up the gravel as he accelerated away.

★ ★ ★

So, he was angry, Merry thought to herself as she made her way down towards the lake. But he was also being completely unreasonable. She'd dressed exactly the same as she always did for these outings. Hat and scarf. Heavy jacket. Jeans and a jumper.

Well, her new skinny jeans instead of the old ripped pair. And a new, fine-knit V-necked sweater instead of the comfortable baggy one she generally selected. But still.

So maybe she was wearing a bit more make-up than she usually did. And some scent. But that didn't mean –

Damn. The butterflies in her stomach, that unmistakable mix of nervousness and anticipation – clearly, some part of her brain had decided she *was* going on a date.

Merry pulled her phone out of her pocket – wondered whether she would have enough time to get Leo to take her back home so she could change – shoved the phone away again.

She knew what seemed to be happening between her and Jack couldn't last. But where would be the harm in pretending, just for a little while?

She might be dead before the autumn.

One more evening. Was that too much to ask?

SEVENTEEN

AT THE LAKESIDE, Merry spread the picnic rug on the grass and sat down to wait, huddling close to the portable heater. In theory, it was spring. There should have been drifts of bluebells in the woods, almost ready to flower, the vivid green of new leaves on the beech trees. The evening air should have been warmer.

But instead, it still felt like winter: damp, cold, dead. Puddles left behind by the endless rain were now thickly glazed with ice. The bizarre weather was gradually spreading north and west, affecting more of the country. The forecasters were talking about the jet stream and the Gulf stream and cold air being sucked down from Siberia; Merry wondered what they would say if she told them it was all due to a dark wizard, trapped under a lake in Surrey.

She got out one of her history books and a torch. Her exams were a little over two months away now; if she was still alive at that point (and maybe she would be, just maybe) then she wanted to do better than last summer. And by herself this time, without relying on magic. She managed to ignore the fluttering, fizzing feeling in her stomach, and got about halfway through a chapter on the European Reformation before the water formed a vortex and Jack stepped out on to the grass.

Merry spoke the words of command: he crumpled to the floor. She carried on reading – glancing at him occasionally, studying the length of his eyelashes and the curve of his lips – until he woke up.

'Hey.' She shut the book. 'How are you feeling tonight?'

'Well, I thank you.'

'Good.' Merry noticed Jack looking around. 'Oh, it's just me tonight. Leo – he's going to a birthday party.' Jack still looked blank. Merry had been speed-reading articles on Anglo-Saxon England, but trying to bridge a fifteen-hundred-year time difference was still almost impossible. 'It's like… a special feast, to celebrate someone being a year older. Do you understand?'

'I think so.' Jack sat down next to Merry and studied her face. 'I am glad. I have been waiting for this: the chance to be alone with you again.'

Merry felt her face flush.

'Me too.'

Jack lifted Merry's arm and slowly kissed the inside of her wrist. His skin felt hot against hers; almost feverish. He reached forwards to tuck a strand of hair behind her ear, and Merry noticed his hand was trembling a little.

'Are you sure you're OK?'

'Yes. Of course.'

Merry raised her eyebrows. Still, if Jack said he was OK... she leant in to kiss him.

But Jack pulled back. 'Not yet... I have something to tell you first.'

Merry groaned.

'What? Can't it wait?'

'I believe you would find the knowledge... useful.'

Jack was definitely different this evening. Perhaps he was nervous. After all, he hadn't been on anything approaching a date in a really, really long time. And they hadn't really spoken since the last time they'd been alone together.

'Fine. You can tell me the story. But let's be comfortable.'

Merry lay down and patted the rug. Jack lay down next to her, leaning on one elbow.

'You understand, do you not, what it is that the wizard sends me out to collect?'

'Yes. People's hearts. The hearts of people who are in love. In the story Gran told us, she said you had to put them in jars.' Merry wrinkled her nose.

'It is true. Row upon row of them.'

'That's disgusting.'

'And do you know how I… obtained the hearts?'

Merry swallowed. This wasn't exactly how she'd hoped the evening was going to go.

'Um, to be honest, I've tried to avoid thinking about it. I suppose you used the…' she waved a hand towards the broken sword. As usual, Jack had unbuckled the scabbard and left it on the grass nearby. 'What happened to the rest of the blade, by the way?'

'It was damaged, when Gwydion fought the witches. He has not yet the power to create a completely new one. But you're right: I had to use the sword. Only the sorcery within its blade allows me to cut out a heart and keep it alive, so Gwydion can use it in his dark magic. The sword is precious to him, and he will not allow it to be used for any other purpose.'

Was that why the King of Hearts hadn't killed yet – did he need a new sword? Merry glanced at the scabbard again.

Still. A magic blade. I wonder whether it would work on the puppet hearts, if we ever get hold of them. I wonder if I need to steal it...

Jack touched her face gently, drawing her attention back to him.

'But it's hard, to cut out someone's heart with such a blade. The skin and the muscle are breached easily enough. But the bone—' He moved his hand, to touch Merry's breastbone, '—it does not break cleanly. It shatters.'

'That's, um...'

'My task began the first time Gwydion allowed me to leave the tower, about three months after he captured me, once the curse was strong enough to hold for a few hours. I was sent to take the heart of a thatcher. The man was about twenty-five, strong and healthy. But no one has ever been able to withstand the power I have. No one apart from you, and one other.' Merry glanced at the braid around her wrist; when she looked back at Jack, he was staring at it too. 'Well... I killed him easily, but loosening his heart from his chest, that was difficult. I had not the skill of it yet. I had to wash myself in the river afterwards.'

'Jack, I don't understand. Why do we have to talk about

this now?' Merry put her hand on Jack's face, but still he continued.

'When I brought his betrothed to the same place, and showed her the ruin of his body, she fainted. But I waited. I waited for her to wake up before I killed her.' Jack ran his fingers through Merry's hair. 'Long, red hair, she had. And the blood bloomed like a scarlet flower against the green of her gown.'

Merry sat up. 'Stop, please. I don't want to hear any more. This is probably the only evening we'll have alone together and—' She took a deep breath: she was supposed to be kissing Jack, not fighting with him. 'Why did you tell me that story? It's horrible. How is it meant to help me?'

Jack swept the back of his hand across her cheek, brushing away the tears she hadn't even realised were there. 'You mourn for them? Even though you did not know them? Even though they have been dead so many years?'

'I'm not mourning. But I feel sorry for them. It must have been terrifying, to die like that. And I wish you hadn't had to… go through it. I hate the thought of you suffering.'

Jack put his arms around her and kissed her, finally, drawing her back down on to the rug. For a long while, she forgot about the dead people and the jars of hearts.

The only thing that mattered was the feeling of Jack's lips on her mouth, his hands on her waist, his body next to hers. Until he murmured in her ear: 'I would have killed that witch in the same way, if I'd been given the chance.'

Startled, Merry pulled away. 'You mean, that's what Gwydion would have made the King of Hearts do, if Meredith hadn't put you into the enchanted sleep?'

But Jack didn't answer. He kissed her harder and slipped his hand up under her jumper, making her gasp. 'Your heart is beating so fast. I can feel it, just beneath my fingers. Such a fragile thing.'

Merry tried to push his hand away. 'Hey, slow down.'

'What should I wait for? We are here together, all alone.' With one quick movement Jack was no longer next to her but on top of her, carefully pinning her to the ground, caging her there. He kissed her again and smiled.

'Jack, stop it! I don't want to—'

But at that moment Merry looked into his eyes and realised – it wasn't Jack at all. It was the boy she'd dreamt about all those weeks ago, the boy walking through her nightmares with cold, dead eyes, his grin that of a wolf about to make an easy kill. She tried to scream, but terror had snatched away her voice.

The King of Hearts, laughed. 'The braid tied around

your wrist, the one you looked at earlier: that must be the source of your power. So why should I wait? I will take the braid, take what I desire, and then – I will kill you.'

He clamped one hand over her mouth, preventing her from speaking the words that would dismiss him, while tugging with his other hand at the braid, trying to break it.

She tried to remember the words of the stinging hex, or to summon up the power she'd been using on the lake water. Her fingernails began to ache and for a few seconds Merry thought she would be able to fight back.

But the King of Hearts didn't falter: he seemed impervious to her attacks. Inside her mind, in the one, tiny corner that hadn't been overthrown by panic and fear, Merry realised she was about to die. The wizard's servant was going to cut her chest open and take her life. There would be no one to stop Gwydion escaping from the lake; no one to stop him sending the King of Hearts out every night; no one to stop him creating an army of loveless, soulless minions, seizing power wherever and whenever he wanted. People were going to die, because of her.

She'd failed.

How much is it going to hurt, when he kills me? How long will it take?

Oh, God –

Merry struggled frantically, but the braid was coming loose – any moment now she would be defenceless, and then –

– and then not-Jack was no longer pinning her down, because someone had dragged him off of her –

– and somehow, impossibly, Leo was standing there above her.

'Get the hell away from my sister, you monster!'

The King of Hearts pushed himself up – snarled – grabbed the sword from where it lay on the grass and ran at Leo.

'Awende on sinnihte, sceadugenga!' Merry hurled the words at the cursed boy.

He stopped instantly. Without looking at Merry, he ran up the slope and jumped back into the lake.

Merry couldn't seem to stop shaking. Leo had been shouting for a while now.

'...and then, after everything I said, to come back and find that he was about to – I mean, really, even by your standards, I can't believe that you would be so stupid, and irresponsible, and thoughtless, and selfish, and – and—' he bellowed and kicked the lantern across the grass. The light flicked and went out.

In the silence, Leo slumped down next to his sister and put his arm around her shoulders. 'He was going to kill you. Seriously, Merry, what the hell were you thinking?'

Merry buried her face in Leo's shoulder and began to cry.

They were back in the car now, driving home. Merry wanted to talk to Leo, but about normal stuff. Definitely not about Jack.

'Um, how was the party?'

'It was great.' Leo glanced over at her before switching his attention back to the road. 'I've got a new plan for getting down to the bottom of the lake. Dan has this cousin who teaches scuba diving. I thought if I took a course, I could borrow some gear. Go into the lake, have a look around, that kind of thing.'

A course? How much time did Leo think they had? What had happened tonight – it must mean that Jack had been taken over permanently by the King of Hearts. So Gwydion was getting stronger, despite the fact that they'd stopped his servant from attacking anyone, despite all the hours they'd wasted at the lake. He was getting stronger and soon he'd be able to do whatever he wanted: create servants, or make new swords or leave the lake – it seemed impossible to stop him. So how was she supposed to destroy him?

All her earlier positivity had vanished. Gwydion was going to kill her. Or he'd send his King of Hearts to do the job for him. Others would die too. And Jack – surely, Jack was gone forever?

But there was no point upsetting Leo.

'Good plan.'

'You think?'

'Sure.'

'You don't sound very enthusiastic.'

'I—' But she was saved from having to think of an answer. They had pulled up in front of the house and the lights were on – almost all of them. 'Is Mum having friends over?'

'What friends?' Leo turned off the engine and sat there, twirling the keys around his fingers. 'Come on. Let's see what's going on.'

The house was quiet. Leo pushed open the door of the kitchen.

Their mother was sitting at the table, the trinket box in front of her. Merry's stomach tensed painfully.

'Where did you get that?'

'You know very well where I got it.' Mum's voice was rigid. 'You surely didn't think I believed Leo's story the other evening, did you? I called the school earlier. Then I had a long chat with Ruby's mother. You've been lying to me. Do the two of you have any idea what you've got involved in? How much danger you're in?'

'Yes, we do, actually.' Merry was too exhausted to feel angry. Too exhausted to feel anything much. She remembered the last time Mum had confronted her like this: when she was twelve, over Gran's proposed witch training. Mum's face had exactly the same look of supressed fury and – and what? Fear? But what did Mum have to be afraid of? She wasn't the one who'd almost been killed. 'You've lied to me – to both of us – for years. You knew about Gwydion, and Jack, and the oath, but you did nothing. You taught me nothing.'

Her mother flushed.

'I had good reasons. When your father left—'

'I don't care. Really. None of it matters now.' Merry turned Leo. 'I'm sorry, but I can't cope with this any more. It's over. Let Jack kill me. Let him kill all of us. I'm not even going to try to stop him.'

'But Merry—'

'Leo, that's enough.' Mum stood up. 'The Easter holidays are only a few days away: I'm pulling your sister out of school early. Go and pack a case each. We're leaving.'

★ ★ ★

In his prison under the lake, Jack opened his eyes. He had a moment of blissful forgetfulness...

...until the recollection of what he had almost done swept over him, drowning him. He remembered the terror in Merry's eyes as she realised what was happening, remembered everything he had said and done to hurt her, remembered how desperately she had tried to escape...

'No!' Jack screamed and tore at his hair.

Somebody started laughing.

'Gwydion?'

'Yes, Jack, I am here.'

Jack heard the scrape of a flint against the wall; light flared in the darkness. Gwydion was sitting on a stool in the corner of the room. 'I've been waiting for you to awake. I thought it would prove entertaining.'

'You devil. I'll kill you!' Jack lunged at Gwydion, but with a flick of his hand, the wizard threw him back against the wall of the cell.

'Now, Jack, you and I both know that is impossible.'

'How? How did you stop her from—'

'From granting you power over your own body again? It was a difficult enchantment to weave, and costly.' Gwydion held up his right hand, and Jack saw that one finger was missing.

'But you failed. Her brother saved her.'

Gwydion growled and spat on the floor.

'Filthy, interfering wretch – I shall enjoy torturing him to death, one day soon. But still, I gained much knowledge. Worth the price, I would say.'

Jack hesitated. Perhaps the King of Hearts had found out something useful. But Gwydion might just be trying to trick him…

The wizard laughed.

'Do you not guess, Jack? Why I am happy? Because I know now that the girl – loves you.' Gwydion grimaced, as though the word was bitter poison in his mouth. 'Yes, she does. Just like Winifred did. And you remember what happened to her.'

Jack did remember

'No, you mustn't—'

'Oh, yes. You will cut out the girl's heart, and I will feed it to you, and your transformation will be complete. And permanent.'

Jack flung himself at Gwydion again, but was instantly pinned to the floor, immobile. Gwydion had set a binding charm on him.

The wizard hobbled over.

'There is no point trying to fight me. The curse that

runs through your blood means that anyone who loves you will suffer grief, because they love you. Your parents, your foster-parents… there is no escape from what you are, Jack. Now, sleep until I require you again.' Gwydion smiled as he pulled out a knife. 'A pity *she* is no longer here, to tend to your wounds.' Jack felt the pressure of the blade explode into pain as the wizard carved a mark into his forehead. 'Sleep, and dream of what you have done…'

Jack sank back into his nightmare, watching the King of Hearts kill and hurt, seeing Merry's face over and over, her eyes wide with horror because of him.

EIGHTEEN

MERRY COULD HEAR the wind gusting, carrying the waves of rain that were bludgeoning the bedroom window. Northumbrian rain, roaring in across the North Sea: they had been up here three days now, after Mum had driven through the night to get them away from Tillingham. Every few hours Leo and Mum would get into another argument; Merry could hear the raised voices through the thin walls. But trying to force their mother to back down was pointless. Instead, Merry stayed in her bedroom as much as possible. Most of the time she slept. When she was awake, her main aim was to stop her brain going over and over what had happened at the lake – and the fact (for she was almost certain, now) that Jack was lost forever. But it wasn't easy.

Honestly, what had she expected? That because she'd kissed him, the monster would change back permanently into the handsome prince?

This is real life, not a fairy tale.

And you're an idiot, Merry Cooper.

The door opened and Leo stuck his head into the room.

'You're awake. Good. I brought you some food.' He inched a tray on to the bedside table – two mugs of tea and a plate of cakes – and sat down on the dressing table stool, which creaked threateningly.

Merry sat up and looked at the cakes. Leo had arranged them in a neat spiral, trying to tempt her, obviously. She picked one up and lifted it to her mouth, but a spasm of nausea twisted her gullet and she dropped the cake back on to the plate. 'Actually, I don't fancy anything. Thanks, though.' Merry sank back on the bed and closed her eyes. A moment later there was a touch on her wrist: Leo was taking her pulse. She pulled her arm away. 'Stop it. I'll be fine.'

'But you've barely eaten anything the last couple of days. Are you feeling sick?'

'A little. It's probably just a cold.'

'You don't know that.' There was an undertone t[o] brother's voice Merry hadn't noticed before. She glan[ced] up at him and saw the dark circles under his eyes.

'I honestly will be fine, Leo; you don't need to wor[ry.] It's just been too much: inheriting Meredith's oath – th[e] training – what happened at the lake. And now this. I guess I need a holiday.'

Leo smiled a little. 'Well, this is a holiday cottage, allegedly.'

They both looked around the bedroom. It was at the back of the house, facing on to a rising slope of scrubby grass and spindly, wind-twisted shrubs that shut out any view of the surrounding countryside. The room itself was small and mostly beige and smelt faintly of damp, overlaid with furniture polish. The cottage belonged to a work colleague of their mum's, and they were staying for free. Merry couldn't imagine anyone actually paying to be here.

'Yeah. Have you spoken to Mum today?'

Leo shook his head.

'Other than to ask her to take this damn spell off me? No.' There was no landline at the cottage, no mobile phone reception and no Wi-Fi. But Mum wasn't taking any chances. She didn't want Leo making his way to the village

bouring farm and contacting Gran from there.
t a spell on him, to stop him going past the
ndary. Merry had watched him from the
terday, trying to get past the invisible barrier
or digging, but nothing had worked. Eventually
emper – kicked – beat his fists against it. Now
of his hands were marked with bruises. 'I suppose
ven't been able to…'

No. Sorry.' Merry had tried to break her mother's spell,
d tried to bewitch Mum into returning the trinket box
and its contents. But whether from shock or exhaustion
her magic, which had seemed to be blossoming only a
few days ago, had withered again. It was like when she'd
broken her leg; that same sense of limitation. 'I'm just lucky
Mum doesn't know how incapable I am, or she'd put a
spell on me too.'

'Does it matter about the magic?' Leo asked. 'If you've
given up, if you're not going to try to stop Gwydion, you
don't need magic any more.'

Merry turned away and began tracing the pattern on
the wallpaper with her fingers.

'Yes. It matters.' She knew Leo was trying to provoke
her. He'd been telling her since they got here that she had
to leave, pointing out that she was putting others in danger,

how she ought to be focusing on the 'greater good'. She still had the braid tied round her wrist, after all – she could still stop the King of Hearts from sticking his broken blade into the locals. But the thought of facing Jack again, or facing whatever he'd become…

I'm not sure I can do it. Even though I miss him more than I thought I ever would, more than it makes sense to. I hardly even know him, but I still dream about him.

The dreams were different, at least: she and Jack weren't killing each other any more. They weren't kissing, either. Instead they were holding hands, running together through long, torch-lit corridors, and they were searching for – for something. Merry didn't know what it was, because they never found it. And all the time fear pursued them, while from somewhere in the distance came the sound of singing…

'Merry,' Leo began, 'I need to—'

'Do you think Jack's really gone, Leo? Changed permanently into the King of Hearts?' Her stomach seized up again at the thought of it: to be trapped like that, maybe for eternity.

'You have to go home. Perhaps what happened the other night with Jack was just a – a one-off. If you go home, at least you'll find out.'

'At least I'll find out? It almost sounds like – like you want me to fight Gwydion, to risk my life.'

There was a knock, and the door opened a little.

'Can I come in?'

It was their mother. Merry nodded fractionally.

'Whatever.'

Mum sat down on the edge of the bed and ran one hand over the tartan blanket, smoothing out the creases, not looking at Merry or Leo. 'You didn't come down for lunch, Merry. Are you still not feeling well?'

'I'm just not hungry, that's all.'

'I've been doing a lot of thinking, since we arrived here. I still believe that taking you away from Tillingham was absolutely the right thing to do.'

'No, really?' Leo picked up his mug of tea and went over to the window, standing with his back to his mother.

'But I want you to understand why,' she continued. 'So, I've realised I need to give you some background.'

'Mum,' Merry said, 'I'm tired. I really don't want to—'

'Meredith.' Mum's voice took on a hard edge. 'For once, will you just...' She stopped for a moment, closing her eyes and pinching the bridge of her nose. 'I'm sorry. I'm not trying to be the baddie here, honestly. I realise I've mishandled things, over the last few years. And some of the things I've done,' she glanced at Leo, 'I know you might never forgive. But please listen. It won't take long.'

Later, when Merry thought about the story Mum told them, she decided it had almost been like listening to a stranger introducing herself. For the first time, as far as she could remember, Mum talked to them about her childhood. She described her early attempts at magic, practising charms with her first cousin, Carys. She talked about the pleasure she took in other activities, especially dancing. Her dancing was good enough for her to think about trying to make a career out of it, and Gran had encouraged her. But then, everything changed. Carys and her mother died in a car crash; at fourteen, Mum inherited her cousin's role as official descendent. 'I inherited the family curse' was how she described it. Gran told her that a career as a dancer was out of the question. She had to stay in Tillingham and focus on her magic.

'So that's how my life was, from fourteen to twenty-four: ten years of grief, and anger that my choices had been taken away from me, and fear that I'd actually have to fight the wizard, that I might die.' Mum pulled a tissue out of her pocket and blew her nose. 'I decided that I wasn't going to have children, that the whole ridiculous saga was just going to end with me, and damn the consequences. But then I met your father. And I thought, or at least I convinced myself, that maybe the whole story of Meredith's oath was a lie anyway, or maybe the sleeping charm would never wear off. I even gave you the same name as our ancestor. Bravado, I suppose; trying prove to everyone that I wasn't afraid of the past, or the future.' She leant forwards, taking one of Merry's hands. 'Your father left me, left all of us, because of the craft. After ten years together, he suddenly decided he couldn't really trust someone who was… "abnormal". I didn't want that for you and Leo. So I tried to cut magic out of your lives, even though I couldn't quite cut it out of mine. I would have moved, if I'd been able to afford it, and if you two hadn't been so attached to your grandmother.' She paused. 'I realise, now, that I've been pushing the two of you away, by keeping so much from you. We're not exactly… close. But I was just trying to protect you. I didn't want you to grow up with fear and uncertainty over something that probably, hopefully, was never going to happen anyway.'

'Probably never going to happen? But it has happened, Mum,' Merry said.

'I know. That's why I've taken you away from Tillingham: I made a mistake, and now I have to fix it. I have to keep you safe. I'd never, ever forgive myself if anything happened to you. To either of you.'

Merry stared at her mother. She was still Mum, still the same person who had walked into the room twenty minutes ago. But she was someone else too, someone with a whole secret history that she and Leo had known nothing about. It was like looking at one of those optical illusion pictures by Escher she'd studied in Year 9.

You stare at it for ages. You think all you're seeing is black demons on a white background. And then some switch is thrown in your brain and suddenly, you're looking at white angels. The same image. Two completely different pictures. So which one is the truth?

Mum stroked Merry's hair.

'Do you understand? Why I need to keep you here? Why you can't be involved any more?'

Merry's head was swimming. She pulled away from her mother's hand.

'I don't know, Mum. I—'

'No!' Leo swung round and slammed his mug down on the tray. 'She doesn't understand. And I don't understand why you're still lying to her!'

Mum jerked back as though Leo had slapped her. 'But I'm not, I didn't—'

'You know what's going to happen. What's already happening.' Leo was shaking – Merry had never seen him this angry, never – not even when he'd been yelling at her three nights ago at the lake. But there was something else in his eyes too: fear. Just like the day Gran had explained what was happening.

Merry hugged her knees to her chest. 'Leo? What's going on?'

'Nothing,' Mum interrupted. 'Nothing, apart from your grandmother's insane meddling. She's blinded herself, Leo, and she's blinded you too. This isn't Merry's fight.' She stood up and pointed at Merry. 'I don't care what magic she's been playing around with, your sister is not a witch. She's a child. By keeping her away from Tillingham I'm going to force the coven to do what they should have done in the first place. I'm going to keep my daughter safe.'

Leo moved closer to his mother, shaking his head.

'No, you're not. You're going to kill her!'

Merry stared at Leo.

Did he just say what I think he said?

Leo sat next to her on the bed and put his arm around her.

'I didn't want to tell you. I – I thought I wouldn't have to.'

'Tell me what?'

'Leo, please don't do this.' Mum stretched out her hand towards him, but Leo ignored her.

'The oath Meredith swore all those centuries ago has a side effect. Gran told me about it, back at the beginning, but – we didn't want to scare you.' Leo paused, chewing on his bottom lip as though unsure how to continue. 'Um, apparently, when Jack woke up, your life somehow became linked to the oath. And now the oath *has* to be fulfilled. Gran said that if you try to run away, to avoid confronting Gwydion, you'll get ill. Unless *you* defeat Gwydion in time, before he escapes from the lake, you'll get ill.'

'What?' Merry pulled away from him. 'What is this, some kind of – punishment clause? How ill?'

'But it's not true,' Mum interrupted. 'She's not ill.'

'Leo, how ill?' Merry repeated.

'Gran said she didn't know. But that we have to… assume the worst. The oath leaves you no way out. You have to go home, straightaway.'

Merry curled up on the bed and closed her eyes, shutting out the sound of Leo and Mum yelling at each other.

Is this it, then? I've avoided being killed by the wizard or the King of Hearts, so that I can just… waste away, shut up in this horrible house?

But surely, Gran would have told her something this important?

Surely it couldn't be true?

She knew, in reality, that she was in bed, feverish and shaking. But at the same time she was also, very definitely, somewhere else: a stone-walled room, with rushes on the floor. And that was real too. She couldn't quite recall who she was any more. Her name, or how she'd come to be here…

She gave up and shook her head, trying to clear the fog that seemed to be clouding everything. Because she had a job to do: that much she did remember. There was a wooden platter of food in her hands. The boy, the one she cared for, was slumped in a chair by the fire.

'Jack? I've brought your supper. Rabbit pie, tonight.' She put the plate on a table by his elbow.

The boy just stared at the food.

'Please try, Jack. You know he'll punish me if he thinks you're not eating.'

He sat up straighter, took a few mouthfuls.

'Do you know what hour it is?' he asked. 'I have slept away most of the day, again.'

'It is late. The wizard made me scrub the floors in his rooms today,' – her mouth twisted as she remembered the bloodstains on the flagstones – 'and it put me behind.' She reached out and

touched Jack gently on the arm. 'He will be here soon. Eat.'

Jack took her hands in his. He turned them over and kissed the pulse points on her wrists, making her shiver, though he still did not look up at her.

'You take too many risks for me. You should flee, while you still can.'

'I do not wish to leave you, Jack. I love you. You know that.'

Jack's shoulders started shaking. She knelt in front of him.

'Don't weep, Jack, please.'

But he wasn't weeping. He was laughing.

'I – I don't understand.' She pulled her wrists out of his grasp. 'I thought—'

'What? That I loved you in return?' He laughed even louder, while her face burned, and her heart beat so fast and hard in her chest that it hurt. 'I would have been a king. And you are just a kitchen maid. How could I possibly love you? You mean nothing to me, Merry, nothing…

NINETEEN

OR LEO, THE next three days were a nightmare. He shouted at his mum until he was hoarse. But Mum still refused to give Merry the trinket box, still refused to accept that Merry's sickness was to do with the oath, still refused to contact Gran – despite the fact that Merry was now rapidly getting worse. She had a fever and double vision. She slept more and more, tossing and turning all the while, muttering to herself about Jack, hearts, the lake. She ate nothing and drank less and less. Leo was watching his sister disintegrate, and he couldn't do anything to stop it.

It was Friday, six days since they had arrived in

Northumberland. Mid-morning, Leo went upstairs to check on Merry and found her trying to stuff her clothes back into her suitcase. She looked flushed. Her bottom lip was cracked and bloody.

'What are you doing?'

'I'm leaving. With or without the trinket box.'

Relief made him dizzy. 'Thank God. The next house isn't too far away. I think you can make it, if you take it slowly. When you call Gran, ask her if she can take this spell off me, then I can come and help you. Otherwise you should get a taxi to Alnmouth, that's the nearest station, but you'll need to stop and get some cash.'

Merry had slumped on to the bed and was wiping the back of her arm across her eyes. She looked far too ill to be travelling anywhere.

'What happened to change your mind?'

She sniffed.

'I had another dream. It was Jack, but not my Jack – the King of Hearts. And he was walking around Tillingham, near the school. He met this guy, and he started talking to him, and then he just – just went for him. He—' she made a stabbing motion with her hand, '—he cut his chest open, Leo, and then he reached in and...' Merry clamped a hand over her mouth, and Leo could see she was gagging.

'Hold on, I'll get something—'

'No,' Merry shook her head. 'I'm OK. I…' She closed her eyes, breathing rapidly. 'I told Mum about the dream. She still wants to stay here. *Still*. But I keep thinking about what Jack said, about blood on his hands. If people die because I fail, well – that's one thing. But if they die because I didn't even try… I have to end this, Leo. For Jack's sake too: I can't abandon him now. I have to… to kill him, if I can't set him free any other way. I have to go back.'

'You do need to go back. But it was just a dream, Merry. I'm sure—'

'It was Dan. Dan was the one Jack stabbed.'

Dan. Leo's best friend. His first love, really. Leo subsided on to the bed next to his sister. Just a dream, he'd said. But in Merry's world dreams were visions and portents. Was it something that was going to happen? Or was it already too late?

'I've got the braid,' Merry continued, 'and I know the words by heart. I can—' a spasm of coughing wracked her, and as she wiped her mouth Leo was sure he saw blood on the back of her hand. 'I can at least keep doing what we've been doing: stop the King of Hearts from attacking more people.'

Leo nodded.

'OK.' He nudged the suitcase with his foot. 'But you need to leave all this.' Merry's bag was hanging on the chair; he checked it for her phone, keys and purse and grabbed the painkillers from the bedside table. 'Right, let's go.' Merry started forwards, stumbled – Leo put an arm around her waist to steady her. Her curves had disappeared; he could feel her hip bone jutting out sharply. 'On second thoughts, you have to eat something first.'

'But Leo—'

'You have to try. Fifteen more minutes won't make any difference.' He put his hands on her upper arms, turned her to look at him. 'Come on. Do as you're told for once.'

She nodded. 'OK.'

The large, open-plan downstairs – kitchen, sitting room and hallway all rolled into one – was empty. Mum had gone to Alnwick earlier to look for somewhere with a free broadband connection (she was still trying to work, in the middle of everything else), which hopefully meant she would be out for a few hours. Leo made Merry sit at the kitchen table, heated up a portion of casserole from last night's dinner and put it in front of her. She wrinkled her nose but picked up her fork and started nibbling at the food. He shook his head and turned away. It would be sensible for her to take some food with her too. He found a carrier bag in one of the drawers and started going through the cupboards.

The back door opened and Mum walked in. Her gaze flicked from Leo to Merry, sitting at the kitchen table, back to Leo and then to the bag, half-filled with food. 'What's going on?'

Leo and Merry looked at each other. There wasn't much point in lying.

'Merry's agreed to leave,' Leo began. 'She's going home.'

'Because of that dream?' Mum turned to Merry. 'But we talked about that.'

'No, we didn't. I talked, and you ignored me.' Merry pushed the bowl away and stood up, though Leo could see she was supporting herself, one hand on the kitchen table and one on the back of a chair. 'I'm leaving. And I want Leo to come with me. You have to remove the spell.'

Mum shook her head. 'Absolutely not. I can't believe you, Leo. You know your sister won't be safe in Tillingham. But you're willing to put her life in danger because of a dream? Because you're more concerned about a school friend?'

'No.' Leo slammed his fist down on the kitchen counter.

'No, Mum, it's not me putting Merry's life in danger. It's you. You say you're terrified that Jack or Gwydion will kill her, but that's exactly what you're doing. You're staying up here, watching your own daughter die, rather than admit that you're wrong. You're doing nothing to help her. Nothing!'

'I'm not doing nothing.' Mum's voice was trembling. She moved closer to Merry, stretching out a hand towards her. 'You're not well enough, darling, to deal with any of this. So I've decided to go to the police. Somebody at work has a friend who—'

'Seriously?' Merry gave a snort of derision. 'The police? What the hell are they going to do? Besides, what exactly are you going to tell them: the truth? You'll end up sectioned. Gwydion won't stop, Mum. Gran said he wants to create an army – an army of creatures just like Jack's become, so that he spreads fear in the place of love. He wants this world to become his. What about all those people who are going to die because we did nothing?' Both Merry and Mum started talking over each other, both waving their hands around to try to get their point across. In some ways they were so alike. But Merry kept one hand on the chair, and Leo could see her shaking now with the effort of standing.

'Shut up, both of you! Right now!' Leo shouted. They turned and stared at him, mouths open.

There was a loud knock at the front door.

'Who the hell can that be?' Mum started forwards, but before she could get there the door slammed open and Gran walked into the room, followed by two other women. Leo recognised them from the morning he and Merry had found the coven outside, putting protective runes around the house. Was it really only a few weeks ago?

'Bronwen Elizabeth Cooper,' Gran began, her hands on her hips, 'what on earth have you done?'

There was crash somewhere behind him. Leo swung round.

Merry had fainted.

They were in the cottage, seated around the fire. A woman stood before them. She was richly dressed: the flames flickered over a gold belt around her waist, played across a jewelled collar about her neck. But they also revealed a face marked with lines of sorrow, and light brown hair streaked with grey. The woman was asking for their help.

'I come to you in great need, Anwen's daughters. There is a wizard—'

'We know,' Carys interrupted. 'Our mother bound us to help break the curse, if we could, and we have been watching Gwydion for many months. A darkness has been festering in the forests of the north.'

The woman shook her head.

'But he is not in the forests. We have searched that whole region and found nothing.'

'That is because you did not know what you were looking for.'

Nia leant forwards, throwing dried bunches of lavender and rosemary on to the fire, watching the flames blaze higher as the herbs filled the room with their scent.

'We can feel him, you know. He throws everything out of balance, like a thorn in your foot, or a broken bone gone bad.' She sighed. 'We realised that something would have to be done about him. Sooner or later.'

'So now you know, my queen.' Carys stood up and stared down at the older woman. 'We are not idle. But ours is a defensive magic, of earth and tree, river and sky. The wizard has a power we neither crave nor fully understand. So, our work progresses slowly, and we cannot see the end. But we hope,' she glanced at Meredith, and the bundle of provisions half-packed in the corner, 'before many more moons have waxed and waned, to find a way of destroying Gwydion. Gwydion, and all the evil he has brought into the world. We have already found the tower from which he spins his webs. What more would you have us do?'

'What more?' the queen asked. 'I want you to save my son. That is why I came.' She sank to her knees on the rush-strewn floor. 'I beg you, save my Jack. He is not evil, I know he is not.'

Carys sat back down, and took her sisters' hands in hers.

'We are seeking for a way to destroy the hold the wizard has over your son. But it will be difficult. More difficult, I think, than you can possibly imagine. Still, we will try. He doesn't deserve what has happened to him.'

'Thank you. I—'

'Wait: there is a condition. We cannot save him unless there is something of him still to be saved. As long as his heart remains true, then we will attempt to separate him from Gwydion and free him. But if, or when, he becomes wholly the wizard's creature, there will be no way back for him. Once the darkness takes him completely, the person who was your son will be dead, even if his outer form still survives.'

'And if that happens?'

'If that happens, we will kill him. Or we will try to. Do you understand?'

The queen still knelt silently.

'Lady, do you agree to our terms?'

'I agree. What do you require in return?'

Nia held out her hand.

'There are two things the queen has that may aid us... aside from those, nothing but peace: to be left alone to carry out our plan...'

Something nearby was clicking. Merry opened her eyes, but she couldn't figure out where she was. The ceiling and the colour of the walls looked wrong. She thought she had gone home, but she wasn't exactly sure where home was any more; she remembered a brightly-lit room with a Union Jack duvet and posters, but she also remembered a cottage, and a hearth with a cooking pot...

In the dim light spilling in through the doorway she recognised her grandmother sitting by the bedside, knitting and talking under her breath.

'Gran? Where are we?'

'Still in Northumberland, dear, though not for much longer.'

Merry thought about this for a while.

'But, I saw a woman. She was kneeling down, and she wanted us – I mean, she wanted them, to – to—' She squeezed her eyes shut, trying to sort the images in her head into some kind of coherent memory. 'It was something to do with Jack...'

'Was it a dream?'

Merry opened her eyes. Gran had stopped knitting and was watching her.

'I thought they were dreams, first of all, but now... I'm frightened, Gran. I keep having moments where I seem to be somewhere else. Or someone else. Meredith, usually, but not always. It happens when I'm awake as well as when I'm asleep. And it's getting worse.'

Gran put a hand on Merry's forehead, then felt her pulse.

'The magic that's being focused through you – it's putting your body and your mind under a lot of strain. What you're experiencing may be a side effect. I don't honestly know.' She patted Merry's hand. 'But, from what I've read, such things are not permanent once the cause is removed. Now, let me help you sit up, and then you have to drink some tea.'

Merry identified the subtle, herby scent that had been nagging at the edge of her awareness: her grandmother's supposedly everyday tea. There was a steaming cup already sitting on the bedside table. Apparently Gran had known she was about to wake up.

The tea was refreshing, and she did feel better. Even a little bit hungry.

'Can I have something to eat?'

'Of course. Just a minute.' Gran went out on to the landing and Merry could hear her giving instructions to Mum. 'Right. Your mother will be up shortly with a tray. But in the meantime I will explain what's been happening.'

'But—'

'Shh. No talking. Just drink your tea.' Gran raised an eyebrow, but Merry didn't have the energy to argue with her. 'Good. First of all, I'm sorry we didn't get here earlier. Your mother used a concealment charm to hide you from me; not a terribly effective one, since she's so out of practice, but it made things more time-consuming. And while you've been up here, there have been two more attacks, one in Tillingham and one in Ashbury. The King of Hearts' range is expanding.'

Merry sat up, nearly spilling tea all over the duvet.

'Then what are we doing here? We have to—'

'Calm down, Merry! You can't do anything, the state you're in at the moment.' Gran took the cup away and pushed her back on to the pillows. 'That's better.' She picked up her knitting again, pulled it out straighter. 'There's a full-scale police hunt going on now, for all the good it will do them. But at least the people who were attacked are still alive, and they're being cared for in hospital.

Hopefully they should all make a full recovery. Though your brother is rather shaken. One of the young men is a friend of his.'

'Dan?'

Gran nodded.

'He lost an awful lot of blood – almost didn't make it, apparently. But at least that vision you had wasn't a prediction. Jack didn't actually cut out his heart.' She frowned and added a few more stitches to the row of knitting. 'What I still can't understand is why, so far, he hasn't attempted to do just that.'

'We asked Jack about that, but he didn't know why either.' Merry shivered and pulled the duvet up higher. 'I wondered whether it was something to do with the sword being broken…'

'Hmm. Well, the important thing is to get you back home as soon as possible. If your mother had just talked to me none of this would have happened.'

Merry yawned. Her limbs felt like the bones had been taken out and replaced with foam.

'Leo was right, wasn't he? What he said about the oath, and me getting sick?'

Gran patted her hand.

'Yes, dear. I should have told you myself, but I honestly

thought it was better for you not to know. I was trying to protect you. Just like your mother was, I suppose. As far as we can work it out, our ancestor swore by the land itself. You're tied to the land that formed the old Saxon kingdom, until you break the curse. Or until Gwydion escapes from the lake. I've managed to slow down the illness, but you can't stay here. Your mother understands that now. We were – discussing things, while you were sleeping.'

Merry picked up the mug of tea again. There was a picture of the Golden Gate Bridge on the outside, and a line of curly writing: *Greetings from San Francisco!* One of a long list of places she wanted to visit when she got older. If she got to be any older.

'Not much of a choice, is it Gran? Stay up here and die, or go back home, try and break the curse, and probably die anyway.'

'No. It's not much of a choice.' As Gran stared at her over the top of her glasses, Merry caught a gleam in her eyes; something behind the love and the grandmotherliness. Something as hard and sharp as a diamond blade. 'Did you think the craft was just something to be used, Granddaughter? That it was an easy way of getting what you want? That there would never be a price to pay?'

'But you and Mum haven't been asked to risk your lives. You haven't been asked to pay.'

'I think your mother would disagree, from what she's been telling me. Besides, if anything happens to you, Merry, then we will most certainly pay.'

And then Gran was just Gran again.

'It's going to be OK, angel. I'm sure of it.'

'I don't know. My magic's stopped working again. I haven't been able to do any spells since I got here.'

'That's probably because you're so weak. I'm sure your ability will return.'

'But we can't even get into Gwydion's hideout. The spell I've been practising to get to the bottom of the lake – it's still not working the way I want it to. I'm just not powerful enough. And there's no way around what the manuscript keeps saying.'

'Then don't try to go around it. Merry, I took the coven to the lake the other day. Tried to replicate what you've been doing. All of us working together did manage to uncover the bottom of the lake, or a small part of it at least, but there was no sign of any entrance, or magic doorway... I suspect it only exists when the King of Hearts wants it to exist.'

'Then what on earth do I do?'

'Do what the manuscript is telling you to do. *Exactly* what it's telling you to do. Have you tried that?'

Merry thought, *I guess not. Not exactly.*

Gran patted Merry's hand.

'Trust yourself, and trust those who have gone before you, Merry. Witches far more powerful than me have been working towards this moment, ensuring everything is in place. You have generations of experience and planning behind you. I've told you before: you're not going to be alone. And remember, Gwydion isn't invincible. If he were, we wouldn't be sitting here right now. That's hopeful, isn't it?'

TWENTY

THE WHOLE FAMILY left Northumberland the next day. Merry slept for the first part of the journey. Slept properly, with no nightmares: no dreams at all. Mum was just pulling into the motorway services near Milton Keynes when she woke up ravenous – hungrier than she had been for days. Not that there was much food available in the service station supermarket. The floods had disrupted supplies. Huge swathes of Lincolnshire and Somerset were underwater, and snow had started falling across Scotland and Northern England. There had been two inches on the ground when they left that morning. And it was only going to get worse: the newspaper headlines were full of warnings about food shortages and photos of frostbitten crops shrivelling in the fields. Merry wanted to talk to Leo about it, about everything. But once they got back in the car Leo put his headphones on and kept his eyes closed pretty much the whole way home. Merry guessed he was worried about Dan.

When they reached the house, Merry quickly dumped her case in her room and went straight to the kitchen, where Mum was making dinner.

'Can I have the trinket box now? I need to look at the manuscript.' But Mum carried on stirring the contents of the saucepan, her back to Merry. 'Mum?'

'Of course. I'll fetch it for you.' As her mother walked over to the dresser, Merry could see the tension in her face and shoulders. Mum put the box on the table and turned back to the stove. 'The key's in the lock.'

Merry lifted the lid; everything was there.

'I was thinking,' Mum said, still stirring, 'when all this is over, we should go on holiday. Somewhere warm. During the school holidays, of course.'

'Er, yeah.' Merry couldn't quite keep the surprise out of her voice. They hadn't been on a proper family holiday for years. Mum was always too busy. 'That would be – fun.'

'And I'm going to look for another job, something more local. So I can be here more. It might be too late for me to fix things with Leo, but while you're still living at home…' She turned to look at Merry. 'It used to be different, didn't it? Better. When you and Leo were little. Before your father left.' She started twisting one of her rings round and round on her finger. 'Can you remember that far back?'

'Not really; a little bit. What happened wasn't your fault. Dad's a jerk. We know that.'

Mum's mouth quirked up a little.

'I can't argue with that. But, the way I handled him leaving, the way I handled the emergence of your abilities, and the fact that your grandmother wanted to train you – I don't know. I suppose I've been thinking a lot about the choices I've made, the last few days. I'd really like a second chance.' Merry pulled her mum into a brief, fierce hug. 'I don't know what's going to happen. But – I have to believe that we're going to get through this. That we'll all get a second chance.'

Mum smiled. 'When did my little girl get so… grown-up? So capable?' She pressed one hand to Merry's cheek. 'We *are* going to get through this. But still, I'm sorry. Sorry for everything I've done over the last couple of weeks, for the risks I've taken.' She sniffed, turned back to the oven and began clattering the pans around. 'Anyway, off you go. Do what you need to do.'

Merry took the trinket box up to Leo's room. He was playing a game on his laptop, but from the way he was jabbing at the keys and frowning he didn't seem to be enjoying it much.

'Hey. Are you OK?'

'Yeah. Why?'

'No reason. Just checking. You ready to tear yourself away from whatever fantasy world you're in and confront some real-world problems?'

'What, cursed Anglo-Saxon princes, wizards, that sort of real-world thing?' He shut the laptop. 'Sure, bring it on.'

Merry opened the manuscript.

'Will the King of Hearts come out of the lake tonight?'

No. But if he walks free again, and is allowed to strike unhindered, the wizard will gain enough strength to escape his prison.

They'd got back from Northumberland just in time. Once Gwydion left the lake, he would surely come after them himself. Merry wasn't certain the braid would work against him as well as against the King of Hearts.

But the manuscript hadn't finished.

Before the waxing crescent wakes, follow the monster into the lake.

While his heart is true, hope still lives: break the curse with true love's kiss.

Merry ran her fingers over the text. 'It still wants us to go into the lake.'

'And are we?' Leo asked.

'Yes. But this time we're going to do exactly what Jack does. We're not going to wade in, or swim in, or faff about with diving suits. I've got an idea about how I can use my magic too. But we're going to have to be right behind him, and we're going to jump.' She took a deep breath. 'I'm through with waiting around. We're taking this fight to Gwydion.'

Leo grinned at her.

'Whatever you say, boss.'

Merry hesitated.

'Um, OK. I thought I'd get more of an argument from you on the whole jumping straight into the water thing. Since last time I nearly drowned.'

Her brother shrugged. 'Clichéd fighting talk aside, I'm with you on this. Literally following Jack into the lake is pretty much the only thing we haven't considered. It makes sense.'

'Oh.' said Merry, relieved that Leo seemed to have confidence in her plan. At least that made one of them. She studied the manuscript again. Something nagged at her memory: Carys, talking to Jack's mother: *we cannot save him unless there is something of him still to be saved. As long as his heart remains true…*'

Perhaps she'd been wrong, in Northumberland. Maybe Jack hadn't yet been swallowed up by the shadow, and there was still a way to separate him from Gwydion.

'What do you reckon this second line means?'

'Er… well,' Leo frowned, 'I guess it means we should be hopeful. That Jack is still in there somewhere. As for the kissing bit, I…'

Merry waited, but Leo just gave an awkward kind of half-shrug.

'Leo, I know you know I've kissed him. I've kissed Jack, and I've kissed… the other guy. The King of Hearts.' Merry swallowed, trying to get rid of the sour taste in her mouth.

'There's no point thinking about that now.'

'Fine. But my point is, kissing Jack certainly didn't break the curse.'

'Well,' Leo plucked the manuscript out of her hands, 'you've kissed him, but this is talking about love. Do you love him?'

Merry wrinkled her brow.

'What, now? Or before he tried to…'

'In general. And bearing in mind that that wasn't actually Jack.'

'I don't know, Leo. I'm so confused. I like him. I *really* like him. And sometimes I have this – impression, I suppose – that we've known each other forever, not just weeks. A… closeness. I think Jack's felt it too. And he has this deep belief in me; more belief than I have in myself. Like, he's decided he knows something about me…' She swung her legs up and stretched out on Leo's bed. 'So, I care about him. I want to protect him from any more harm. But does that add up to "true love"?' She sighed. After what had happened, the thought of Jack touching her made her insides knot up with tension. But… she was still dreaming about him. Still couldn't get him out of her head. She'd always wanted to believe in love at first sight; was this what it felt like? Something else occurred to her. 'Wouldn't Jack have to be in love with me, too?' Maybe her kiss hadn't saved him because he just didn't feel the same way about her. Her heart plummeted.

Almost as if he'd read her mind, Leo squeezed her hand.

'It doesn't make any sense, anyway,' Merry continued. As far as they knew, Jack was gone: completely and finally taken over by the King of Hearts. And even if he wasn't, the manuscript had always seemed to suggest that Merry was meant to destroy him, from the first day they'd talked to it. Where was true love – and kissing – supposed to come into that? 'I give up. I suppose we'll have to figure it out if – when – we make it down there. When do you think we need to go?'

'Aha. There, my young apprentice, I can help you. It must be to do with the phases of the Moon. I've got an app for it.'

'Course you do.'

Leo grinned and pulled his phone out of his pocket.

'So – before the waxing crescent comes the new moon. And the next new moon is... the day after tomorrow. Tuesday night.' His smile faded. 'Doesn't give us long.'

Only forty-eight hours. Forty-eight hours more of normal life – normal-ish, at any rate – and then –

Success. Or death. Or worse.

Merry took a deep breath in, let it out slowly.

'OK. Tuesday it is.'

Late Tuesday morning, the coven turned up. Some of the women Merry recognised, and there were some more she hadn't met before, but a sudden stab of happiness quickened her breath when she saw Mum walk into the sitting room and join them. Over the last few weeks Merry had become aware of the barrier between her and her mum, like a sheet of glass that let them see but not hear each other. The glass was still there, but now at least it had cracks in it.

As Gran had predicted, Merry's power had returned – she'd tried the stinging hex on Leo, and it had worked really well – but the other witches were going to put some protective charms on her too. They finished setting up the room (closed curtains, candles, various magical implements), then Gran made a shooing motion with her hands. 'Off you go now, Leo dear. This is not for outsiders.'

Leo and Merry frowned at each other.

'But we're both going,' Leo said. 'We agreed.'

There was a murmur of disapproval from the other witches.

'Oh no, dear.' Gran shook her head. 'This task is appointed to Merry, and to her alone. You have no training—'

'But neither does she!'

'That's not the point.' Gran put her hands on her hips and advanced on Leo. 'She has a latent ability which you

lack. She is the focus, the end point of centuries of planning.'
She reached up and took Leo by the shoulders. 'I know
you mean well, Leo, but it just won't do.' She sighed. 'I
knew that first evening you called me that I would have
to put a stop to your involvement at some point. When
Merry gets under the lake tonight – and she will – you'll
end up being a distraction. A liability, even.'

'He won't Gran, he's been brilliant,' Merry broke in. 'I
wouldn't have lasted this long without him. I'd be dead
by now.'

Gran ignored her.

'Furthermore, you ought to be thinking of your poor
mother. It's bad enough that she has to watch her daughter
go off and risk her life. Trust me, Leo, you can be of more
help here.'

Leo turned to Merry.

'But you want me there, don't you Merry? Tell them
you want me there.'

Merry could hear the pain in Leo's voice. But she could
see the agony on Mum's face too. What would it do to
her mother, if neither she nor Leo ever came back?

And maybe it will be easier, if I know Leo's safe.

'Um, actually, I think maybe Gran's right, Leo. I think…'
She looked down at the flowery rug in front of the fireplace,

tried to keep her voice steady. 'I'd like you to stay here this time.'

'No, Merry, I don't believe you. I want to—'

'Please, Leo.' She held up a hand, silencing him. 'Don't argue with me. You should stay here. You're not a witch. You're not… one of us. You're just going to be in the way.'

Leo threw his hands up in the air.

'Fine. Have it your own way. I won't go with you.' He glared at Gran, who pursed her lips.

'You have to *promise* me, Leo, that you're going to stay away.'

'Oh, I promise, Gran. Scout's honour. After all—' he glanced at Merry '—she doesn't want me there.' He stalked out of the room, slamming the door behind him.

'Leo—'

Gran put her hand on Merry's arm. 'Leave him be. He'll calm down soon enough.'

Merry had no real expectations of how her grandmother and the others would work their charms. She had briefly considered spell books, and magic words, and perhaps a cauldron. She had certainly not anticipated quite so much singing. Or so much jewellery. Standing in a circle around her, the witches chanted musical phrases in a language she didn't understand. They drew strange symbols on her chest, her palms and the soles of her feet, marking her with inks that smelt strongly of herbs and spices she couldn't identify. They gave her bracelets of multicoloured gems, and tied ropes of small, scarlet stones around her waist, next to her skin where they would be hidden by her clothing. Mrs Galantini insisted on hanging a large cross on a chain around her neck – Merry decided she would have to ask Mrs Galantini how she reconciled Church doctrine with witchcraft later, if she ever got the chance. They cut off sections of her hair, tied them to twigs and burnt them on the open fire Mum had set burning in the hearth. And then, Gran brought out a long, black-bladed knife.

'I'm afraid, Merry dear, this is going to be a bit uncomfortable.'

Merry backed away.

'What's with the knife, Gran?'

'I want to put a concealment charm on you. We still don't know exactly how that braid of hair works,' she gestured to Merry's wrist, 'so this will provide reinforcement. But unfortunately, we need some of your blood.'

For a moment, Merry had to remember to keep breathing. The singing, and the beads – it had all seemed a bit like a dream. But the black knife Gran was holding was the most solid thing she had ever seen. This was actually happening.

'Just give me your hand, darling. I promise I'll be as quick as I can.'

'Mum?'

'It's alright, sweetheart.' She came and stood next to Merry. 'Your grandmother's just trying to make sure you're as safe as possible.'

'OK.' Merry forced herself to stretch out her hand. Gran took it and held it steady above a bowl that Mum was holding. The other witches started to sing, their voices becoming part of one, multi-harmonied chorus, while Gran drew the very tip of the blade carefully across Merry's palm. Merry gasped – held her breath to stop from crying out. The cut burned like ice. Blood welled up, a streak of scarlet against the paleness of her skin, and ran down into the bowl.

Gran tipped something else into the bowl, some kind of powder. Dipping her finger into the bowl, she drew a symbol on the back of Merry's uninjured hand: a straight vertical line with diagonal lines at the top and bottom, almost like a backwards zed. The singing ended.

'This is an Anglo-Saxon rune for defence and protection. Each witch here has contributed some of her power to the charm, the better to guard you. So you will have a little bit of all of us with you, when you face the wizard.' Gran spread some ointment on to the cut. It stung for a moment, then the pain faded a little. 'Better?'

'A bit. Thank you, though.' Merry looked round at the other witches. 'All of you.' She blinked and stifled a yawn. 'Um, can I go now?'

'Yes. We're finished. Go and rest.'

Merry escaped to her bedroom, pushed the cats off her bed and lay down carefully, so as not to disturb any of the charms. She was physically exhausted, but the cut on her hand still hurt and the beads round her waist dug into her skin. Sleep wouldn't come. Time ticked away as her mind went round in circles, trying to plan for every unknown eventuality, going over and over possible scenarios. Most of them involved Jack killing her, or Gwydion killing her, or worse.

Eventually though, her eyelids grew heavy. She let them close, and sank thankfully into oblivion…

She followed him at a distance through the dim corridors, keeping to the shadows. Eventually, the wizard stopped by a small door. She hurried to catch up – was just able to conceal herself within the room as Gwydion began lighting the candles set in niches along the walls. He seemed suspicious – kept looking around and over his shoulder – but he didn't discover her hiding place.

Once the candles were lit, filling the room with the rancid smell of tallow, Gwydion turned to the hearth and set a fire burning. He muttered under his breath the whole time: ugly words that she didn't recognise. He kept adding more wood to the fire, building up the flames until the very air was burning in her throat. Finally, he took up a large pair of tongs and lifted out of the fire a silver box, glowing red with the heat.

Gwydion opened the box and tipped something out on to the table next to him. She could not see clearly through the woodsmoke, but it looked like two lumps of dark wood, carved all over.

He stripped to the waist then and took up a knife. All his movements so far had been sure and quick; but now he hesitated, staring down at the black blade. Peering more closely, she saw that his chest and arms were disfigured all over with scars and scabs, and she had to swallow back the acid that rose in her throat.

The wizard took one deep breath – and another – and drew the blade across the left side of his chest, grunting with the pain of it. He leant forwards, and she thought he was about to faint –

– but then she saw, and she understood. He was leaning over so that his blood would drip on to the lumps of wood, muttering the same phrase over an over; an incantation of some sort. He *was feeding them. And as they began to twitch and swell she pressed her hand to her mouth so as not to cry out in horror.*

She was too late. She'd come here expecting to have to kill Jack. But instead, she'd fallen in love with him. So she had thought to strike direct at Gwydion, and had summoned the others — was waiting for them even now. But the enchantment she had just witnessed... She had no weapons with which to fight such magic. The wizard and his King of Hearts were now invincible. It was too late, and all those she loved were in danger, because of her...

There was a creaking sound. In the dim light, Merry could see Gran peering round the edge of the door.

'I thought you would be asleep.'

'I was, but I had a nightmare.' Merry scrunched up under the duvet, pulling her knees close to her chest.

Gran came and sat down on the edge of the bed. 'Tell me about it. It might help you feel better.'

Merry explained what she'd seen. '...and then he put the lumps of wood back in the box, and I woke up. It was Gwydion. I know it was.'

'I believe you. And the two lumps of wood, I suspect, are the puppet hearts that the manuscript has been talking about. One for Gwydion and one for Jack, fed with the wizard's own blood…' Gran shuddered. 'At least now you know what you'll be looking for.'

Merry didn't reply; knowing what the puppet hearts looked like didn't seem much of a comfort. If she'd been seeing something that really happened… the anguish that she'd just felt had been someone else's emotion, not hers. The person following Gwydion had to be the kitchen maid Jack had mentioned – his former love. But a kitchen maid wouldn't have recognised the type of magic Gwydion had been using. Only a witch would know that…

Was it possible Jack had been lying to her?

'What are you thinking about, sweetheart?' Gran asked.

'Um… the knife Gwydion used. It looked a lot like the one you used on me earlier.'

'A magic knife is a magic knife. It's the intention of the user that's important.'

'I s'pose. But – I did feel a tiny bit sorry for him. For Gwydion, I mean. That's crazy, right? I must be losing it.'

'It's not crazy, angel.' Gran took off her glasses and started polishing them on the end of her scarf. 'I dare say he wasn't always a monster; he must have had a heart once, for it to have been broken. But,' she lifted a finger for emphasis, 'he had free will, as all men do. He chose to follow that path, and he's no more human now than that alarm clock. When you face him, Merry, *if* you have to face him, don't take the risk of offering him mercy.'

'Vengeance,' she murmured, more to herself than Gran. 'We shall have vengeance.'

'What did you say?' Gran was staring at her, eyes narrowed.

'Oh, nothing. It just popped into my head. That's the kind of thing you're supposed to say, isn't it? If you're going on a quest?'

TWENTY-ONE

MERRY WAS IN the hallway with Gran and Mum. It was time to leave: Gran was standing with her car keys in one hand and the other on the front-door latch. Merry had said goodbye to her mother – hugged her tightly and told her not to worry, that everything was going to be OK. Mum had smiled – though the smile looked odd, like she was trying to stop her face crumpling into tears. But there was still no sign of Leo.

Merry couldn't quite believe it. He, of all people, knew what she was facing. He knew how unlikely it was that she would actually make it back alive, even if she succeeded in defeating the wizard. How could he not be here? Sure, she'd upset him earlier, but still…

He should have understood.

'We really have to go.' Gran opened the front door. 'It's nearly sunset.'

Merry didn't answer. From where she was standing, she could see the empty spot on the driveway where Leo usually parked his car.

'Sweetheart,' Mum began.

'It's OK, Mum. I guess I'll see him later.'

Mum nodded. 'Of course you will. We'll be waiting for you.'

They drove in silence to the small car park near the lake. Merry expected it to be empty as usual, but instead the whole coven was waiting on the gravel, some in tight knots, heads down, talking; some stamping their feet against the cold, watching the crows wheeling overhead. As she got out of the car the other witches gathered near the entrance to the woods. Merry turned to Gran.

'What's going on?'

'We can't go with you, angel. But we all want you to know—' Gran's eyes filled with tears. 'We want—'

One of the witches stepped forwards.

'We want you to know that we, your sisters,' she gestured

to the other witches, 'will be with you in sprit, Merry. There will be some of us here in the woods every minute until you return. And you will return.'

'Of course she will.' Gran had recovered her composure, more or less. Merry looked round at the girls and women standing near her. All of them were nodding in agreement. Flo had all her fingers crossed. Despite the fear lodged in the pit of her stomach, Merry smiled at her.

I'm – I'm actually part of this. Maybe it's not just me any more. Or even just me and Leo. Maybe now it's all of us.

'Thanks everyone, really. I'll, um, see you afterwards.' She hugged Gran, took a deep breath, and forced herself to walk away, and not to look back.

Too soon, Merry was standing by the edge of the lake. The air was freezing. Frost crunched under her feet, and the scent of smoke from a bonfire somewhere nearby made her think of autumn, but at least it wasn't raining. The western sky was still light, just about, the unseen sun backlighting the thick cloud with a faint, pink glow. But in the east, night had already fallen. A night with no Moon and no visible stars. Merry shivered and checked her pockets again for the manuscript, key and sword hilt.

The coven was out there somewhere, among the still-bare trees, but she couldn't see them. The burst of warmth and fellowship she'd experienced only minutes earlier had faded; she felt like the last human being left on an empty planet.

Despite what had happened the last time she'd been at the lake, it was almost a relief when Jack emerged from the water. Merry spoke the words that rendered him unconscious then stood at a distance, waiting.

He woke, and took a step towards her.

She raised her arm with the braid tied around her wrist. 'Stop. Don't come any closer.'

Jack stopped and sank to his knees. 'I do not dare to ask your forgiveness. But please – don't be afraid. I am myself, I swear.'

Merry edged a little closer, holding the torch high, trying to see the expression in Jack's eyes. 'How did the King of Hearts stay in control of you, last time? Tell me.'

'Gwydion placed an extra enchantment on me, before I left the lake that night. It enabled the shadow within me to resist your command. But it cost him dear, and he has not repeated it.'

Merry peered at the figure kneeling before her. His voice was different: it had lost that tense, urgent quality she'd noticed last time. He sounded like her Jack again – only utterly defeated. She moved a little closer still, and saw the scarring on his forehead. 'What has he done to you?'

Jack ducked his head. 'It is of no matter. I just wish he would hurt me enough to kill me.'

'Oh, Jack.' Merry sat down and Jack slumped sideways, his shoulders sagging.

'I did try,' he murmured a few minutes later. 'When the wizard first started sending me out to kill. I did try to take my own life. But he placed enchantments on my skin: no knot would hold, no knife would bite. I prayed every day for death.'

Merry didn't know what to say. To long for death, and have even that choice taken away; it was a miracle despair hadn't driven Jack to madness.

'I asked her to kill me,' Jack continued. 'Meredith. But she refused, first of all. And then later… she told me Gwydion had placed another enchantment on me, one that protected us both and linked my life to his. She could not overthrow the enchantment, so she could not harm either him or me…'

He was talking about the puppet hearts; that had to be the enchantment Jack meant, even if he didn't know the details. The witches had realised they hadn't the power to destroy the hearts, therefore they could no longer destroy the wizard. So they'd taken the only other option and put the wizard and his King of Hearts to sleep.

Three fully trained witches failed to stop Gwydion, and now it's up to me...

Jack spoke again.

'You must finish this, Merry. Promise that you will find a way to put me to death.'

She hadn't learnt any spells for murdering people. It would have to be done by hand. Maybe she would have to stick a sword into his chest, just like in her dreams. Her stomach churned with the thought of it.

'I don't think I can, Jack.'

'You must. If Gwydion captures you, he will kill you.' Jack looked at her intently. 'He will make the King of Hearts kill you...'

'But – I care about you...' Merry got up, started to walk towards Jack. She really wanted to feel his arms around her right now.

'No.' he put his hand out to stop her. 'You mustn't. Because, I cannot – I *do not* – care for you. Not in the way you want.'

'But that evening, at the lake—'

'It was one evening, a pleasant way to pass a few hours.' He shook his head. 'It meant nothing to me. Do you understand? There is no reason why you should not do as I ask, and take my life. Kill me, then forget about me – as I would forget about you.'

Merry thought her knees were about to give way. Staying upright, not giving in to the tears building in her eyes, not screaming at him… it was almost more than she could bear. But to allow Jack see to see her cry would have been worse.

At least now I know. However many times I kiss him, it won't make any difference. He doesn't love me. He doesn't care about me at all. Will that make it easier, in the end? Easier to kill him?

'Merry?'

The voice came from behind her. It was Leo.

Merry turned and ran to him. 'Leo! I thought I'd made you too angry, that you weren't coming—'

'Don't be daft. That was just an act, to get Gran off my back. I can't believe you thought I wouldn't show.' He peered at her. 'Are you OK?'

'Yeah, I'm… I'm fine.' Merry tried to look… normal. She couldn't let herself think about what Jack had just said to her. Not now. 'Nervous, that's all.'

Leo looked unconvinced, but he just said: 'I'd have been here sooner, but I had to take a massive detour to avoid her and the rest of the coven. Sending you in there alone is nuts. I can help you. I know I can.'

'Oh, thank God for that.' Merry sighed with relief. 'I realise I should be self-sacrificing and think of Mum, and you, but… there's no way I can do this on my own.'

'Good. That's settled then.' He paused. 'Though if I'm honest, I was expecting a bit more—' he put on a high-pitched voice, '—"Oh no, Leo, I can't let you risk yourself!" That sort of thing.'

'Yeah. If I wasn't scared absolutely witless then maybe… But – there is one thing you have to do for me.'

'What?'

Merry glanced back at Jack, and drew Leo a little further away. 'You have to wear this.' She unknotted the braid from her own wrist and tied it around Leo's. He tried to pull his arm away when he saw what she was doing.

'No, Merry, stop it. You need to keep wearing it. It protects you.'

'But you're going to need protection too. Gran and the others have put all sorts of charms on me, and I can't concentrate on whatever it is I'm supposed to be doing if I have to worry about you. Plus, I've got a plan. Sort of a plan. The King of Hearts knows that I've got the braid, yes?'

'Yeah.'

'So, he won't expect you to have it. It will... confuse him.'

Leo shook his head. 'That's one of the worst plans I've ever heard, even coming from you. Really. It stinks. Take the braid back. I can look after myself, you know.'

'Leo, come on! Take the braid, or go home. I mean it.'

Leo looked at her doubtfully, but he stopped arguing.

Merry tightened the braid on his wrist a bit more, and frowned. 'What happened to your hand?'

Her brother looked down at his bloodied knuckles and flexed them, wincing.

'I hit Simon.'

'What? Why?'

'Merry, I really think we're going to make it out of this. But, if there's even a small chance of something bad happening... I decided, if I'm going to die, I want people to remember me as I really am. So while you and the coven were doing your stuff, I met up with Simon and Matt and some of the others. I told them. About being gay.'

'And?'

'I shouldn't have been so worried. Everyone was surprised, but none of them actually seemed to care. Apart from Simon.' Leo looked up at the starless sky. 'I can't believe I thought he was so great, all these years. Turns out he's just a poisonous, homophobic…' He stopped and took a deep breath. 'Anyway, the upshot was, I decked him. Then I left. Really, if the others want to stay friends, that's great. If they don't, screw them. I'll make new friends.'

'Course you will.' Merry hugged him tightly. 'I'm so proud of you.'

'Thanks.'

'Did you visit Dan?'

'No. He's still not allowed visitors, apart from family. I'll go when we get back. If we get back. I'd like to talk to him properly.'

'Dan's lovely. He's not going to care.'

'I know.' Leo sighed. 'Come on. We should go back and check on Jack.'

Nobody seemed inclined to chat. Merry wasn't surprised: the last time the three of them had been together was not a moment any of them wanted to remember. Jack's earlier rejection made it too painful for her even to look at him. And the knowledge of what she and Leo were about to attempt sucked at her attention like a sore tooth. Without true love, success could only mean one thing: this would be the last time Jack ever saw the sky. The sadness of it almost took her breath away.

She started yanking closed-up daisies out of the grass, trying to split the stems enough to thread them into a chain. Not that easy in the dark. Beside her, she heard Leo shift position, grunting slightly as he massaged his hand.

So when I get into the water –

She took a deep breath.

When I get into the water, I mustn't forget. It would be very easy to panic, and forget…

As Gran had suggested, she and Leo were going to do *exactly* what the manuscript had been telling them to do all these weeks: follow Jack into the water, his way. At the same time, however, Merry was planning to use the magic she'd been working on. The King of Hearts would jump into just the right part of the lake, he would open the secret entrance to the space under the lake, and she would magically keep the water from rushing back into place after him. It would be easy for her and Leo to follow.

Huh. I'm not sure the word 'easy' can be applied to any of this…

Leo nudged her. Jack was grimacing with pain – the King of Hearts was regaining control.

'Ready?' Leo asked, swinging his backpack on to his shoulders.

She nodded, and said the words to return the wizard's servant to the lake.

And there was no time for anything more. As Jack ran up the small cliff they sprinted after him, close on his heels, and at the exact same spot that Jack threw himself out above the lake. Merry vaulted after him into the darkness, plunging down into the churning waters, concentrating on holding the freezing water at bay. And as she fell her power ignited, surging up from her fingertips and arms until it ran across her whole skin like electricity...

Air. Dry, dusty, stale air, but air nonetheless. Merry was taking great gulps of it, her head between her knees, her mind somewhere between terror and relief. They were still alive, her magic had worked, and they were under the lake.

She knew they were under the lake, because when she looked up she could see a fluctuating but roughly circular hole above her head, and above that, water. It was dark, but Leo's torch showed up bubbles and bits of plant floating around in it. They had definitely been above the water – Merry remembered holding her breath as the lake rushed up towards her, desperately trying to focus – and now they were under the water, but they didn't seem at any point to have actually been in the water.

At least now they knew why Jack's clothes were never wet.

There was a touch on her shoulder: Leo, hunched down next to her.

'Hey, are you feeling better?'

Merry nodded.

'Yeah.' She smiled. 'We did it.'

'We did. But if you're up to it, we should start moving.'

Merry nodded and stood up, clinging to the wall beside her.

Leo shone the torch downwards. Next to the small, stone platform on which they were standing was a shaft, leading down into the earth. Rough stone steps were set into its sides, a sort of spiral staircase disappearing into the depths.

'I wish there was a bannister. Or at least more light.'

'Oh, hold on a second.' A violet glow slowly lit up the staircase. Leo gazed, mouth open, at the sphere of blue-purple fire hovering above Merry's open hand. She smiled at him

'It's witch fire. I've only just learnt how to do it.'

'Wow. Impressive.' Leo grinned. Then he frowned.

Merry frowned back at him. 'What's the matter? You're looking at me funny.'

'Have you dyed your hair? It looks… darker…'

'Like I've had time to get my hair done?'

'And your eyes look greener…'

'You're imagining it. Or the witch fire makes things look different.'

Leo rubbed his eyes. 'Guess you're right.'

There was a dull thud above them. The hole had disappeared, leaving only solid rock. Merry swallowed, tried not to think of the word *trapped*, and grabbed Leo's hand.

'Come on. Let's go.'

The staircase ended in a wide tunnel. The first part of the tunnel was rock, but they soon came to a more open section, the sides of which seemed to be partially collapsed. Merry turned aside from the path to investigate. The light of the witch fire, together with Leo's torch, revealed not rock, but trees. A broad wall of dead, petrified holly trees, which once must have been enormously tall but were now broken by the weight of the roof above them. Huge leaves still clung to the thick branches, long, curved thorns gleaming in the soft light.

'What on earth is that?' Leo put out his fingers to touch one of the leaves. Merry grabbed his wrist.

'Black holly. It used to grow round the outside of Gwydion's tower. I've seen it before. It's poisonous.' She pulled Leo away from the trees and the deadly thorns before he could ask any more questions. 'We'd better hurry.'

They caught sight of Jack, or not-Jack, ahead of them, walking towards a pair of enormous doors that started to swing open as he approached. Leo and Merry sped up, sprinting along the uneven floor – but the doors swung silently shut just a fraction of a second before Leo reached them.

'Damn!' Leo ran his hands rapidly over the carved and pitted surface in front of him. He leant against the doors, shoving until Merry could see the veins standing out on his neck, but the doors didn't give a millimetre.

There was no handle or keyhole that Merry could see. But something about the doors felt familiar... Merry let the witch fire fade.

'Leo, it's OK. We've got a key.'

He turned around, panting.

'No. There's no keyhole. And that's just the key for the trinket box.'

'But – I feel like I've been here before. Like I've done

this before.' Merry shrugged her shoulders. 'I think I have to try.' The silver key that had once dangled from her charm bracelet was now larger than her hand. She hesitated, her eyes closed, before pressing it against the centre of one of the doors. For a moment nothing happened. But then the edges of the doorway began to glow with a muted orange light, and the doors swung open again. 'OK.' She led the way through the doors. 'Well, we'd better – oh, crap.'

There were five corridors leading away from the doors, all dark, all identical: stone-built, with fragments of rotting tapestry still hanging in places. The air had a thick, powdery quality; it hit the back of Merry's throat and made her cough.

'It's like a maze. What are we going to do?' The dense silence forced her to whisper.

Leo switched his electric torch back on – just in time, as the doors swung shut behind them.

'Um… I reckon we should follow Jack, for now. At least it's somewhere to start. And maybe we'll get lucky and he'll lead us straight to the puppet hearts.' He shone the torch down the corridors. 'But try the manuscript too – ask it if it can tell us where the hearts are, and direct us from here. I'll have a scout around.'

Merry pulled the manuscript out of her pocket as Leo started examining the entrances to the corridors.

'Manuscript, where are the puppet hearts?'

Under the lake.

'Yes, I know. That's really not enough detail right now. Can you—'

'Hey.' Leo waved her over to the right-most corridor. 'Look.'

'What am I looking at?'

'Footprints. Just a trace of them, in the dust – there.' He pointed. 'Jack's still human, after all. At least on a part-time basis.'

'Genius. Come on then.'

The corridor twisted and turned and dropped down sudden flights of steps. Other dark doorways, some of them half-blocked with rubble, opened to the left and right. The air grew cold and the trail of footsteps sometimes disappeared altogether, but each time they eventually rediscovered it. Finally, the trail ended at another door. This one was ajar. Slowly, Merry pushed it further open.

The room beyond the door was huge. There was no sign of decay here. A fire was burning in a long trench down the middle of the floor, yellow flames casting twisted, flickering shadows on the walls. The air had an odd, metallic taste. Shelves covered the wall at the far end of the room, filled with containers of some sort, many of them glowing. Merry remembered Gran's story, remembered what the King of Hearts had told her, and realised what must be inside the jars. She clamped a hand to her mouth. And then she noticed a chair facing the fire. More than a chair – a throne.

Jack was sitting on it, motionless.

Merry ran towards the throne, ignoring Leo's hiss of warning behind her. When she got closer, she saw Jack was bound to it with thick cords around his arms, legs, waist – even his neck and head. He was pinned fast. But he was clearly himself again: there were tears streaking his face.

Leo caught up with her.

'Oh, no—' He pulled his Swiss Army knife out of the back pocket of his jeans.

'Leo – wait.' Merry moved closer to Jack and waved a hand in front of his face. Jack didn't react at all. 'He can't see us. Why can't he see us?'

'I don't know. Seems he can't hear us, either.' Leo glanced down at the braid round his wrist. 'D'you think this thing works differently here?'

'Maybe.' She thought back over everything Gran had told them, everything Jack had said, everything she seen in her visions.

Meredith obviously made it, and I still don't know how. But I do have an idea whose hair it might be...

Leo was watching Jack again.

'But why can't he see you?'

'Um, Gran put a concealment charm on me.' She held up her hand and showed him the dark, spiky symbol inked on to her skin. 'Quick, cut him loose.'

Leo raised his knife, then paused.

'What're you waiting for?' Merry asked.

'It might be better if he doesn't know we're here. We still don't know whether the King of Hearts can read his mind.' He closed the knife.

'I suppose, but—'

Leo held up a hand. 'Hold on: do you hear something? Like—'

'Footsteps.' Merry gasped; suddenly there didn't seem to be enough air in the room. 'Gwydion. He's coming.'

TWENTY-TWO

NEITHER OF THEM wanted to rely on magic for concealment. They managed to squeeze themselves under a table in the corner of the room, creeping as far back into the shadows as possible. Just in time: a small door nearby opened a minute or so later and a man walked stiffly into the room. His hair was dark, streaked with grey, and as he passed the table Merry caught a glimpse of black eyes and a narrow, scarred face.

She felt Leo's grip on her hand tighten.

The wizard walked up to where Jack was imprisoned. He clicked his fingers; the cords around Jack's head and neck curled back, waving like tentacles before falling lifeless around his shoulders. Gwydion started speaking to Jack, his voice rusty from disuse, but Merry couldn't understand the words, or Jack's replies. The language sounded tantalisingly close to English, but – she glanced at Leo. He was frowning, clearly as confused as she was.

Of course. They're speaking Old English. If only I knew a translation spell…

Except…

Except in all her dreams and visions, Meredith, her sisters, Edith – they must have been speaking Old English, and she'd understood that. She thought about the coven meeting, and the water she'd made boil, just by fantasizing about coffee.

Yes, but that was all… unofficial. Unnatural.

She hesitated for a moment longer. But Gran had said she should trust herself. And there really wasn't any other choice.

Come on. Just imagine. Imagine you can understand, you and Leo…

It was like someone had suddenly switched on subtitles in her head: the words Gwydion and Jack were saying sounded the same, but now she knew exactly what they meant. She reached forwards and touched her brother's forehead; Leo gasped. Merry spent a couple of seconds enjoying the surprise on his face before focusing back on the wizard.

'...no point in trying to lie to me, boy. She is back again, is she not?' Even in translation, Merry could detect the loathing in Gwydion's voice. 'How else is it that you return to me without having completed your task?'

'Torture me all you like, wizard. I will tell you nothing further.'

Gwydion waved his hand and Jack grunted with pain as his head jerked sideways. Blood trickled from a long red welt on his cheek.

'Oh, but you are brave now,' Gwydion snarled. 'That will not last. And soon, even with this girl's interference, we will be ready to proceed. My King of Hearts has not been idle.'

'I have killed no one. Those I attacked are recovering.' Jack held himself up straighter, despite the bonds restraining him. 'Your enchantments are failing, old man.'

'Really? I think not.' Gwydion reached around and pulled the broken sword from the scabbard hanging at Jack's waist. Merry leant forwards, trying to see more clearly.

The sword had grown.

It was impossible. She remembered seeing the blade lying on the grass by the lake, some weeks ago now: then, at least half of it was gone, the shattered edge discoloured and eaten away. But the blade Gwydion now held in his hands was almost whole. Just the tip was missing. Gwydion made a strange, croaking sound, and Merry realised he was laughing.

'Still, you do not understand, do you? Idiot boy. The first sword I gave you was destroyed when you failed to kill your brother. This second blade was almost lost to the meddling of those cursed witches—' Gwydion turned his head and spat on the floor, 'but enough survived that it could be remade.' He stroked the hilt of the sword, and it was almost a caress. 'My King of Hearts knew what to do. He has been feeding the blade, bathing it in living blood, and it is nearly whole again. One more meal, I think, will be enough to complete it. I shall send you out tomorrow night. Then I will be strong enough to leave this prison, and you—' he waved an arm towards the shelves at the end of the room, '—you have a lot of empty jars still to fill, Jack. Together, we will show this new world of yours what power really means.'

'No! I will not submit to you! I will not—'

'Silence!' Jack froze, and the leather cords settled back

across his face and neck, even over his mouth. Gwydion gripped Jack's jaw in his fingers. 'A life for a life, Jack. Your mother took my life away, and I have taken yours. You belong to me.' He stepped away from the chair, staggering slightly. 'I must rest now. The enchantment of the black holly still lies heavy on me while I am trapped here. In the meantime, you can stay shackled there until I send you out again.' He turned away and started limping back towards the door, then stopped and looked over his shoulder at Jack. 'If you defy me further I will cut out your tongue. Think on that, boy.'

Merry waited, holding Leo's hand, until she was certain – as certain as she could be, anyway – that the wizard wasn't coming back. They both ran over to Jack. She put her hand out to touch his injured cheek – but forced herself to stop, to lower her arm.

'I wish we could help him. But we're running out of time.' Merry dug her fingernails into her palms, trying to subdue the panic building in her guts. They had to find the puppet hearts, quickly. She pulled out the manuscript.

'Where are the puppet hearts?'

Hidden.

'Brilliant.' Leo was craning over her shoulder. 'Really helpful. So where do we start searching? Here?'

Merry thought for a moment, then pointed to the door though which the wizard had recently appeared.

'If I were Gwydion, I'd keep them hidden somewhere near me. But you're the smart one, Leo. Tell me I'm wrong. I'd really kind of like to be wrong.'

'I really wish I could.' While Merry conjured another ball of witch fire, Leo switched on his torch and pulled a compass out of his jacket pocket. 'Let's go.' He paused. 'Jack, I know you can't hear me, but we'll be back soon. I hope.'

Minutes became hours, hours became a day, and hope faded away. Merry didn't know exactly how long they had been searching in the labyrinth of rooms and corridors under the lake. Her phone and Leo's were both out of charge, and there was neither daylight nor moonlight to give any sense of time passing. The twisting, turning passages made the compass almost useless. She tried to summon the puppet hearts using a powerful finding spell Gran had shown her, but – whether because her magic was still erratic, or because there was something else interfering with the spell – absolutely nothing happened. At one point they found themselves back in the hall with the throne, and Jack was gone.

'I can't believe it. It must be Wednesday evening already,' Leo said. Merry just nodded. She didn't want to think about what Mum and Gran were going through. She didn't want to think about what Jack – controlled by the King of Hearts – was doing somewhere up above them, or what that meant for the growth of Gwydion's powers.

There was nothing for it but to keep going. They slept a little, and eked out the food and water Leo had brought with him in the backpack. If there was anything to eat down here, they hadn't discovered it so far.

They were just finishing examining another room. Leo was lying on his stomach and groping with his fingers inside a compartment hidden in the window frame. Merry was sitting on the floor by the door, hugging her knees and watching him. There was dirt on his face, and the back of his arm was streaked with dried blood from a cut on his forehead. Merry was sure she looked at least as bad. She certainly felt pretty terrible. The dust made her throat sore, and her ankle ached from tripping down some stairs.

Leo pulled his hand out of the compartment.

'Nothing. Just more desiccated spider corpses.' He sat up and wiped his hands on his jeans. 'You doing OK?'

'Yeah, except I can't stop thinking about how much I

want a shower.' Merry started running her fingers through her hair, trying to get out some of the tangles.

'And you're not getting any feelings of déjà vu, like back at the doors?'

'If you mean do I think we're going round in circles, then yes. I'm sure we've checked this room already, at least once. But if you mean any helpful images, then no.' She closed her eyes for a moment. 'This dust is really getting to me.'

'Here, drink something.' Leo passed her the last bottle of water. It was already half empty. 'We need to keep moving.'

'What's the point? Even if Gwydion can't see us to kill us, we're going to die of dehydration. Or starvation. Or blood poisoning, or—'

'Stop it. We're going to find these puppet hearts, whatever they are, and we're going to get out of here. I've got stuff I want to do with my life. I'm sure you have too.'

She shrugged. There was no point in arguing. She could say something about self-sacrifice, about taking Gwydion down with her and making a difference – but they would just be words.

I'm only sixteen. I accept I'm probably going to die down here, and that maybe my death will help other people. But that doesn't mean I'm happy about it.

She pushed herself to her feet.

'Let's get on with it then.'

Merry went to pick up the empty water bottle, stopped herself – *Am I seriously worried about leaving rubbish behind?* – then frowned.

Is it my imagination, or is that bottle trembling?

'Leo? Look at this.'

Leo put his hand between the bottle and the wall.

'There's a draft. There must be a room or a passageway behind this wall.'

Merry already had the key in her hand. She slapped it on to the wall. Almost instantly there was a grinding sound, stone on stone, and the entire section of wall sank vertically into the ground below.

Behind the wall was another spiral staircase.

For a moment neither of them spoke. Then Leo gave a sigh of relief.

'See? How easy was that? The heart things have got to be up here, and it only took us, what, thirty-five hours to find them. Give or take.'

Merry managed a smile.

'Yep. Not a bad result for Team Cooper, all things considered. Turn off the torch. I'll go first.'

Merry conjured a globe of witch fire, ordered it to become as dim as possible – and was somewhat surprised when it obeyed – then tiptoed up the stairs. She was expecting to come to a door, but the staircase opened directly into a room. A room hung all over with tapestries of the black holly trees, dark leaves bearing silver, needle-like thorns that shone out of the gloom. And in the centre of the room was a wide low bed, draped with furs and richly embroidered cloths. It was like a scene out of Sleeping Beauty except…

Gwydion was in the bed, snoring.

Merry, virtually immobilised on the top step, twisted round a fraction and motioned Leo to be silent. She tried to think.

If the heart things are in here, where are they going to be?

She scanned the room. Apart from the bed, there was a large wooden chest in one corner and a door that presumably led to another room. No other furniture.

No way am I going anywhere near his bed. So that leaves the chest, or that door over there…

She felt a prod in the small of her back: Leo, wanting to know what was next.

Come on, Merry – make a decision.

She took a couple of long, slow breaths.

OK. I guess starting in the wizard-free room is sensible. If it is a room, and not just a cupboard.

Gesturing to Leo to follow her, Merry moved as quietly as possible towards the door. It opened as soon as she touched it with the key. The hinges creaked a little and Gwydion snorted and shifted in his sleep, but he still didn't wake.

There was a room on the other side of the door: a cramped, smelly room. Merry increased the strength of the witch fire and sent the globe of light upwards, to hover near the ceiling. The increased radiance revealed shelves, covering every wall. And every shelf was crammed with – stuff, basically. Merry didn't know how else to think about it. There were gold and silver plates heaped with jewellery, bolts of woven cloth, weapons and bits of armour she had no chance of identifying. There were piles of parchment rolls, drinking horns, tarnished bronze hand mirrors and bunches of keys. And then there were things that made her flesh goose pimple: bits of wood carved into hideous shapes, the dried-up corpses of animals, a leather bucket full of bones. She turned to Leo. He had his hand over his nose and mouth, and looked like he was trying not to gag.

'Open any boxes you can find,' she whispered, 'but be careful. The puppet hearts are made of wood, roughly ...' she held her hand out, indicating a size.

Leo nodded and turned to the nearest shelf. Merry did the same – wishing she had brought a pair of gloves – and started poking around amongst the detritus in front of her. She knew she had to be thorough, not miss anything important, but with Gwydion just next door she was also very aware of every passing minute. The voice in the back of her head was getting stronger: *How much longer until he wakes up? How much longer until you're caught? How much longer until it's too late?*

Merry moved on to another set of shelves. They contained more variations on the old and/or revolting theme.

This is crazy. We just don't have time…

She tried to put herself into Gwydion's position. Who would he fear might try to find the hearts? Another wizard, or a witch – someone magically powerful, to have got this far.

Yeah, right.

So perhaps the puppet hearts were protected from powerful spells. But... would they be protected from simple ones? Especially simple ones that rely on the spellcaster knowing exactly what she's looking for? Feeling slightly ridiculous, Merry shut her eyes and started to sing, ever so quietly, the words of the basic charm for finding lost things, trying to recall as she did so all the details of the puppet hearts that she had seen in her vision.

O Sun by day and Moon by night, shine on the thing I seek, a light...

An image leapt into her mind: a carved horse's head. She peered around the room. In one corner, right up by the ceiling, there was something that could be a horse's head, though it looked as if it was just part of the roof beam...

'Leo,' she whispered, 'see if you can get that down.' Leo raised an eyebrow, but he stood on a wooden chest and pulled at the carving. After a few moments of effort it came away in his hand, revealing a compartment in the wall behind. He reached in and pulled out a box, which he passed to Merry before replacing the horse's head in the wall.

The box had a smudgy black surface – heavily tarnished

silver – with a pattern of ugly, lizard-like creatures embossed on to the lid, all claws and bulbous eyes and gaping mouths. Merry pulled the top away from the box; inside were two identical lumps of dark wood, carved all over with more of the hideous snakes.

'This is it. We've found them.'

'Oh, thank God.' Leo put his arm around her shoulders and gave her a quick hug. 'Ask the manuscript how to destroy them.'

'Somehow, I doubt it's going to be straightforward,' Merry muttered. But she held up the parchment.

'We've found the hearts. How do we destroy them?'

Words blossomed on the page.

When the time comes, true love's kiss will end the strife.

'No.' Leo jabbed at the manuscript. 'Oh, no. You're not doing this to us now, stupid booklet. Give us some proper information. Ask it again, Merry.'

Merry asked again. But the same exact words appeared again further down the page. And again, and again. Leo got out his lighter and ignited it. He snatched the manuscript from Merry's hands.

'Leo, what the hell are you doing?'

He waved the lighter at the manuscript. 'I'm going to burn this damn thing if it doesn't start being a bit more helpful. How would you like that, Manuscript? Fancy starting a new career as a torch?'

'Seriously? Just give it back to me and stop being—'

There was a fit of coughing from the adjacent room. Leo dropped the lighter.

Gwydion was awake.

TWENTY-THREE

MERRY WONDERED IF this was an appropriate moment to panic.

The monster I'm supposed to destroy is waking up next door, and my brother's decided now is a good time to go gaga and start menacing pieces of paper. No one would blame me if I did panic, surely?

She dimmed the witch fire and went on tiptoe to whisper into Leo's ear.

'We have to get away from here. Pick up the damn lighter and give the manuscript to me.'

Leo bristled, but he passed her the bundle of parchment. They both looked around the room, but Merry couldn't

380

see any other exit. How long before Gwydion came in here?

'Try the key thing again,' Leo mouthed.

'But where? There is literally no wall space.' Merry got the key out anyway and held it up in front of her face.

'How do we get out of here and back to the hall without Gwydion seeing us?' She shook the key. 'How?'

Great. Now I'm talking to inanimate objects too.

The key twitched. Merry let go with a yelp.

'Shh!' Leo threw his hands up in a *What the hell are you doing?* gesture.

'It moved.' Merry glared at him. She went to where the key lay on the floor, tried to pick it up – and frowned. The key was hard to lift, almost as though it was magnetically attracted to the floor. She pushed away the dirty rushes with trembling hands. There was a trapdoor underneath. She beckoned to Leo.

'Let's go.'

'Hold on.' Leo squatted down on the floor next to her. 'Gwydion can't see you because of the concealment charm and he can't see me because of the braid. We think. So maybe we should stay here a bit longer, look around for something to destroy the hearts?'

'No, Leo. We need to get out while we can.' Merry

381

couldn't shake the feeling that the wizard was somehow staring at her through the wall. 'Maybe we can set fire to the hearts? They're made of wood,' she whispered, as she reached for the trapdoor edge to lever it up.

'We could try. Though I thought you wanted to figure out—'

'I can feel you, witch.'

Merry stared at Leo, her own shock mirrored in his face. The voice had come from the other room. She looked at the concealment charm on the back of her hand.

The rune had changed. The carnelian ink had faded, and the end of one of the diagonal strokes had vanished. And of course, she wasn't wearing the braid.

Leo grabbed her hand.

'Can you fix it? You did that translation spell earlier, you must be able to fix it.'

'No, I don't think so. That was different, I don't know how to make this—'

'I know you are there, witch. I cannot hear you or see you yet, but you will not be able to hide from me for much longer. I am coming for you.' Gwydion's singsong voice was just the other side of the door.

Leo pulled the trapdoor up and almost threw Merry down the stairs below.

'Run!'

Merry held the key out in front of her.

'Take us away from Gwydion!'

She felt a slight tug from the key, and started running in the direction it seemed to want them to go, Leo at her heels.

The key led them along corridors and down stairs. They ran as fast as they could, but still they could hear Gwydion behind them in the distance, laughing. Merry glanced at the rune on her hand: it was half gone. She sped up.

Leo tapped her on the shoulder.

'Where – where are we going?' he panted.

'Dunno. I'm following the key.'

They sprinted on in silence, until Merry's blood was pounding in her ears and she could hardly drag enough air into her lungs to keep her legs moving. They turned one more corner, went through one more doorway and found themselves back in the room with the throne.

Jack was still missing.

Merry pulled Leo back beneath the table they had hidden under before.

'What are you doing, Merry? We have to get out of here. Why did you stop?'

'Because the key stopped.' Everything seemed to keep

coming back to this room. She guessed it made sense; what Gwydion did here was at the heart of what he was doing to Jack.

'This is crazy.' Leo grasped her shoulders. 'We've got the hearts, let's take them back—'

'No. We've… *I've* got to finish this. Now.' Merry peeked out from their hiding place. The wizard hadn't found them – yet. 'Listen, I don't know how much time I have. There's something I need to tell you.'

'But Merry—'

'Please, Leo.' She scanned his face, remembering the countless times he'd looked out for her, cheered her up, been there when she'd needed him. 'I haven't been honest with you, about the witch stuff. About what I used to do, before—' She took a deep breath, trying to stop her voice from wobbling. The thought of Leo finding out the truth after she was dead, and thinking the worst of her, made her feel sick. 'I got in over my head. I did things to Ruby, and to Alex especially – terrible things. What happened to Alex, what he tried to do – it was all my fault. He hates me, and I'm pretty sure Ruby doesn't like me much any more either. I don't blame them. I just – I want you to know that I'm sorry. I never meant to hurt anyone.'

'Of course you didn't, but—'

'And that I love you, and Mum and Gran. And—'

'Merry – I know that. But you're wrong about Ruby. She's been really worried about you. She's been texting me non-stop for days, 'cos you've had your phone turned off so much. Something about feeling guilty, and that she knows you'd never dump her for a bloke....'

'Oh.' This whole time, she'd had it wrong. Ruby still wanted to be her friend; even without being magically forced into it.

Leo started to tug the braid off.

'Here, you should take this.'

'Absolutely not. You have to keep it on. Promise me. Gwydion doesn't know you're here and neither does Jack.' Merry pushed Leo's fingers away from the braid. 'Stay here, and figure out what to do with the puppet hearts. Figure out how to end this. You know, preferably before he kills me.' Though nothing was likely to stop that now.

Leo didn't answer. He just pulled her into hug and buried his head in her shoulder. She could feel his tears on her neck.

Gwydion limped into the throne room. Merry's heart started thudding violently in her chest.

'Come out, come out, wherever you are.' Gwydion moved further into the room. 'I can hear you, witch. I can hear the blood pounding through your veins. I can smell your tender, young skin. Come out now, or it will be the worse for you.'

Merry let go of Leo and forced his arms away from her, pressing the key, the sword hilt and the parchment into his hands. She put a finger to her lips, scrambled out from underneath the table and went to stand in the middle of the room. The rune on the back of her hand had disappeared – Gwydion could see her. He stepped closer.

'What is your name, witch?'

'Merry. Meredith.'

'Meredith…' Gwydion began to laugh. 'The one who escaped. I see… yes, now I see. How clever. She wanted revenge. And so, fifteen hundred years later—' he shook his head, as though he could still not believe how much time had passed, '—here you stand.' He raised a finger, beckoning, and Merry stepped forwards, no longer in control of her own body, no longer able to speak.

Is this what Jack feels like the whole time?

Gwydion stopped her right in front of him and ran one blackened fingernail down the side of her face and neck. She shuddered.

'You are quite like her. And you will die here, just as her sisters did.'

Carys and Nia had died here?

Vengeance...

The word whispered through her mind, just as it had done in Northumberland.

Gwydion turned and looked through the doorway opposite. 'You have returned, my servant?'

Jack walked back into the throne room.

Merry felt the wizard watching her as Jack... the King of Hearts... walked towards them. Gwydion's black gaze got under her skin, into her bones, and for one horrible moment she wondered whether he could read her mind, whether he was going to find out about Leo. She forced herself to keep staring at his servant, not to let her eyes wander towards the corner where Leo was hiding.

Gwydion stepped back, allowing not-Jack to come face-to-face with Merry. He was the boy from her nightmares again, the boy who had attacked her at the lake: there was no recognition in Jack's gold-flecked eyes, no gentleness. They were dead and cold. Grief weighed down on her chest like a gravestone: grief for Jack, grief for herself.

Gwydion laughed again.

'I knew it. You know what he is, what he has done, and still you love him. Just like she did.'

'The kitchen maid?'

'Kitchen maid, witch, whatever she called herself. Your ancestor. She lost her sisters because of her love for him. Did you not know?'

Merry stared at Jack.

Meredith. Meredith was the one he loved, all along. And she loved him too, to the point of risking everything dear to her...

All the dreams, the visions – they had been real. Glimpses of how Meredith and Jack had met and fallen in love, how she had hesitated, hoping to save him, until it was too late. Until she'd watched Gwydion create the puppet hearts and had understood that he was now too powerful to be stopped...

Jack must have felt so guilty...

The ache inside her grew. The feeling she'd had, that she'd known Jack for ages; the way she'd been drawn to him –

I wish I'd had the chance to tell him. That I do love him. That Meredith still loved him, even when she realised what her delay might cost her, even at the end...

The wizard leant forwards to speak into Merry's ear, and she could feel his breath on the side of her face. 'But love is a lie, little witch, an empty trick. I learnt that lesson long ago. And now you will too. Search her.'

Merry tried to back away, but she couldn't make her arms and legs obey her. The King of Hearts lifted her hand, almost as though he was going to kiss it – but she realised he was examining the bracelets on her wrist.

He's looking for the braid.

He yanked the bracelets off. He looked at her other wrist – tore the bracelets off that, too – ran his hands over her body, found the ropes of tiny pebbles Gran had tied round her waist and cut them away. The red stones scattered across the floor like drops of blood...

Leo thought he had been frightened when Gwydion walked into the throne room. But now Jack had reappeared, and he was striding towards Merry, and Leo realised that what he had felt before hadn't been fear, not really, because *this* was fear, this sudden, horrifying realisation that his sister was standing out there in front of a walking, breathing nightmare, and that he might actually not be able to save her...

Get a grip, Leo. You have got to get a grip.

He took the puppet hearts out of the box and placed them gently on to the floor.

Right. Let's be scientific about this...

He pulled his lighter out of his pocket and quietly

ignited it, trying to shield the flame so it wouldn't be noticeable. But which heart to choose? If there was any way to give Jack a happy ending…

Let's hope this one belongs to Gwydion.

He picked up one of the hearts, held the lighter under the lump of wood and waited.

Nothing happened.

The wood didn't start to smoke, or blister; it didn't even get hot.

OK. Plan B.

He got the Swiss Army knife out of his bag, flicked the blade open, put the point against the centre of the heart and pressed.

Nothing happened. Again. Not a dent, not a scratch.

Leo pushed harder. The tip of the knife slid sideways, slicing into his thumb. Just in time he bit down on his lower lip, stifling a cry of pain – and horror: as he peeked out from under the table, Leo saw not-Jack strip the bracelets from Merry's wrists.

Clearly, nothing non-magical was going to work on the puppet hearts. Leo took a deep breath and picked up the manuscript again. It wouldn't respond to him, but maybe there was a clue he had missed.

★　★　★

'The braid of hair is not here, Master. She is defenceless.'

Hearing the King of Hearts using Jack's voice, calling the wizard 'Master' – he may as well have just kicked her in the chest. Gwydion studied her face.

'But what has she done with it, I wonder?'

'I saw another with her at the lake.'

'Oh yes, the brother. So she gave the braid to him, perhaps, hoping to protect him from us. How noble. You see, witch, Jack is truly my servant. My King of Hearts could not hear your words, but he told me everything he saw: how you prevented him from carrying out his task, how you comforted him, fed him. How you kissed him.' Gwydion lingered on the word kiss. Merry's stomach lurched and acid burnt the back of her throat – but the wizard moved away from her again. 'I do not yet know what this braid was, or how it protected you, but since you were foolish enough to come here without it… Give her a sword.'

Merry felt the lifting of the spell Gwydion had used to control her body. Ignoring the cursed blade still hanging at his waist, Jack pulled two swords from a rack on the wall and threw one to her. She almost caught it – dropped it – grabbed it from the floor. This was no fencing foil; the balance and weight of the sword were completely different to the ones she used to use in the school club.

But at least it was a weapon. She moved quickly into the on guard stance she'd been taught.

Gwydion laughed.

'Now, *Jack*, show her what your love means. Hurt her.'

The King of Hearts lunged forwards.

Leo dropped the wooden heart he was holding and grabbed the large kitchen knife from his belt as not-Jack attacked Merry. He had to protect his sister.

Or, much more likely, he had to die trying.

He was about to charge out from his hiding place when he heard a faint rattling.

Behind him, his bag seemed to be having some kind of a spasm; he lifted it up slowly. Underneath was the sword hilt. It was vibrating.

Leo's gaze flicked from the hilt to Merry and back again. He had forgotten about the hilt – it was the one thing in the seven-sided box that hadn't grown in size. It seemed to be non-magical and basically completely useless. Clearly, the non-magical bit of that assessment needed to be reviewed. But what use could a hilt on its own possibly be? If he waited to find out, he would have to leave Merry out there alone.

Leo heard his sister scream.

★   ★   ★

It was not a match she could possibly have won. Merry had parried, recovered, parried again. But she never got close to a counter-attack. The King of Hearts wasn't using a blunt-tipped foil, and he wasn't obeying any rules. He had driven her backwards, slamming his blade down on top of hers again and again until, with a flick of his wrist, he had forced the sword out of her grip.

Now, she was losing track of time. There was no past, no future: just the next breath and the next wave of pain. Too much pain and too much fear: she couldn't recall any of the spells Gran had spent so many hours teaching her. Meanwhile, the wizard's servant was playing with her. He wasn't hitting her hard enough to knock her unconscious. He hadn't stabbed her. But when she tried to grab the cursed sword still hanging at his waist he had slashed her arms and hands. He'd dragged her up by the hair and thrown her against the walls of the throne room until she'd stopped trying to get up. Now she was lying, curled into a ball, while not-Jack stood above her. She peered up at him through the tangle of her hair.

'What's the matter?' Her voice was no more than a sigh. 'Why have you stopped? Why don't you just kill me?'

'Because this pain is your punishment, witch.' Gwydion

came into her field of vision. 'You have hindered my servant and delayed my plans.' He held up a hand from which one finger was missing. 'You have cost me dear. But now it is time for us to begin our work again, and we are going to start with you. My King of Hearts will cut out your still-pumping heart, and then I will feed it to Jack, just as I did the heart of the first girl he loved. Thus, the renewal of my power will be completed, Jack's transformation will become permanent, and we will be free of this prison. Free to harvest more hearts, to summon more power from the shadow realm, to destroy all love—'

'No! the magic sword isn't complete. You can't collect hearts without it. They die…'

'The sword is rebuilt. Show her.'

The King of Hearts forced Merry on to her back and drew the sword out from its scabbard. He held the tip in front of her eyes.

The blade was whole again.

The thing standing above her grinned.

'I went to the place where you tend your sick people, witch. I found the one I almost killed before, when you were not there to stop me, and this time I took his life. I plunged my sword into his heart, and as he died his heart's blood completed my blade.'

Dan. He had gone back, and found Dan in the hospital, and now –

Merry started crying. She couldn't help it. Dan, whom Leo had known since he was five, who had crashed at their house only a few weeks ago – how could he be dead? It was her fault – she hadn't been quick enough…

The wizard bent over her again.

'Do not weep, witch. Save your pity for yourself. Bring her.'

The King of Hearts picked Merry up and carried her, almost gently, to edge of the long fire pit running down the centre of the room. He laid her down next to the hearth stones, straightened up and pointed the sword at her throat.

It's almost funny. All those dreams I had about Jack killing me in different ways, and I never once imagined it would end like this.

I was supposed to be the one with the sword.

Out of the corner of her eye she could see Gwydion moving his hands about, creating strange, brightly-coloured streaks of light in the air. He was muttering in a language Merry didn't understand; an ugly, guttural language that wormed its way into her brain. She wanted to put her hands over her ears. But with not-Jack holding the sword above her, she didn't dare move. Was there anything of the human Jack still left, or had the completion of the blade finally destroyed him? Merry closed her eyes. She didn't want to look at him any more.

It might be too late for him. But it's not too late for me, not yet. Don't let me down, Leo.

He will not let you down, and neither will I, daughter.

Merry's eyes flew open. There was no one else there: just Gwydion, Jack and her. But the voice had been so clear. A woman's voice.

The King of Hearts glanced at Gwydion, then spoke a single word in the same grotesque language that Gwydion had been using. Merry couldn't move; it was as if she had become part of the granite flagstones beneath her, one complete structure set fast into the earth. And then she understood: her brain knew she was about to die, so she had hallucinated her mother's voice.

I guess it is too late for me, after all.

The tears ran across her temples into her hair, but she couldn't wipe them away.

The King of Hearts pressed the point of the sword to the base of Merry's throat and drew the blade slowly downwards towards her breastbone. She felt a trickle of blood against the side of her neck; would have screamed if she'd been able to.

Not-Jack made a strange, gasping sound.

Gwydion came to stand next to his servant.

'Yes, you want to kill her, don't you? Well, now you can. Cut out her heart. Slowly.'

Merry dragged her gaze away from the blade of the sword and tried to focus on Jack's face. It was just a trick of the firelight, but he looked almost like her Jack again, the Jack who had held her in his arms that night at the lakeside.

He knelt over her and pressed the tip of the blade up under her ribs, leaning forwards to bring his face close to hers. The wizard laughed.

'Yes, kiss her as you make her bleed. Show her how much you love her.'

But Jack didn't kiss her. He whispered to her instead.

'Forgive me, Merry. If you can.'

Then he hurled the sword at Gwydion.

TWENTY-FOUR

THE **SWORD STRUCK** Gwydion in the shoulder. The wizard screeched and staggered backwards – but he didn't fall. He dragged the sword out of his flesh, gasping with the pain of it, tossed it aside, and jabbed his hands in the air, creating a seething ball of multicoloured light that he hurled towards Jack. Jack threw his arms up, but he couldn't stop the strands of light settling on him. He screamed, struggling, trying to twist away. The smell of burning filled the air and Jack collapsed. At the same instant, Merry realised she could move again.

'Jack?' she whispered, inching her fingers sideways, trying

to reach him without the wizard realising she was free. 'Jack, hold on—'

Wait, daughter. Wait and see.

The same voice. Merry risked turning her head a little.

'Hello?'

The moment for our revenge approaches. Wait…

Gwydion staggered over to them. His face was dark, twisted with fury.

'How is this possible? What have you done, boy?'

Jack groaned as the wizard kicked him in the stomach.

'No matter. If you do not wish to serve me, you shall be the sacrifice.' The wizard knelt down and ripped Jack's tunic open, exposing his chest. 'The witch here shall carry out my wishes in your stead. I will cut out your heart and force it down her throat, and she will become my servant.' He tore the golden wolf's-head brooch off Jack's cloak and pinned it to Merry's T-shirt. Grasping the boy's jaw in his fingers, Gwydion forced Jack to look at him. 'She will do all that you were going to do, and more. Think on that as you die!'

He struck Jack across the face and spoke the same word that the King of Hearts had used earlier, the one that had pinned Merry to the ground.

But the paralysis didn't take effect again, at least not for her. Merry lay as still as she could, terrified that Gwydion would realise his magic had not worked, uncertain what she should do next.

Now, daughter, now is our chance. Seize your power. Open yourself to it. Use it against the wizard.

Gwydion retrieved the sword that Jack had thrown at him. Moments later Merry could hear a rasping sound: he was sharpening the blade, preparing to slice open Jack's chest.

Daughter, you must get up. Now.

She had to get up, she had to get up, she had to —

But I can't do it — I can't —

Fear smothered her, the tombstone weight of it crushing the life out of her.

Gwydion was muttering to himself now: '...kill the boy first, then send her after her brother... yes... get the braid from him, and find out what power it has... I wonder, will brotherly love be enough to make the enchantment permanent, if she eats his heart too...'

But still, she could not move. Gwydion was going to kill Jack, then he was going to change her into a monster, and there was nothing she could do to stop him, nothing —

The voice in Merry's head sighed.

If you do nothing, all those you love will surely die...

'...it is too late for us, Meredith. You have to take the key and go. Now!'

She was in the same room, but in a different time. She was watching Nia push Meredith away. Meredith, tears running down her face, took one long, last look at her sisters before she turned and ran. Nia went to stand by Carys. There was Jack, already asleep, and there was Gwydion, writing fire runes in the air, attacking the two remaining witches. They were singing a shielding charm, pouring all their power into it, but Merry knew it wasn't going to be enough. The intensity of the fire runes increased; Gwydion, realising that Meredith had escaped with his master key, bellowed with rage. Carys screamed and sank to the floor, white fire looping around her arms and torso like living chains. A tongue of flame lashed the side of Nia's face – but she kept her arms raised, kept chanting the words of power. Gwydion slumped against the wall behind him. The fire runes began to fade, but with a last effort he hurled a single blazing rune towards Nia. It hit her square in the chest, spreading glowing embers across her skin and clothing. The wizard toppled forwards on to his face. There was a thunderous rumble from somewhere up above and wind and dust swept through the room, extinguishing all light except for the fire in the long hearth. By the dull gleam of the flames Merry watched as Nia, breath gurgling in her chest, dragged herself slowly towards Carys.

'Carys?'

There was no answer. Nia laid her head on her sister's broken body, and the fire died.

Oh, my sisters…

Merry gasped and opened her eyes. Meredith's sisters had died, in agony, because Meredith had not acted when she had the chance. Because she had neither killed Jack, nor summoned her sisters to attack the wizard, before Gwydion created the puppet hearts.

But…

But Merry still had a brother. And a mum and a gran. A best friend.

Help me, Meredith. Help me save Leo.

The power is already within you, daughter. You just need to believe that you can, that you should, use it…

Gwydion came and stood above her.

'The blade is sharp enough now. Less painful, perhaps, but this way he will still be alive when I hold his heart in front of his eyes.' He grinned. 'Go, sit on your throne. I want you to have a good view.'

For the first time in weeks, Merry knew with absolute certainty what she needed to do.

Leo saw Merry get up.

'Oh, no—' He tried to gather everything up – fumbled – dropped the puppet hearts – threw everything down again. The shock of Dan's murder had left him reeling. But he couldn't allow himself to think about it, not now. He had to help his sister. If he ran, maybe he could still get to her before she reached the throne.

But Merry wasn't moving towards the throne. Instead, she stretched both hands out in front of her, fingers spread wide. Gwydion, who was standing with the cursed blade poised above Jack's chest, yelped as the sword twitched out of his grasp and flew through the air, the hilt smacking into Merry's open palm. Leo choked back a cry of surprise: because it wasn't Merry any more. Or not just Merry...

The wizard was staring at her, his mouth open.

'You? How? How is this possible?'

Merry smiled.

'Magic, Gwydion. Did you think you were the only one with power?'

Leo rubbed his eyes and stared at his sister again. It

403

was like looking at a double exposure on a photograph. The girl facing Gwydion had dark brown hair, but also light brown hair. She had deep hazel eyes, but also eyes that shone a vivid green, even in the dull light of the throne room. When she spoke, it was almost as though there were two people speaking at once, perfectly synchronised.

The wizard bellowed, overturned the table next to him, and stood there, breathing hard, fists clenched.

'I still have Jack. And your power is nothing compared to mine. You are going to die here, witch. Alone.'

Gwydion opened his hands. Leo saw twisting black shapes, edged with red fire that seared itself into his retinas. The shapes poured out into the air, coalescing into a dark, churning mass.

He dashed out from his hiding place.

'She's not alone, you bastard!'

Colour bled from Gwydion's face. Merry frowned. How was he able to see Leo – could it simply be that Leo now wanted to be seen? And, more importantly, how had her brother got hold of a sword?

The sword looked almost identical to the one Merry held, the King of Hearts' own sword. Leo placed the puppet hearts on the floor and knelt with the blade held above them.

The wizard snarled.

'Why, you—' He raised his arms and hurled the seething mass of black runes at Leo.

'No—' Merry gasped and started forwards, but the black shapes were already rippling around Leo, encasing him, hiding him. 'Leo, no…'

The darkness melted away.

Leo was still there, kneeling, his wrist held up in front of him. The wrist with the braid on it. He was pale, and there were streaks of what looked like ash on his hair and face, but he was alive. Merry started breathing again.

'How…?' Gwydion muttered. He looked at Merry, and for the first time she saw fear in his eyes.

'How? Because you once loved somebody…'

The wizard looked confused now, as well as frightened; Merry sensed the stirring of that pity she'd felt for him once before. 'Do you still not get it? The braid that has protected us was woven from Edith's hair. Edith, whom you loved so deeply that even fifteen hundred years later the vow you made to protect her holds fast. Your love has proved stronger than your hate, Gwydion. Love always is, in the end.'

'No. It is not possible.' The wizard began backing away and Merry moved forwards to protect Jack. 'But – but even if it were true, you don't know which puppet heart is mine, boy.' His voice was almost a whine. 'Would you kill Jack?'

Leo glanced at Merry.

'I'll take a chance.'

He plunged his blade down into the first heart. It cracked, splintered and disintegrated into dust.

Gwydion staggered, pawing at his chest. His fingers came away red: blood was soaking through the front of his clothes. Merry stared in horrified wonder.

Is this it?

Was this all they had to do: destroy the wizard's puppet heart, and the wizard would die automatically? Had they really done it?

But as Merry watched, the bleeding stopped.

The wizard laughed.

'Ha. You guessed right, but it will do you no good. You should leave now, while you still can.' He held out his other hand to Leo. 'Come, give me the second heart. Save yourself.'

'No.' It was Jack.

Merry's heart began to race. Jack dragged himself up to look at her.

'You must… destroy the other heart too, so I can die.' He paused, gasping for breath. 'Please, Leo. It is the only way…'

Gwydion started hobbling towards Jack, but Merry raised the sword she carried. He stopped, sneering.

'She will never kill you, you fool. And do you know why? Because she is selfish. Both of them are. They would let the world burn rather than willingly suffer such a loss.'

Merry shook her head.

'We made that mistake once, Gwydion, a long time ago. My sisters paid dearly for that error. I do love Jack. We all do. And that is why we're going to kill him.'

She nodded at Leo. His face was taut and white, but he took a deep breath, steadied his hand, and plunged the sword down into the second puppet heart.

Jack groaned and sank back, his eyes wide. Blood spurted from a gaping wound that had opened across his chest. His lips moved, but through her tears Merry could not tell what he was saying. She dropped on to her knees next to him, pressing one hand to his torn flesh, trying to hold the sides of the tear together, trying to stop the bleeding.

'Jack, I'm so sorry, I'm—'

'Do not... do not weep. This is... the way it should be.' Jack's voice was barely a whisper; she leant in closer. 'Forgive me. Earlier, above the lake... I... I wanted only to protect you. Meredith lost everything... because she loved me. I could not see you suffer in the same way.' He gasped and shuddered. 'I wish... I wish I could hold you, one last time, my love...'

She sobbed and pushed harder on his chest, but her hands were wet with his blood.

'No... please – we should have been able to save you...'

Jack shook his head.

'You have saved me...' One more breath, and one more, flinching with the pain of it. 'You loved me enough... to come back for me, you and Meredith, despite everything... so you have... set me free...'

He smiled at her, and was still.

Jack...

Jack...

Her voice echoed round the room.

Gwydion's scream of rage and pain broke through her

grief. He was bleeding again, scarlet dripping from the front of his tunic, but still he stumbled towards her, his face contorted, his arms raised, dark red fire runes pulsing at his fingertips.

Merry rose to her feet. Fury flowed through her body and the pain of her injuries faded into the background.

In that instant, she felt her own power as she had never done before. She could sense all the potential within her, the raw ability that was hers to harness. It was almost tangible: liquid fire flowing through and around every vein and artery, every synapse, every blood cell. Her own personal energy source to be summoned at will.

For such a long time, she'd been afraid of her magic. But she wasn't afraid any more.

Gwydion spat at her.

'You shouldn't have given away the braid, girl. Your ancestor is just a kitchen maid, a – a hedge witch with a smattering of knowledge, crumbs stolen from the tables of her betters.' His lip twisted into a snarl. 'She is nothing. You are *nothing*.'

'You're wrong, Gwydion. Meredith did not follow her sisters to that which lies beyond. Through all the long centuries, through all her descendants, she worked towards this moment: vengeance for her sisters, vengeance for Jack, vengeance for all you have harmed. And now our time has come.'

Merry stretched her right hand out and concentrated. Magic sizzled across her skin as threads of silver light began to cascade from her fingertips, weaving a shimmering shield between her and Gwydion.

Gwydion screamed and hurled the fire runes at her.

The runes crashed into the silver net. The filaments blazed more brilliantly, forcing Merry to screw up her eyes against the light. Brighter and brighter it grew, until –

– until there was nothing left. No runes, no net: just grey ash, drifting down through the air.

Merry brought up the sword in her left hand like a javelin – tightened her grip on the hilt – took aim at Gwydion, and threw –

The blade thudded into the centre of his chest.

Gwydion grasped the hilt. For a moment he looked down at it, eyes wide, mouth open, disbelieving. Until, hands still around the sword, he toppled backwards and hit the floor.

Silence. Followed by a strange, high-pitched humming sound. Merry spun round; it almost seemed to be coming from the –

'Merry, look out!' Leo ran over and pushed her to the ground, throwing himself on top of her.

Behind them, the glass jars of hearts exploded.

★ ★ ★

Merry opened her eyes. There was a girl sitting on the floor next to her, a girl about her own age, with dark brown hair and green eyes, and a long dress belted at the waist. The girl looked real enough – Merry could see her chest rising and falling as she breathed – but everything around them was pale and out of focus. They still seemed to be in Gwydion's hall: there was the ugly chair that Jack had been strapped to, there were the now-empty shelves, and there was –

Leo. Kneeling next to a body, crying.

Her body.

Merry swallowed.

'I am dead then, Meredith?'

The girl shook her head.

'No. Your body is somewhat damaged, but you have no injuries that will not heal in time. Your body, and your heart, will both mend.'

Merry pressed her hand to her chest.

411

My heart…

Meredith sighed.

'Many people, you included, have suffered because of my choices. I am sorry.'

Merry looked over at Leo. She knew she would take any number of risks to save someone she loved.

'Don't be. Love is a far better reason for doing something than most other reasons I can think of. Besides, you killed Gwydion in the end.'

'No, Merry – you killed him. It is true that my blood runs through your veins. A part of me has continued on through each generation, tied to the lifespan of the curse. And I always intended to be present at the moment of Gwydion's defeat. But the power to defeat Gwydion – that was yours. All the work and sacrifice that has gone on across the generations, to bring us to this point: that accumulated power is your inheritance. A power that sets you apart. It's just that, up until this moment, you've never really trusted yourself to use it.' The girl smiled. 'You will have to be properly trained, Merry, and soon. Unless… you still would rather you were not a witch?'

'No—' Merry stopped, surprised by her own vehemence. Losing her ability now would be like – losing her hearing,

412

or a limb. It was part of who she was. 'No thank you, Meredith. I will stay as I am.'

'As you wish. No more questions now. It is time for me to rest, finally.' She gazed at Jack, lying nearby, and sighed. 'And it is time for you to wake up...'

★ ★ ★

'Wake up, Merry. Please wake up...'

Merry tried to focus on the face hovering above her. 'Leo?'

'Oh, thank God.' And his arms were around her, crushing her to his chest. 'Thank God. I really thought you were dead this time.' He scuffed the back of his hand across his eyes. 'Are you OK? And are you... I mean, has she—'

'Yeah. She's gone. Gwydion?'

'Dead as an extremely dead thing.'

She hesitated. Leo understood.

'Jack's gone as well. I'm sorry, Merry.'

She knew he hadn't made it. She'd watched him die. But still – it wasn't the fairy-tale ending she had imagined. It didn't make any sense.

'Where is he?'

'Over there, but—'

She clambered to her feet and limped across to Jack's body.

'Merry—'

'The manuscript, Leo – don't you remember? True love's kiss, it said. True love's kiss to break the curse. We owe it to him, and to Meredith.'

And I must love him too, even now Meredith's gone. Otherwise, I don't understand why this hurts so much –

She knelt next to Jack, smoothed his hair back off his face. He looked like he was asleep, not dead.

Please, let him not be dead.

Merry leant forwards and let her hair fall around Jack's face, shutting them in together. She studied his features, trying to remember how it had felt, that night they had kissed by the lake: the way their fingers had intertwined, the way Jack's body had moved under her hands. Closing her eyes she bent closer still, until her lips were grazing Jack's, and she kissed him.

She kissed him for herself, and she kissed him for Meredith.

Please, come back...

Pulling away, she looked at him again, willing there to be a flush of colour blooming on his cheeks, warmth returning to his lips. Willing his eyelids to flutter open.

That's how it should work. The brave princess kisses the sleeping prince, he wakes up, and they live happily ever after...

'Jack?'

There was a touch on her shoulder.

But it was Leo, not Jack.

'Merry, he's dead. You have to let him go.'

'But – the manuscript—'

'Look.' Leo had the sword in his hand, the twin sword he had used to destroy the puppet hearts. There were words etched into the blade. The language was not modern English, but the meaning was clear. 'I can still read it.'

'Me too.' True love: that's what the words said. Merry ran her hand over the ornately curved letters. 'True love's kiss. So the manuscript was right.'

'Yeah. If your dictionary defines "kiss" as "to stab with a sharp implement".'

She sat back on her heels.

'I really thought we could save him.'

'We did save him.' Leo leant forwards and touched Jack's face gently. 'I hope he's with her now, with his Meredith. That would make him happy. I think she really was his true love.'

'I hope so too.' Merry stopped. There were no words she knew of to express the churning mixture of sorrow,

415

relief, anger and happiness she was experiencing. So she gave up trying, and burst into tears.

It took quite a while for the tears to dry up. Leo had been crying too, at the same time as trying to fix up her injuries as best he could without any kind of medical supplies.

'OK.' He wiped his nose on his sleeve. 'I can't do any more. And we ought to get out of here. The fire's dying, and unless you're feeling up to creating some witch fire, we've only got one working light source left.' He stood and held out a hand to pull Merry to her feet. 'I've got the manuscript.'

Merry noticed the hilt from the trinket box, protruding from the top of Leo's backpack.

'When did it grow a blade?'

'Oh – when Jack produced his regrown blade, ours started growing a blade too. It was weird.'

Merry touched the hilt lightly. It must have been part of the first cursed sword, the one that had shattered when Jack tried to kill his brother. Gwydion probably thought he was so clever, making puppet hearts that could only be destroyed by the King of Hearts' own blade.

But Meredith was cleverer. She worked it out. Realised that with enough time — an awful lot of time — the remnants of that first sword could be turned against its creator.

Leo took her hand.

'Let's go.'

Merry shook her head.

'We can't just leave him here. We've got to take him back, bury—' The word choked her. She tried again. 'Bury him.'

'I wish we could, but we'll never get him back up to the lake.' Leo sighed and looked around the hall. 'I suppose we could at least move him out of this horrible place.'

Merry found a small, bare room off one of the corridors. Leo had to drag Jack's body – he was too heavy for Leo to lift that far, and Leo said she was too injured to help – so it took a while. Eventually Leo manoeuvred the body through the door and stood up, breathing heavily and rubbing his back.

'So, do you want to say something? I—' There was a noise like a gun going off, a shower of tiny bits of rock. 'What the hell's happening?'

Merry stared at her brother.

'I think we're out of time.'

Leo quickly knelt next to Jack, straightened his tunic and his sword belt and crossed his hands over his chest.

'We should go, but—'

'I know.' Merry crouched next to him. 'I don't want to leave him down here in the dark, either.' There was another loud crack. She glanced up: above them, a split had opened in the ceiling.

But Jack's not here any more. And — I want to live.

She kissed Jack's forehead, wiped her tears away from his face.

'Ready?'

Leo nodded.

'We'll miss you, Jack. Rest well.'

The ground underneath them shook and ruptured. Leo put his arm around Merry's waist.

It was time to go home.

It seemed to take forever to reach the great entrance doors. The ceiling was falling away in chunks; both of them were covered in dust and scratches. Merry hobbled ahead to slam the key against the dark wood. The doors swung open; only at that point did she realise she had been holding her breath.

'Keep going!'

They hurried down the long tunnel, found the bottom of the stairs and started climbing. Merry's legs were cramping up, and she could see the sweat running down Leo's forehead. She paused for a second and glanced down: behind them, the stairs were falling away.

'Faster! Hurry!'

'You go first!' Leo stopped to push her in front of him. She saw why: the top of the staircase was still sealed. Behind her, Leo leapt forwards on to the platform just as the stair he had been standing on slipped down into the abyss.

Merry thrust her arm upwards, slamming the key against rock above them. Leo staggered as the edge of the platform started to crumble.

Jack had said the King of Hearts used a word to open the lake bed – was the key even going to work? Because if it didn't, they were going to be plunging to their deaths any second now...

The rock dissolved, revealing a swirling, rising whirlpool of water. But it wasn't opening. Merry shoved the key into Leo's hand and flung her arms out, visualising the water moving away from them, forcing a way through to the air above.

I can't let us drown, not now, not after everything else –

The rising air currents grabbed her, dragged her upwards, and then –

– and then she and Leo were standing at the shallow

edge of the lake, gold-flecked clouds above them shading away to grey.

It was dawn.

Leo seized her hand, and as they stepped on to the grass she turned, ripped the golden brooch away from her shoulder and hurled it out over the seething waters. The brooch spun and fell, glinting in the first gleams of sunlight, until it plunged into the lake.

The waters stilled, and the sun rose.

Merry smiled. It was a new day.

TWENTY-FIVE

THREE WEEKS LATER

ODAY, EVEN THE Black Lake looked beautiful. It sparkled, reflecting the sunlight and the cornflower blue of the sky. Merry took off her cardigan, lay back on the picnic blanket and closed her eyes for a moment, letting the warmth soak into her skin. After such a winter – such a long, terrifying, blood-stained winter – summer had come as suddenly and forcefully as a wrecking ball.

She should have been happy. And, for the most part, she was.

There was a grey feather lying on the grass nearby. Merry hummed the musical phrase she'd learnt, then sang it, the words telling of migrations and air currents and the freedom of flight. The feather trembled, rose upwards and floated off towards the lake. She smiled. She was finally starting to enjoy discovering her abilities, and training in both 'proper' witch magic, and the more... unusual stuff that she could do too. Her power felt like an instrument now: something that didn't control or define her, but that she could use if she chose to. She knew she would make mistakes. But, that was OK.

I'm not the wicked witch, but I don't have to be the perfect good fairy, either. I'm just me: a normal, complicated human, who happens to have a talent for witchcraft.

A complicated person from a family of complicated people: she'd learnt things about Mum, and Gran, that had changed her perception of her family. Changed it in a good way. Another reason for her to be happy.

If only Leo were happy too. Her big brother was in pain. They both missed Jack. Both carried the scars of what had happened over the last few weeks. Merry's left arm was still bandaged, and she still had nightmares about Gwydion. But Leo was also grieving for Dan; grieving much more deeply than Merry had expected. Of course, he said he was fine. But she could see the confusion and loneliness in his eyes. He hadn't been given the chance to say goodbye, and it was hurting him.

Merry sighed, grabbed a bottle of water from her bag and took a couple of sips.

Leo was at Dan's funeral today. Maybe that was why she'd come here.

Because, despite the tranquillity Merry saw around her, the lake was a place of suffering. A place of death. Jack, Carys, Nia, all those people whose hearts had been stored in jars beneath the shimmering water: they all were still there, somewhere, mingling with the dust.

A large cloud drifted in front of the sun, casting a shadow over the lake. At the same time a breeze sprang up, cold in comparison with the heat of a moment ago. The surface of the water rippled, spiralling –

Merry leant forwards, her heart beating faster –

But in another minute the cloud passed, the heat returned and the lake was still again. She sat back and took a deep breath.

Get a grip, Merry, for heaven's sake.

The water was still glinting in the sunlight. But for a second, she'd really thought that –

No. She'd imagined it, that was all. Jack was dead, and

the nightmare of the last couple of months was over and
done with.

And in an hour's time she was meeting Ruby for
shopping and pizza. Life was good. Merry picked up her
bag and headed for home.

ACKNOWLEDGEMENTS

THE WITCH'S KISS began life in June 2014 as an idea, when the plot fell virtually fully-formed into our collective subconscious (probably through a rip in the space-time continuum). As we write this, nearly two years later, our book is just over three months away from publication. Obviously, we couldn't have got to this point without a huge amount of support, advice and time from a lot of people. We'd especially like to thank the following wonderful individuals:

Ruth Alltimes, our editor at HarperCollins, for lots of utterly brilliant ideas, and for forcing us to polish and polish until we were left with something gorgeous and sparkly. We're lucky to have her.

Claire Wilson, our agent at Rogers, Coleridge & White, for being completely lovely and incredibly supportive. Claire's belief in our writing kept us going during the most difficult moments on our publishing journey. She is the best.

Georgia Monroe at HarperCollins, and Lexie Hamblin and Rosie Price at Rogers, Coleridge & White, for helping to organise us and staying unfazed in the face of mild (and sometimes not so mild) authorial hysteria.

Lisa Brewster at Blacksheep Design Ltd, for capturing the essence of our story with her stunning cover art.

Ruth Brandt, tutor and confidence-booster extraordinaire.

Our families, scattered across the UK and the US. We love you and we couldn't have done any of this without you. Special shout-outs to Auntie Gill, who first suggested that maybe, just maybe, other people might like to read some of the stuff we were writing; to our dad, for passing on his writing genes; and to Hattie, who gave us just the pep talk we needed to start submitting to agents.

Our last 'thank you' is the most important. To Laurence, who loved *The Witch's Kiss*, even though he didn't get to finish it. To Neill, for his unstinting love and generosity of spirit. To our children: Georgina, Victoria, Rebecca and Sam. Thank you for putting up with the excitement and the drama, the late-night writing sessions and the oh–Lord–we've-run-out-of-milk-and-I-forgot-to-do-any-washing moments of neglect. This is for you.